The Mara Conspiracy

Philippe Faucon

Dedication

To those who fight on the front lines to protect our world's wonders, both natural and human-made, against the forces of greed and destruction. And to my mother, who, despite her flawed personality, inspired me always to research and understand more. I think she would have been proud.

Acknowledgment

I would like to extend my heartfelt thanks to everyone who made this book possible. To my publisher, editor, and team — thank you for your guidance and for believing in this story. To the conservationists, researchers, and journalists whose work inspired the novel's backdrop, your dedication is humbling and a reminder of what it means to truly protect. And to my marvelous children, Christophe, Anni, and Pierre — your love and encouragement bring joy to every chapter I write. Finally, to my readers, whose enthusiasm fuels each new story — this book exists because of you. Thank you for joining me on this journey.

Dedication

To those who fight on the front lines to protect our world's wonders, both natural and human-made, against the forces of greed and destruction. And to my mother, who, despite her flawed personality, inspired me always to research and understand more. I think she would have been proud.

Acknowledgment

I would like to extend my heartfelt thanks to everyone who made this book possible. To my publisher, editor, and team — thank you for your guidance and for believing in this story. To the conservationists, researchers, and journalists whose work inspired the novel's backdrop, your dedication is humbling and a reminder of what it means to truly protect. And to my marvelous children, Christophe, Anni, and Pierre — your love and encouragement bring joy to every chapter I write. Finally, to my readers, whose enthusiasm fuels each new story — this book exists because of you. Thank you for joining me on this journey.

Table of Contents

About the Author

Philippe Faucon was born in France but has lived in Arizona and sometimes in Peru. With a family background in all kinds of military careers, including a brother who has worked as a real-life spy, Philippe brings a unique insight into the world of espionage and intrigue. Writing allows him to explore the difficult choices people face when confronted with only bad options, and he aims to keep his novels grounded in reality. While the characters and storylines are fictional, the background information is meticulously researched and real.

Prologue: Maasai Mara

The first light of dawn swept over the Maasai Mara, a golden savannah stretching endlessly, punctuated by acacia trees and the silhouettes of roaming wildlife. Crisp, cool air carried the distant calls of birds, heralding the start of another day. Known as "the Mara" for the "spotted" look created by the scattered, short, bushy trees, this was one of Africa's last bastions of unspoiled wilderness—a sanctuary for wildlife and a timeless landscape. The Mara River cut through the terrain, its murky waters sustaining life across the reserve. Crocodiles lay in ambush near its banks, while hippos rose and submerged in a calm rhythm, the serene backdrop belying the recent brutality that had scarred this place.

Naomi Mwangi stood atop a small hill, her face etched with shock and fury as she looked over the scene below. Twenty-three elephants lay scattered across the savannah, their lifeless bodies hacked for tusks, and, disturbingly, other parts. Blood darkened the grass around them. Even the babies hadn't been spared; only one calf, huddled beside its fallen mother, had survived, nudging her lifeless form in a heartbreaking display of confusion.

The poachers had flown their helicopter low, raining death from the sky. Naomi could still hear the faint echoes of gunfire in her mind, the panicked screeches of the elephants. This was not the work of ordinary poachers; it was something far more sinister. Organized crime.

Naomi's eyes narrowed. She'd heard whispers of crime syndicates pushing into Kenya, exploiting security gaps and corrupt officials, but this was a ruthless escalation. She pulled out her satellite phone and dialed Kamau Mbugua Gikandi, the director of the Anti-Poaching and Security Unit at the Wildlife Preservation Alliance. His voice came through gruff and concerned despite the early hour.

"Naomi, what happened?"

"We have a massacre, Kamau. Twenty-three elephants were killed by poachers in a helicopter. This was coordinated organized crime on a scale we've never seen. We can't handle this alone."

There was a weighted pause, and Kamau answered. "We need someone who can go beyond the limits. I'll make the call."

Naomi closed her eyes, steadied by Kamau's words yet aware of what was at stake. "We're ready."

As she ended the call, Naomi looked back over the savannah, the morning light casting long shadows over the lifeless forms. The Mara, usually so vibrant with life, now felt heavy with loss. But her resolve was steeled. They would fight back—protect the Mara from those who sought to exploit it, even if it meant risking everything. The world was changing, and so were the threats to this land. But as long as she stood here, she would not let the Mara be torn apart. Not without a fight.

Chapter 1: Arrival in Nairobi

Arrival

Dennis Bellamy sat back in his seat as the plane descended into Nairobi's Jomo Kenyatta International Airport. It had been a long journey. He had left the US from Hartsfield-Jackson Atlanta International Airport in the evening. After 8 hours of transatlantic flight, he arrived late in the morning at London's Heathrow Airport. His next and last flight was going to be a Kenyan Airlines in the late afternoon at 5:25 PM. Finally, he arrived at Jomo Kenyatta International Airport (NBO) at 5:00 AM, two days after leaving the US.

Dennis needed to be ready for action immediately upon arrival, and resting was crucial. That was a good excuse to travel in first class, and with the comfortable seats, he had managed to get some reasonable sleep. As he reclined in his seat, his thoughts drifted to Naomi Mwangi, the ranger he would soon meet. He had read her file multiple times—her passion, dedication, and bravery were apparent even in the dry language of reports. He wondered how she would react to him, an outsider claiming to understand the complexities of her work. He knew he needed to win her trust, and that wouldn't be easy.

Dennis found a quiet corner in one airport lounge during his layover in London. He ordered a pint of English cider, savoring the crisp taste—finding good cider in the US was challenging. As he sipped his drink, he continued thinking about his mission, reviewing his notes, and reminding

himself of what was at stake. Kenya was beautiful, with sprawling landscapes and chaotic energy, but the stakes were higher this time.

Dennis, a senior executive at IRIS—a global intelligence and risk assessment agency—had been pulled into this mission because the poaching network wasn't just about endangered wildlife. Intelligence indicated that the same criminal syndicate involved in poaching was also tied to arms smuggling to northeast Africa, refugees and drug smuggling from northeastern Africa, money laundering, and even funding extremist groups in East Africa. The mission had grown beyond a conservation effort; it was now about destabilizing a network that threatened regional security.

As the wheels touched down, Dennis thought about his cover story. As an environmental consultant working with a high-profile conservation NGO, Wildlife Preservation Alliance (WPA), he had the credentials, the backstory, and even the right gear. His job was to blend in and earn the trust of those who would otherwise see him as an outsider. He reminded himself that first impressions were critical in Kenya, like anywhere else, especially when powerful people were watching. The airport was bustling with travelers worldwide, tourists in safari hats, businesspeople, and locals waiting for loved ones.

Dennis had gotten his e-visa a few days before, went flawlessly through immigration, collected his luggage, and made his way outside, where the surprisingly cool 55 degrees Fahrenheit (12 C) dry morning air hit him immediately. One would think that Kenya is always hot, and that's true of the coast, but Nairobi is at almost 6000 feet

elevation (1800 m.) He squinted in the early sun, taking in the sights of Nairobi—the sky was clear and blue, but there was a haze in the distance, hinting at the city's pollution. He scanned for his contact—an unassuming Kenyan man named Daniel Muriithi Mwangi, who had been assigned to drive him to his accommodation.

Daniel found him first. "Mr. Bellamy?" he asked, his eyes darting around, a hint of nervousness in his voice. "Welcome to Nairobi. I'm Daniel, your driver."

Dennis smiled, offering a handshake. "Thanks, Daniel. Good to meet you."

The two men walked to the car, a dusty Toyota Land Cruiser fitting with Dennis's role. Daniel loaded Dennis's bags into the back while Dennis glanced around the busy pick-up zone, watching for anyone who might be interested in his arrival. It all looked normal, but experience had taught him that normal was often where trouble began.

"First time in Kenya?" Daniel asked, starting the engine and merging into the chaotic flow of Nairobi traffic.

"Not quite," Dennis replied, keeping his tone light. "But it has been a while."

The drive took them through the heart of Nairobi, past colorful matatus packed with commuters, their blaring horns and vibrant graffiti making them impossible to ignore. Street vendors lined the sidewalks, selling everything from fresh fruit to bootleg DVDs, their calls mixing with engines' roar and the bustling city's hum.

Dennis observed the contrast between the modern high-rises' glass facades and the sprawling, chaotic markets full

of life and noise. This was a city of layers—wealth and poverty, progress and struggle—and he knew that his mission would force him to navigate all of it.

Nairobi was founded in 1899 as a supply depot for the construction of the Uganda Railway, which was being built by the British to link Mombasa on the coast with Uganda. At the time, the city was a small, swampy area known for its freshwater, and the name "Nairobi" is derived from the Maasai, the phrase "Enkare Nairobi," meaning "cool water."

As the railway expanded, the cooler Nairobi quickly grew into a key administrative and commercial hub, replacing the hot, tropical, Mombasa as the capital of British East Africa in 1907.

Its strategic location on the railway line, along with its central role in colonial administration, contributed to its rapid development. Nairobi continued to grow throughout the 20th century, becoming the capital of the Republic of Kenya after it gained independence from Britain in 1963. Today, it remains the country's political, economic, and cultural heart.

The streets were a blend of dusty, dry roads in some areas and lush vegetation in others. The scent of grilled meat from roadside stalls and the smell of exhaust fumes created a unique aroma distinctly Nairobi. Dennis could see children playing by the roadside, women carrying baskets of goods, and men gathered in small groups, talking animatedly.

The Guesthouse

After navigating through the early morning traffic, Daniel drove Dennis to a small guesthouse on the edge of the city. It was a modest place, chosen by Kamau specifically for its unremarkable appearance and quiet surroundings—perfect for someone who wanted to keep a low profile. Daniel pulled into the narrow driveway, and they got out of the vehicle. The neighborhood was quiet, with only a few children playing in the distance. The guesthouse owner, in the front yard, greeted Dennis warmly but with little interest, quickly handing over the keys to his room... Room. 201, right in front of the staircase.

Daniel helped Dennis unload his bags from the car. "This place was Kamau's choice," Daniel said, giving Dennis a knowing smile. "He thought a regular hotel might draw too much attention. Here, you can come and go without anyone asking too many questions."

Dennis nodded, appreciating the thought that had gone into the arrangements. "Makes sense. Thanks for the help, Daniel."

Kamau has negotiated a multi-month deal, in case you need to stay longer, but in any case, this is your stable lodging while you are in Kenya.

Daniel shook his hand firmly. "If you are not too tired, I'll pick you up later in the morning to take you to the office. Let me know a little later. Meanwhile, welcome in Nairobi, Mr. Bellamy."

Dennis watched as Daniel drove away, then turned to observe the guesthouse. It was a modest, two-story building

situated on the edge of the city. It was surrounded by a small garden with a few flowering shrubs and potted plants, giving it a quiet, secluded feel. The exterior was painted a faded yellow, and a wrought iron gate separated it from the narrow street beyond.

It was not a luxurious place, but it was comfortable and functional—perfect for someone who wanted to avoid drawing too much attention. Inside, the guesthouse had a simple but welcoming atmosphere. The common area had office space and was furnished with worn but clean couches and a small television.

There was a dining table with mismatched chairs and a few local art pieces hung on the walls, adding a touch of character to the otherwise unassuming interior. The scent of fresh-brewed chai often lingered in the air, a reminder of the hospitable nature of the owner, who was always ready with a cup for her guests. A cursory check found that all the windows and doors could be secured, and there was a small safe in the office area.

Dennis's room was on the second floor, overlooking the quiet street. It was small, with just enough space for a single bed, a wooden wardrobe, a desk, and a chair. The en-suite bathroom was basic, with a small shower, a toilet, and a sink. A ceiling fan rotated slowly above, stirring the cool morning air. Dennis appreciated the simplicity—it allowed him to focus on the task at hand without unnecessary distractions.

Dennis dropped his bags, unpacked quickly, and took a long, hot shower. The fatigue of the journey was setting in, and he knew he needed to rest and get settled before diving into his work.

He set up a few essentials—a laptop, a notebook, and a basic surveillance kit—then sat at the small desk, glancing at the clock. He still had a few hours before he needed to meet Kamau, so he decided to catch some rest. He lay on the bed, his body sinking into the mattress, and closed his eyes, letting the exhaustion take over.

When he woke, it was late morning. He felt a little more refreshed after the short nap. Dennis splashed cold water on his face, combed his hair, changed into fresh clothes, and took a deep breath. He had a meeting soon, and he needed to be sharp.

Lunch with Kamau

Around 11:30, Daniel arrived to pick Dennis up, and they headed to the WPA office, a modest but well-equipped office building in Kilimani. Even at that hour, the Wildlife

Preservation Alliance (WPA) office was busy, with people coming and going, preparing for field operations, and making calls to coordinate with rangers in the field. Dennis was greeted by Morah, the receptionist, a young woman who always seemed to be smiling.

"Good morning, Mr. Bellamy," Morah said warmly. "Welcome. Mr. Kamau expects you for lunch, but feel free to make yourself comfortable in the lounge area until then."

Dennis nodded, returning her smile. "Thank you, Morah. It looks like a busy day already."

"It always is," she replied, her eyes sparkling. "But we're used to it. Everyone here knows the importance of what we're doing."

"How big is WPA?" asked Dennis.

"About sixty persons are in the organization, about fifteen are working from this office, and the rest are in the field. We have the complete floor," answered Morah. "Everyone is very nice and correct. I love working here." She added.

Dennis settled in, taking the time to observe the office environment. The WPA office was bustling with activity—staff members were on phones, others were huddled over maps of the Maasai Mara, and some were preparing gear for upcoming field operations. It was clear that these people were dedicated to their mission, and Dennis felt a sense of admiration for them.

He and Kamau went for lunch in a quiet, elegant restaurant in Westlands. The place had an understated charm—dim lighting, rustic wooden tables, and a bar stocked with an impressive selection of local and international spirits. The menu featured a mix of traditional Kenyan dishes and continental cuisine.

Kamau was already seated at a table in the corner, his eyes scanning the room. He waved Dennis over, a polite smile on his face.

"Mr. Bellamy," Kamau said, standing to shake Dennis's hand.

"Welcome. Please, have a seat. I hope you don't mind—I ordered some Nyama choma for us. It's the best in Nairobi, I assure you."

Dennis smiled, taking a seat. "Sounds perfect. Thank you, Kamau."

A waiter arrived with a platter of sizzling grilled goat, accompanied by sides of kachumbari—a fresh tomato and onion salad—and ugali, a staple maize dish. Dennis could feel the tension in the air as they began to eat, both men aware that this was more than just a friendly lunch.

Kamau took a sip of his Tusker beer, his eyes meeting Dennis's.

"The situation in the Mara is getting worse, Dennis. Naomi will tell you more, but the poachers are becoming bolder. They're better equipped, and they seem to know our every move. It's almost as if they have inside information."

But it's not just about the poachers. The entire ecosystem is under threat—economically, politically." He paused, his expression growing more serious. "Tourism is a major part of Kenya's economy. The Mara alone brings in millions of dollars each year. However, with the rise in poaching, fewer tourists are willing to visit. It affects everyone—hotels, guides, local businesses."

Kamau set his beer down, his eyes narrowing slightly as he spoke again. "And it's not just poaching, Dennis. Have you heard about human trafficking? The drug runs?"

Dennis frowned. "Not much. Tell me."

Kamau leaned over the map, tapping a finger against the well-worn paper spread across the table. "Look, Dennis, it's not just ivory and guns. Drugs are a huge part of their network. They've got routes mapped through Kenya, like veins, which all come down to control. Entry points, exits, and even protection along the way. It's all strategically placed."

Dennis nodded, glancing at the familiar sprawl of Kenya and its neighboring countries. "Mombasa is their main anchor, right? It's the most accessible port for getting products in and out, mostly undetected."

Kamau gave a curt nod. "Right. Mombasa is critical for heroin coming in from Afghanistan and Pakistan. They hide it in shipping containers, blending it with legitimate cargo, often bound for Europe and Asia. It slips under the radar."

Dennis looked up, brows furrowed. "But how do they keep customs and law enforcement off their backs? Random checks, inspections—they must come across this stuff occasionally."

Kamau's eyes narrowed. "Bribes, mostly. And intimidation where bribes don't work. These syndicates have paid off customs officers and, occasionally, the police. They work quietly, only through trusted channels. Their shipments are controlled every step of the way. But Mombasa is just one part of the chain. Once inside Kenya, they move it out. Mombasa's like their distribution hub." Dennis leaned closer, intrigued. "What about the exit points? They aren't just dumping it all here, are they?" Kamau traced a line along the map with his finger. "No, they move it. Land routes take it into Tanzania, Uganda, and even South Sudan. They use Jomo Kenyatta International Airport in Nairobi too. They've got people there. From Nairobi, it's smuggled to Europe, the Gulf States, sometimes even down to South Africa."

Dennis crossed his arms, thoughtful. "So this isn't just an isolated network. Everything's interconnected." Kamau's expression hardened. "Exactly. And the same people

running the drugs are running everything else. Trafficking people, ivory, even weapons. They use the same routes and the same bribes. One operation props up the next. Drug money supports the arms trade, arms protect the traffickers, and human trafficking. That generates capital, and they reinvest in smuggling."

Dennis considered this. "So, if we're dismantling this, we can't just focus on one aspect. Drugs alone won't cut it."

Kamau nodded. "You're right. We must take down every operation, hit the ports and the airways, and take out their contacts in customs and the police. Without drugs to finance the syndicate, they'll lose their grip. If we can dent in Mombasa and Nairobi, it'll send a shockwave through their entire network."

Dennis clenched his jaw, feeling the weight of the mission settle in. "And we're up against people who won't hesitate to protect their operation. We'll need resources, Kamau. But if we can break their hold on Mombasa, it could cripple everything else."

Kamau's gaze was steely, his voice low and resolved.

"Exactly. We'll have to tread carefully, but we strike hard. Mombasa, Nairobi—they're the heart. We take down the heart, and the rest will crumble."

He leaned back, his tone lowering. "And then there's the influence of foreign investments. The Chinese have poured money into infrastructure projects, and with that comes a certain level of leverage. They've also created a demand for ivory and rhino horn that fuels the poaching crisis. The

government is caught between needing the investment and trying to protect what's left of our wildlife."

Dennis could see the frustration in Kamau's eyes. "And local politics?" he prompted. Kamau sighed. "Corruption runs deep. Some officials are on our side, genuinely trying to help. But others are either turning a blind eye or actively profiting from the trade. The lines are blurred, and knowing who to trust is hard. That's why people like Naomi are so important. She's not afraid to stand up to them, even if it puts her in danger."

Dennis took a moment to absorb everything Kamau had said. It was a complex web—poaching, politics, foreign influence. And in the middle of it all were people like Naomi, fighting to protect what was left of Kenya's natural heritage.

Dennis nodded, listening carefully. "Naomi seems like someone who knows what she's doing. I've heard good things about her work."

Kamau smiled with a hint of pride in his eyes. "Naomi is one of the best. She grew up near the Mara and dedicated her life to protecting it. Thank you for reaching out.

Naomi Mwangi was well-known in conservation circles. She had grown up near the Maasai Mara, and her passion for wildlife protection was rooted in her childhood. She had worked on various conservation projects across Kenya, earning a reputation for her bravery and relentless pursuit of poachers.

Dennis had read about her before arriving—her name frequently appeared in articles and reports on anti-poaching efforts. She was respected but also had powerful enemies,

especially among those who profited from the illegal wildlife trade.

Dennis had exchanged several emails with Naomi before his arrival. Their communication had been brief, but Naomi had agreed to meet him after the NGO contact introduced him.

However, she had made it clear that she was wary of outsiders. She had seen too many foreign consultants come and go, making promises they never kept. Dennis understood her hesitation, but he hoped his experience and genuine interest in her work would win her over.

Kamau sipped his Tusker beer, his eyes meeting Dennis's.

"The situation in the Mara is getting worse, Dennis. Naomi will tell you more, but the poachers are becoming bolder. They're better equipped, and they seem to know our every move. It's almost as if they have inside information."

Meeting Dr. Mugo

After lunch with Kamau, Dennis returned to the Wildlife Preservation Alliance (WPA) office. The office was busy as usual—phones ringing, staff bustling with documents, and rangers preparing for field operations. It felt like the pulse of a war room, a reminder that every day was a battle for Kenya's wildlife. It was almost 3 PM, and he was scheduled to meet with the executive director, Dr. Isaac Mugo. Dr. Mugo greeted Dennis with a firm handshake. "Dennis, I'm glad you could make it on such short notice. We need you more than ever." Dennis smiled, nodding. "It's good to be here, Doctor. What's the situation?"

Kamau was already seated, and the tension in his posture was evident. He exchanged a look with Dennis, signaling they were about to delve into something serious. Dr. Mugo began, his tone grave. "We're facing a crisis, Dennis, and it's more than just about poaching. Poaching has been a persistent threat for decades, but the fight is shifting. We're not just dealing with rogue hunters anymore. It's bigger, more organized—an evolving criminal syndicate." Dennis listened closely as Dr. Mugo continued, "The Maasai Mara, with its world-renowned wildlife, is under siege. According to the latest census, we have 2,595 elephants in the Mara ecosystem, and they are key targets for poachers. We've got around 150 KWS rangers employed in the Maasai Mara National Reserve. The authorities are hiring all the time, but it's insufficient. Most of the poaching happens in the surrounding conservancies, which comprise most of the Mara ecosystem.

In these conservancies, community rangers—local Maasai men— are the ones fighting the poachers. They're not government employed like the Kenya Wildlife Service (KWS) rangers, but they're doing the best they can with limited resources." Dennis shifted in his seat. "What exactly are these conservancies? How are they different from the National Reserve?" Dr. Mugo explained, "The Maasai Mara National Reserve is a government-protected area managed by KWS and local authorities. It's where most tourists go and where a significant portion of Kenya's conservation budget is focused. However, the conservancies are private or community-owned lands, often managed in partnership with tourism operators.

They make up 83.7% of the wildlife population in the Mara. In these conservancies, wildlife moves freely, but so do poachers. The conservancy rangers don't have the same legal authority or resources as KWS rangers in the National Reserve, but they're critical to keeping the wildlife safe." Dennis frowned, absorbing the information. "And these community rangers, they're the ones on the front lines?" Mugo nodded. "Exactly. But they're underfunded and outnumbered.

It's a dangerous job, and the poachers are becoming more ruthless. We're seeing more sophisticated operations—poachers armed with automatic weapons, working in coordinated groups. These aren't just desperate men trying to make a living anymore. The people at the top of these operations are well-connected, well-funded." Kamau jumped in, "What about the law enforcement here? Who's in charge of stopping these syndicates?" Mugo sighed, rubbing his temples. "We're working closely with the Kenya Wildlife Service, but their reach is limited, again, especially in the conservancies.

Most of the time, by the time KWS gets involved, the poachers are long gone. There are reports that some local officials are even being paid off. We've heard whispers of a big player behind all this—a figure people are starting to call The Broker. He's someone who's not just controlling poaching but running a network that includes illegal arms and other criminal enterprises. We don't know who he is yet, but we need to find out." Dr. Mugo sighed, rubbing his temples. "We're working closely with the Kenya Wildlife Service, but their reach is limited, especially in the conservancies.

Most of the time, by the time KWS gets involved, the poachers are long gone. There are reports that some local officials are even being paid off. We've heard whispers of a big player behind all this—a figure people are starting to call The Broker. He's someone who's not just controlling poaching but running a network that includes illegal arms and other criminal enterprises. We don't know who he is yet, but we need to find out." Dennis leaned back, his mind already racing with possibilities. "It sounds like this is about more than just wildlife." Dr. Mugo nodded. "It is.

The poachers may be the foot soldiers, but there's a larger network at play. The destruction of wildlife is tied to a much darker undercurrent—corruption, arms trafficking, and money laundering. The sad truth is that Kenya is also a major transit point for illegal wildlife products. Ivory and rhino horns from other African countries—Tanzania, Mozambique, and the Democratic Republic of Congo— often move through Kenya's borders to Asia. The port of Mombasa is a well-known hub for smuggling, and much of what passes through goes undetected by customs." Kamau looked uneasy. "So, we're not just fighting local poachers. We're dealing with a global operation."

Dr. Mugo nodded gravely. "Exactly. Kenya's strategic location and developed infrastructure make it a key gateway for traffickers. They take advantage of weak enforcement and sometimes complicit officials to move their goods out of Africa. Ivory, rhino horn, and pangolin scales are part of a wider trade network, and Kenya plays a crucial role in that." Dennis tapped his fingers on the table thoughtfully. "We need to map out this network. Start with the local poachers and work our way up. If we can gather enough evidence, we

might be able to cut off the head of the snake. But it won't be easy. We'll need to build trust with the community rangers, gather intel from the field, and figure out who The Broker is." Dr. Mugo leaned forward, his eyes locked on Dennis.

"Whatever you need, Dennis, we'll ensure it's in place. But be careful—these people are ruthless and won't hesitate to eliminate anyone threatening their operations. "Dennis felt the task's weight settling on his shoulders, but he was ready. "I understand the risks, Doctor. But we can't let this syndicate destroy what's left of Kenya's wildlife or its future." Dennis stood as the meeting wrapped up, exchanging a firm handshake with Dr. Mugo. The stakes were clear, and so was the path ahead. This wasn't just about saving animals but about dismantling a criminal empire, one piece at a time. Kamau walked Dennis out of the office, giving him a reassuring pat on the shoulder. "Get some rest, Dennis. Tomorrow will be a long day. We're leaving early for the Mara."

Dennis sighed, feeling the exhaustion from the long journey. The jet lag was catching up to him, and he knew rest was essential. "Thanks, Kamau. I think I'll head back to the guesthouse and turn in early." Back in his room, Dennis took a long shower, and swallowed a melatonin pill, hoping it would help him adjust to the new time zone. As he lay down, his mind drifted. He was soon pulled into a restless dream—a dream where poachers were shooting at elephants while he operated a drone, swooping down to attack them.

He saw a mother elephant fall, her eyes wide with pain as her calf stood helplessly by her side. The scene shifted

and blurred, the chaos of gunfire mixing with the cries of the animals. Dennis's heart pounded in his sleep, the dream all too vivid, a harsh reminder of the reality he was stepping into.

Chapter 2: Visiting the Mara

Leaving Nairobi

At dawn, Daniel picked Dennis up from his guesthouse, the streets of Nairobi still cloaked in the quiet stillness of early morning. The city, often buzzing with energy, was barely waking up, giving them the rare chance to see it at rest. They navigated through sleepy roads onto the Nairobi Expressway, Kenya's only toll road, and swiftly made their way out of the city limits. The expressway, a sleek contrast to Nairobi's congested streets, offered them a smooth, fast escape from the city, merging onto the A104—a divided highway that connected Nairobi to the countryside beyond.

After about an hour on the road, with daylight beginning to warm the horizon, Daniel steered off the main highway toward a small roadside "hotel" he frequented on his journeys out of the city. The term "hotel" might have suggested a place with rooms for rent, but in Kenya, these humble establishments serve as local eateries, catering to travelers with simple, satisfying food. This one was no different—just two tables and a handful of wooden chairs arranged on a small patio that opened up to the vast countryside.

Daniel grinned as they entered. "Best maandazi on this road, I swear," he said, waving at the owner, a plump, pretty Kenyan woman with an easy smile. She nodded warmly at Daniel, clearly recognizing a regular. The scent of freshly fried maandazi filled the air, the sweetness mixing with the aroma of strong, dark Kenyan coffee. They sat by the window, and Dennis noted the place's charming

simplicity—a few hand-painted signs on the walls, a modest counter, and the soft murmur of the radio playing an old Swahili tune in the background. When the maandazi arrived, golden brown and steaming, Dennis took a bite, savoring the crisp outside and soft, pillowy inside. "She's right; these might be the best I've had," he said, nodding appreciatively to Daniel.

Back on the road, they continued along the A104, which was well-maintained but busier as they moved deeper into Kenya's interior. The tall buildings of Nairobi had given way to clusters of tin-roofed shops and modest homes, interspersed with stretches of lush, green farmland. As they drove, the landscape continued to shift. They reached the intersection with the B3, a narrower, crowded highway leading towards the Maasai Mara, western Kenya, and Uganda. Here starts the Maai Mahiu Escarpment, located along the Great Rift Valley in Kenya.

The Escarpment is a dramatic geological formation that marks the descent from the highlands near Nairobi to the lower Rift Valley plains. It presents a striking view, with steep, rugged cliffs. The B3 is now a winding road that takes travelers on a steep descent to the Rift Valley floor. Daniel slowed down and stopped on the edge of the road at a lookout point overlooking the Great Rift Valley, next to kiosks selling Kenyan curios. They stepped out into the dry air and gazed across the expansive landscape.

The view from this vantage point was breathtaking— its expansive vistas over the Rift Valley, where, on clear days, one can see Lake Naivasha and beyond. It is one of the best places to truly take in the scale of the Rift Valley, an

ancient fault line running over 6,000 kilometers from the Middle East in the north to Mozambique in the south. The Rift Valley was formed by powerful tectonic forces as the Nubian and Somali plates slowly pulled apart, splitting Africa in two and leaving this colossal depression in their wake. The valley stretched endlessly, with terraced hillsides carved by local farmers and distant acacia trees, their iconic flat-topped canopies casting faint shadows on the dusty red earth.

"The Rift Valley," Daniel explained, his gaze sweeping across the horizon. "It's where Africa is slowly being torn apart, piece by piece. A million years from now, they say it'll split the continent." After a few minutes of taking in the view, they climbed back into the car and resumed their journey down the steep, narrow, busy road. This required Daniel's constant attention as huge trucks and buses jostled for space until they reached the bottom and the city of Maai Mahiu itself. The road occasionally dipped and rose over small hills, and Dennis watched as patches of farmland gave way to dry open plains, the dry grasslands spreading in endless golden waves. Eventually, they reached Narok, the last major town before the Maasai Mara.

The town had a vibrant energy, with market stalls set up along the roadside, Maasai women selling colorful beads and textiles, and herders guiding cattle and goats through the busy streets. They stopped at a small fuel station to refuel and pick up supplies, watching as locals mingled and traders called out to potential customers. Once stocked up, they pressed on, now taking the even narrower C12 road, its pavement dusted with the distinctive red earth of the savannah, requiring Daniel to slow down for livestock and

the occasional pothole. Beyond Narok, the scenery grew wilder, with giraffes grazing near the road and herds of impalas darting through the sparse underbrush.

"The paved road ends soon," Daniel noted as they neared the edge of the Maasai Mara. "After this, it's just us and the wilderness." As they approached the entrance to the Maasai Mara National Reserve, the pavement dissolved into a dirt road. The untamed beauty of the Mara stretched before them, a vast expanse of golden savannah where wildlife roamed freely. Dennis spotted zebras grazing close to the path and a group of warthogs trotting by. Their tails held high as they disappeared into the grass.

The journey had brought them from the urban sprawl of Nairobi to the wild, open plains of one of Africa's most iconic landscapes, and Dennis could feel the pull of Mara's allure settling deep within him. They were now in the reserve. The road was unpaved, and the car bumped over potholes and loose gravel. "Like I said," Daniel muttered, gripping the steering wheel tighter, "it's no highway out here." Dennis winced as they hit another deep rut. "You weren't kidding."

Dennis leaned back in his seat, watching as the savannah spread out before them, endless and untamed. "I think I'll like it here." After passing the Mara River on a metal bridge, one needs to show a passport and hotel reservation to enter the park. There was a prominent warning that wild animals could be dangerous. Daniel, however, showed them Naomi's official invitation letter, and soon, they were in the park. The Mara was home to some of the most magnificent wildlife in Africa, but it was also a battleground, and Dennis could feel the tension even as he took in the beauty around him.

Naomi's lodge was nestled on the Maasai Mara National Reserve's eastern edge near the Talek River, near

the Talek Gate, one of the main entrances to the Maasai Mara with easy access to both the central Mara and the Mara Triangle. The lodge was surrounded by acacia woodlands and open plains, offering an immersive experience in the natural environment. The lodge's proximity to the Talek River gave it a unique advantage. Guests, including Naomi, frequently witnessed wildlife visiting the river for water, especially during the dry season.

The lodge was also located close to one of the migration routes, which offers incredible opportunities to see the annual Figure 1 Wildebeest. Great Migration of wildebeests, zebras, and other herbivores and the predators that follow them. The location made it a perfect base for wildlife conservation efforts and allowed Naomi to monitor activities and poaching threats within different reserve parts. Daniel drove to the small outpost where Naomi was based. It was a modest camp with a few structures, tents, and vehicles, clearly more focused on function than comfort.

Naomi

Naomi was waiting for him when they arrived. She was tall, in her late twenties, with a determined expression and eyes that seemed to miss nothing.

She wore the standard ranger uniform—a khaki shirt, dark green cargo pants, and a hat to shield her face from the sun. She watched as Dennis stepped out of the car, her gaze appraising. "Dennis Bellamy, right?" Naomi asked, extending a firm handshake. "That's me," Dennis replied, matching her firm grip. "Naomi, it's great to meet you in person finally." Naomi gave a curt nod. "We'll see about that. Let's get started." She led him away from the vehicle,

past a few rangers busy loading supplies. Naomi was all business, and Dennis appreciated that. He had expected no warm welcome but someone who took her work seriously. They walked to a shaded area with a simple table and two folding chairs. Naomi gestured for him to sit as she unrolled a large map of the Maasai Mara, detailing the regions that were known hotspots for poaching. She wasted no time diving into the grim reality of what they were facing. "I called for help three weeks ago. In a freak attack, we had 23 elephants killed. But his week, for instance, a more normal week, we still lost five elephants," she began, her voice steady but laced with anger. "Tusks taken, bodies left to rot.

The poachers are getting bolder. They're well-equipped, and they seem to have intel on our movements. They're always one step ahead." Dennis leaned in, studying the map as Naomi pointed out locations. "Military-grade weapons, right?" Naomi glanced at him. "That's right. This isn't just some local operation. These people have backing. They're organized— more than we've ever seen before." She paused, her eyes locking on his. "And they're ruthless. They aren't afraid to kill anyone who gets in their way—rangers, locals, anyone."

Dennis nodded, absorbing the gravity of the situation. He had read about the poaching crisis, but Naomi's expression and the exhaustion in her voice made it clear just how dangerous things had become. "What about the local communities? Are they helping, or are they too scared?" Naomi sighed, leaning back in her chair. "It's complicated. There are two types of poachers we deal with. First, there are the well-organized groups, mostly Kenyans, who are after ivory and rhino horns. They're dangerous, armed with

automatic weapons, and tied into international smuggling rings. These are the ones funded by powerful syndicates, and they have deep pockets.

They come for the big prizes—elephants and rhinos, and they'll do whatever it takes to get them. They don't hesitate to shoot at rangers or anyone standing in their way." She paused before continuing, "Then, there are the bushmeat poachers. Most of them come from local villages or cross the border from Tanzania during the migration season. They're after food—wildebeests, zebras, giraffes. They hunt to feed their families, and their tools are basic—bows, arrows, and spears. Most of the time, they're just trying to survive. It's rare for them to fight back when confronted by rangers, but their methods are devastating.

They set up hundreds of snares during the day, and when they come back at night, they've often caught more than just their target. We lose lions, leopards, and elephants in those snares too." Dennis leaned forward, absorbing the grim details. "So, the ivory poachers are the real threat, but the bushmeat hunters are adding to the pressure?" Naomi nodded. "Exactly. The ivory poachers are funded and armed, and their operations are about big money. They're the ones driving the elephant and rhino populations to extinction. But the bushmeat poachers, while less organized, are still a huge problem. When the wildebeest migration crosses from Tanzania into Kenya, it's like an open invitation.

Thousands of animals and just as many poachers sneaking across the border. It's hard to catch them, especially at night." Dennis sighed, the weight of the situation settling in. "And the populations of animals just

keep dropping?" Naomi's face grew somber. "The wildebeest numbers have decreased for the past two years because of poaching. Between 40,000 and 100,000 wildebeests are killed every migration season, and when those snares are set, they don't discriminate. Lions, elephants, and even endangered species like the cheetah get caught in them. It's relentless." Dennis shook his head, thinking it through. "So, you've got the organized crime syndicates targeting the ivory and horns, and then the local poachers who are just trying to survive."

"That's right," Naomi replied. "The problem is, when you combine both types of poaching, it's overwhelming. We're outmatched."

"What about the NGOs? Are they able to support you?" Dennis asked. Naomi shrugged. "They try, but resources are limited. We're outgunned.

That's why you're here, isn't it? To try to change that balance?" Dennis met her eyes, knowing he had to be honest without giving too much away. "I'm here to help, Naomi. Not just poaching. There's a larger criminal network behind this; we're trying to figure out who's pulling the strings. We must disrupt the flow—the money and the weapons." Naomi listened, her expression softening just a fraction. She took a deep breath. "If you're serious about this, I'll take you out to see it yourself. It's one thing to talk about poaching; it's another to see the consequences up close." She stood, folding the map. "Get some rest today. We'll head out at dawn tomorrow. I'll show you what we're up against."

Dennis nodded, grateful for her willingness to let him in. He knew this was just the beginning, but it was a start.

As Naomi walked away to speak with one of her rangers, Dennis looked out across the vast savannah, the horizon stretching endlessly. The beauty of the Mara was undeniable, but so was the danger lurking within it. Tomorrow, he would see the harsh reality— the carcasses, the blood, the fear that gripped the people. And he would begin to understand just how deep this network went. He watched Naomi, her movements deliberate and confident, and he knew that if he were going to succeed in this mission, he would need her trust and her expertise. The sun was sinking lower now, casting long shadows across the camp. Dennis felt a mix of anticipation and unease. This was not just about protecting wildlife—it was about dismantling a criminal empire that stretched far beyond the Maasai Mara, and it was a mission that could get him killed.

Dennis's tent was modest, equipped with a cot, a mosquito net, a small table, and basic supplies. It was far from luxurious, but it served its purpose. As Dennis lay on the cot after dinner, staring at the canvas ceiling through the net, he thought about the challenges ahead. The Mara was beautiful, but it was also a battlefield, and tomorrow, he would be stepping right into the heart of the conflict. Evening at the Ranger's Camp That evening, after settling into the small guest tent provided for him within the rangers' camp, Dennis was invited to join the rangers for a simple meal.

The camp's communal kitchen was basic—a fire pit surrounded by a few benches and a table where the rangers

shared stories and discussed their day. Dennis ate quietly, listening to their conversations. Without understanding all the Swahili, he was still getting a sense of the camaraderie that held this group together despite the daily dangers. Naomi returned later that evening, sitting beside Dennis by the fire. She seemed to have relaxed slightly, the earlier tension replaced by a sense of camaraderie with a shared purpose. Dennis's curiosity about her grew. "Naomi, how long have you been working here?" Dennis asked, keeping his tone conversational.

Naomi glanced at him, then back at the fire. "Almost ten years now. I started when I was twenty-one, right out of university. I grew up not too far from here, in a small town near Narok. My family has always been connected to the land. My father was a herdsman and, later in life, a ranger, and my mother ran a small shop in the village. The Mara has

always felt like home to me." Dennis nodded, intrigued. "So, you have a long connection to the Mara."

Naomi smiled faintly. "Very personal. My family depended on the land, and I saw firsthand how poaching and exploitation affected not just the wildlife but also the communities around it. I wanted to do something about it, to protect what was left." She paused, her gaze growing distant. "It's not easy. I've lost friends to poachers and seen things that would make most people give up. But I can't walk away. Not now, probably not ever." Dennis could hear the conviction in her voice, the deep-rooted passion that drove her. He knew that she was the kind of ally he needed—someone who wouldn't back down, no matter the cost.

"Thank you for trusting me enough to bring me in, Naomi. I know it's not easy to let an outsider into something like this." Naomi looked at him, her eyes searching his face for a moment before she nodded. "Trust is earned, Dennis. But you're here, and you seem willing to fight. That's a start." She stood, brushing the dust from her pants. "Get some sleep. Tomorrow is going to be a long day." Dennis watched as she walked away, disappearing into the darkness of the camp.

He leaned back, staring at the stars that blanketed the night sky. He knew that with people like Naomi by his side, they would fight back and wouldn't stop until they had dismantled the network threatening the Mara.

Chapter 3: Poachers

An Abandoned Poacher's Camp

The sun had barely risen when Naomi rapped on Dennis's tent. He was already awake, dressed, wondering about the complexity of what lay ahead. He stepped outside, greeted by the cool dawn air and the sight of Naomi waiting, her eyes steely with determination.

"Ready?" she asked.

Dennis nodded. "Let's go."

Naomi led him to a jeep where a young ranger was loading supplies. They set off shortly after, the camp disappearing behind them as they drove deeper into the Maasai Mara. The sun climbed steadily, casting a golden hue over the savannah as they passed herds of zebra, gazelle, and wildebeest.

The poacher's camp was in a secluded area near the edge of a dense thicket, where the terrain made it easier for illegal activities to go unnoticed. As they approached, Dennis could see the aftermath of a recent raid—tents torn down, supplies scattered, and a sense of disorder that spoke of a hurried escape.

Naomi parked the jeep a few meters away and cut the engine. "We raided this place two nights ago," she said, her voice low. "There wasn't much time; we had to move fast when we got the tip-off. They seemed to know we were coming but left a lot behind. I thought you might want to see for yourself."

Dennis stepped out, surveying the scene. The air was still thick with the acrid smell of burnt wood, and the ground was littered with debris—discarded food, ammunition casings, and remnants of their makeshift camp. Naomi gestured for him to follow, and they carefully moved through the abandoned site, picking their way through the chaos the poachers had left.

"Most of them got away," Naomi continued in frustration. "We managed to capture two, but they haven't been talking. They were more scared of whoever is running this operation than scared of us."

Searching the Camp

Dennis knelt beside a charred tent, something shiny catching his eye. He reached out and pulled a half-burned

cell phone from beneath the ashes. It was damaged but still intact enough that there might be something recoverable. He held it up for Naomi to see.

She raised an eyebrow. "Think you can get anything off that?"

Dennis nodded. "It's worth a shot. These guys are getting bolder, but they're not always careful." He examined the phone, turning it over in his hand. "If we're lucky, we might find contacts or messages—something to give us a lead."

Naomi crossed her arms, watching him. "There's more. Over here." She led him to another area of the camp where several crates lay smashed open. Dennis could see the remnants of military-grade ammunition, and Naomi pointed to a pile of shattered wooden boxes. "These were full of rounds. Some of it's gone, but we recovered enough to know they're getting serious backing. This isn't just about ivory or rhino horn—it's bigger."

Dennis studied the crates, a frown settling on his face. He stood up, dusting off his hands. "I think it's time we bring in some extra help." Naomi tilted her head, curious. "What kind of help?"

Dennis pulled out his satellite phone, his fingers moving swiftly over the keypad. "I need to contact my office back in the U.S. We're going to need surveillance equipment— drones, cameras, anything to track these guys without them knowing we're on to them. We can't do this alone, not with what we're up against."

Naomi nodded, her expression unreadable. "You think they'll send it?"

"They'll send it," Dennis replied. "This operation goes far beyond poaching. If we can link it to arms smuggling and drug trafficking, it becomes a priority for many people back home." He pressed the call button, waiting as the phone connected. He turned away slightly, speaking in low tones as he relayed the details to his contact.

Naomi stood back, her eyes scanning the horizon as Dennis spoke. She knew the risks of involving outsiders but knew they were outmatched. Against her team, the poachers were too well-armed, too organized, and too well-informed. They needed every advantage they could get if they were going to have any hope of dismantling this network.

When Dennis ended the call, he turned back to her. "They're sending a package—drones, surveillance cameras, the works. We'll need to set it up as soon as it arrives." Naomi nodded. "Good. The sooner we get eyes on them, the better." She looked back at the camp, her gaze lingering on the destroyed crates. "We need to move fast. The longer we wait, the more time they have to regroup."

Dennis agreed. "We'll set up a perimeter once the gear arrives. In the meantime, I'll see if I can get anything off this phone." He held up the damaged device, a small glimmer of hope in an otherwise bleak situation.

Naomi gave a curt nod, her expression hardening. "Let's get back to camp. We've got work to do."

They walked back to the jeep, the task's weight settling over them. Dennis knew that this lead—however small—could be the key to unraveling the network. But he also knew they were dealing with dangerous people who would stop at nothing to protect their interests.

As they drove away from the raided camp, Dennis glanced at Naomi. She was focused on the road. He could see her exhaustion, the toll this fight had taken on her. But he also saw resilience, a resolve that would not be broken easily.

They were up against a mighty enemy with deep pockets and dangerous connections. But Dennis was determined to see this through, to help Naomi and the others fighting on the front lines. They had found their first lead, and now it was time to follow it, no matter where it took them.

Back at camp, Dennis set up his laptop and used his ever-present toolkit to access the phone. It took a few hours, but eventually, the screen flashed with success. Despite the damage, most of the phone's data had been salvaged.

Dennis opened the messaging app and began scrolling through the recovered messages. There were several exchanges with a contact listed only as 'Ziad.' The messages were written in a mix of English and Arabic, and after a few minutes of reading, Dennis realized that Ziad was a Lebanese businessman operating in Nairobi. The conversations were cryptic but spoke of 'shipments' and 'delivery times,' as well as payments being made in cash.

Beyond the exchanges with Ziad, Dennis found a dozen other contacts, all with local Kenyan numbers. These seemed to correspond to different members of the poaching

operation— most messages were logistical, detailing meeting locations, quantities of supplies, and payment arrangements. Dennis noted the numbers; with a Stingray IMSI catcher, they might be able to track these individuals in real time.

Among the more personal messages, Dennis found conversations with two women—' Amina' and 'Faith.' The messages with Amina were affectionate, detailing plans to meet in Nyawara, while those with Faith were more explicit, including compromising photos. Dennis grimaced, knowing this information could be useful but hating the invasion of privacy it represented. The conversation between the poacher and both Amina and Faith didn't contain references to any of the poacher's illegal activities. Neither girl might have been aware of the extent of the man's involvement in these crimes.

A pattern emerged—most of the contacts, including the poachers and the women, seemed to come from Kisumu and its surrounding areas in western Kenya, particularly from a small village named Nyawara. This was significant; it suggested that the operation wasn't just local to the Maasai Mara but spanned other regions, likely with different groups contributing to the larger network.

Dennis copied all the relevant data onto an encrypted drive. He knew this information could be a good start. With surveillance equipment on the way and the recovered phone data, they might finally be able to map out the connections and start putting pressure on the people behind this sprawling operation.

The Maasai Village

Dennis had seen some Maasai people gathered outside the ranger's station, their tall, lean figures adorned in the traditional red shukas. They were standing near the rangers, talking quietly amongst themselves. The Maasai were an integral part of the Mara, and their knowledge of the land was invaluable to the rangers' efforts. Naomi had mentioned earlier that some of the Maasai were informants, providing tips and information whenever they spotted poachers. It was a delicate relationship that relied on trust and mutual respect.

Dennis knew that gaining the trust of the Maasai, much like Naomi, would be crucial if he wanted to make any real progress. They were the eyes and ears of the Mara.

The Maasai village stood in a wide, open expanse of the savannah, surrounded by acacia trees and tall grasses. At the center were the enkangs—traditional Maasai huts. Made of simple, natural materials, the huts formed a circular arrangement, with the larger cattle enclosure in the middle. Each enkaji, or hut, was small, rounded, and low to the ground, built from a framework of sticks and branches carefully woven together, then coated with a tightly packed mixture of mud, cow dung, and ash. The materials gave the huts a natural brown hue, blending perfectly into the earth as if the structures had grown from the land itself. They also provide a surprising amount of insulation from the extreme temperatures of the Mara.

Inside, the space was divided into two or three small sections, the largest reserved for sleeping. A small fire pit sat in the middle of the room, the scent of wood smoke lingering faintly in the air. The floor was earthen, worn smooth from

years of use, and there were no windows, only small holes in the walls to allow some light and ventilation. The only door was a narrow, low opening that forced visitors to stoop as they entered—a sign of respect and protection from the outside world.

The entire village, with its huts and communal areas, felt intimate and timeless, as though the past and present had merged in this one place. The richness of the Maasai culture thrived within the bounds of these humble walls. Women moved gracefully between the huts, carrying water and food, while children played nearby, their laughter carrying on the wind. The village was alive with tradition, a place that pulsed with the rhythm of a way of life unchanged for centuries.

Naomi greeted one of the elders, Ole Nkoitoi, a tall Maasai man adorned with colorful beadwork who was wearing a traditional red shuka. He welcomed them with a warm smile, his eyes full of life, and spoke to Naomi in Maa, his voice resonating with the lyrical quality of his native tongue. Naomi translated for Dennis, explaining that Ole Nkoitoi was pleased to welcome them and eager to share their   culture.

It was clear from the start that Dennis was being particularly well-received because Naomi was vouching for him. The villagers trusted Naomi, and her presence was enough to assure them that Dennis was an ally who respected their culture and way of life. This kind of welcome was not something that anyone would receive—Naomi's connection to the village opened doors that would have otherwise remained closed.

They were invited into an enkaji where a group of Maasai women sat, their hands busy weaving bead necklaces, their laughter filling the small space. The cool and shaded air inside provided a welcome respite from the warm morning sun outside. Naomi introduced Dennis, and the women nodded warmly, their colorful ornaments jingling softly as they moved.

One of the women handed Naomi a strand of beads, and she smiled at Dennis as she explained the meaning behind the intricate designs. "Each color has a different significance," she said, running her fingers over the red, blue, and white beads. "Red represents bravery. Blue is for the sky, and white stands for purity—usually symbolizing milk and the connection with cattle."

Dennis marveled at the complexity of the beadwork and the rich symbolism. He watched as Naomi spoke comfortably with the villagers. Her warmth was evident in every interaction. It was clear that she had a deep respect for the Maasai and their way of life.

One of the young girls in the village caught Dennis's attention. She was a "beaded girl," Naomi explained quietly to him. In Maasai culture, a beaded girl wore specific necklaces gifted to her by a male relative or suitor, symbolizing that as a preadolescent girl, she was not yet available for marriage, but was still preparing for adulthood. The beads were a mark of honor and tradition, showcasing her family's pride and her role in the community.

After a while, Ole Nkoitoi led them to a village's central area where a group of young morans, the Maasai warriors, were gathered. They wore vibrant shukas, some holding spears as they practiced traditional dances. As they began to leap into the air, their bodies were rising effortlessly in rhythmic jumps that seemed to defy gravity. Naomi explained that these dances were part of the initiation ceremonies—a way for the warriors to demonstrate their prowess.

A Young Cattle Herder

Naomi and Dennis sat beneath the shade of a large flat-topped acacia tree, the mid-morning sun already beginning to heat the Mara. Ole Nkoitoi stood nearby, speaking animatedly with a group of elders, his tall frame towering over the others. They took some time to absorb the community's daily life before continuing their work. "Do you see that young man over there?" Naomi said,

pointing to a young Maasai boy standing among a group of cattle, his stick in hand. He wore a bright red Shuka, the traditional Maasai wrap, and his eyes were filled with excitement and nervousness. "That's Ole Nkoitoi's son, and this is the first year he's migrating with the cattle."

Dennis raised an eyebrow, intrigued. "Migrating with the cattle? You mean they move them around?"

Naomi nodded, her face softening with a smile as she looked at the boy. "Yes, it's called transhumance. The boys and men take the cattle from the village yearly and lead them to new grazing grounds. They follow the rain and search for the fresh grass that grows after the rains. It's a way of life that has been passed down through generations. They must

do it because the grass around the village is seasonal. It's a tough life—the boys camp out in the wilderness, with only the stars above them, and they must protect the cattle from predators."

"Sounds like a rite of passage," Dennis said, watching the boy rounding up a group of cattle, his movements purposeful.

"Exactly," Naomi agreed. "It's an important step towards adulthood. It teaches them responsibility, endurance, and survival skills. The young boys learn from the older men how to take care of the cattle, navigate through tough terrains, and face the dangers that come with it—whether dealing with predators or surviving the harsh environment." She paused, then added, "The cattle are everything to the Maasai. They're not just livestock but a measure of wealth, food source, and an essential part of their cultural identity." The Maasai culture intertwined with their cattle, and Dennis could see how it shaped their identity.

Naomi took a deep breath before approaching Ole Nkoitoi. She greeted him in Maa, the Maasai language, and her words were smooth and respectful. Ole Nkoitoi turned to her, his face smiling as he listened to her question. He nodded slowly, his eyes glancing towards his son.

"This is a big year for my boy," Ole Nkoitoi said in Swahili, his deep voice carrying a note of pride. "He's going on his first migration. He will be out for many weeks, maybe months. He'll follow the rains and take the cattle where there is fresh grass. It is not easy. There will be dangers—lions, leopards, even snakes. And the journey is long. They sleep

out in the open, always watching, always protecting the herd."

Naomi translated for Dennis, and Ole Nkoitoi continued, "They learn to be men on this journey. They learn what it means to care for the herd and to face danger without fear. When he returns, he will no longer be a boy. He will be a warrior—a moran."

Naomi thanked him for sharing, her voice soft with understanding. Ole Nkoitoi smiled, his eyes crinkling at the edges. "It is our way," he said simply. "Our cattle are everything to us. Without them, we are nothing. The boys must learn this, and they must learn how to be strong."

Naomi translated softly for Dennis, her eyes lingering on Ole Nkoitoi's expression. Dennis listened carefully, taking in every word. There was a weight to the elder's voice that spoke of tradition, of pride, but also of the fears that any father might have for his son.

"Is it common for the boys to go alone?" Dennis asked, his curiosity piqued. "Do they ever bring someone with them?"

Naomi posed the question to Ole Nkoitoi, and he chuckled, shaking his head. "Ah, the boys often go alone or in groups with other young men. Sometimes, when a young man has a beaded girl promised to him, she might join them for a time. She helps with the camp, cooking, and tending to whatever needs they might have, but this is rare. It is mostly the boys' journey, a time for them to grow."

Dennis nodded as Naomi explained. He could see the significance of such a journey, not just in practical terms but

in its symbolism—a young man stepping out into the wilderness, facing its challenges, and returning home changed, and matured.

A Marriage Proposal

Their conversation was interrupted by a soft voice behind them. Naomi turned, and her expression softened as she recognized Ole Nkoitoi's daughter, Leila, standing a few steps away. She was carrying a bowl of fresh milk, her eyes lowered shyly as she approached. Naomi smiled warmly, gesturing for her to come closer.

Leila was young, probably no more than eighteen, with delicate beauty and the confident grace of someone who had grown up in the savannah. Her neck was adorned with beaded necklaces that glimmered in the sunlight—red, white, and blue beads woven into intricate patterns that spoke of her family's pride and her role within the community.

"Ashe oleng," Naomi said in Maa, thanking Leila as she accepted the bowl. She noticed Leila's gaze flicking towards Dennis, curiosity evident in her eyes. Naomi exchanged a glance with Dennis, then turned back to Leila. "Would you like to join us, Leila?"

Leila hesitated, then nodded, sitting beside Naomi, her hands resting on her knees. Naomi began to speak with her in Maa, and the conversation flowed easily. Dennis watched, understanding only a few words of what they said, but he could tell from Leila's glances and the way she spoke softly that she was curious about him.

After a few moments, Naomi leaned closer to Dennis, her voice almost a whisper. "Leila wants to know about you—if you are married, to know if you have a family. She's curious about why you're here."

Dennis smiled, his eyes meeting Leila's. He spoke slowly, allowing Naomi to translate. "I am not married, and I have no family. I'm here because I am fighting the poachers."

Naomi translated, and Leila listened, her eyes widening slightly. She looked at Naomi, then back at Dennis, a hint of hesitation in her gaze. She spoke again, her voice so soft that Naomi had to lean in to hear her. Naomi's eyes widened slightly in surprise, but she nodded, turning to Dennis.

"Leila is asking something personal," Naomi said, her tone cautious. She has been watching you since we arrived. She asked me if I would ever consider marrying someone from the village—specifically, her. "

Dennis blinked, caught off guard by the question. He looked at Naomi, then at Leila, who watched him with hope and uncertainty. He could see how much courage it had taken for her to ask, and he didn't want to dismiss her feelings out of hand.

He took a deep breath, choosing his words carefully. "Please tell her that I am honored by her question. She is a wonderful, extremely pretty young woman, and I can see how much she loves her family and home. If I were to marry someone in the village, I would consider her."

Naomi nodded, translating his words with care. Leila listened, her expression unreadable at first, but then she

nodded slowly, a small smile touching her lips. She spoke again, her tone more relaxed, and Naomi smiled in response.

"She says she understands," Naomi said, turning to Dennis. "And she appreciates your honesty. She knows that things are different for you, and she hopes that, if nothing else, you will always think of her and her family as friends."

Dennis smiled, his heart warming at her response. He nodded to Leila, his voice gentle. "I will always consider you and your family my friends. And I am grateful for your kindness."

Leila's smile widened, and she bowed her head slightly before rising to her feet. She said something to Naomi, who laughed softly, and then she turned and walked away, her beaded necklaces clinking softly with each step.

Dennis looked at Naomi, raising an eyebrow. "What did she say?"

Naomi grinned. "She said that if you ever change your mind, she will be here—and she hopes that you would think she deserves a good dowry."

Dennis nodded, his gaze thoughtful but smiling. "Was she seriously asking me to marry her?"

Naomi met his eyes, her expression serious. "Marriage here is about more than just two people. It's about families, about the community. Leila's question might seem sudden to you, but to her, it's a natural part of life. She's seen her friends get married and wants to be part of that. You look honorable and kind."

Naomi smiled, her eyes sparkling. "All this sounds like Leila. She's not shy about knowing what she wants, and a good dowry would be a serious part of any Maasai marriage."

Dennis leaned forward, curious. "Tell me more about that. What does a Maasai marriage involve? Naomi leaned back, considering Dennis's curiosity about Maasai's marriage. "It's a long process," she began. "The bond isn't just made in a single ceremony. There are stages, and each one deepens the commitment between the families and the community."

She looked out toward the vast savannah as if pulling the memories from her surroundings. "First, it all starts with negotiations. The groom's family must approach the bride's family with a dowry offer, usually cattle. It's a symbol of the groom's ability to provide. The negotiation can take a long time, and the more valuable the bride is perceived, the more cattle are required. It's not unusual for a Maasai groom to offer ten or even 20 cows, sometimes more. This negotiation stage is really important because it's a sign of respect and commitment."

Dennis listened carefully, intrigued by the depth of the process. "What happens after that?"

Naomi smiled. "Once the dowry is agreed upon, there's a ceremony, but it's not a typical wedding like you'd imagine. No pastor or priest is presiding. Instead, the elders of the community are in charge. The marriage is considered official after the dowry has been delivered, but the actual living together—the final step—doesn't happen until after several rituals and blessings."

"I'm not sure how well I'd do herding cattle or living in a Maasai village."

Naomi grinned, teasing him. "Yeah, I don't see you fitting into that life too well. But if you ever change your mind, Leila's waiting."

Dennis laughed, shaking his head. "I think I'll stick to what I know.

She paused and then added, jokingly, with a wry smile, "Of course, if Leila's father asked for too many cows, you might need to start saving."

Dennis laughed. "I'll keep that in mind. What about you? How many cows do you think I would need if you were the one I choose?"

Naomi's grin softened, she blushed, and her tone turned more reflective. "If I married a foreigner, he'd have to live here also. I couldn't imagine leaving Kenya—this is home." She paused, glancing at him with a playful glint in her eye. "But if the foreigner were cute, I wouldn't mind being his girlfriend for a while. That doesn't require moving away, does it?"

Dennis laughed, shaking his head again. "You make it sound so simple."

"It is," Naomi said with a smirk. "Some things don't need to be complicated. But a real marriage? That's serious business."

The playful exchange made Dennis relax further, reminding him how grounded Naomi was in her world. He

admired how she belonged to her land and her people, even in the face of all the danger and responsibility she carried.

The conversation shifted back to lighter topics, but Dennis couldn't shake the thought of what it meant to belong to a place the way Naomi truly did.

"Thank you for helping me navigate that," Dennis said, his voice sincere. "I wouldn't have known what to say without you."

Naomi smiled, her eyes warm. "That's what I'm also here for, Dennis: to help you understand this place, these people. And maybe, along the way, help you find a place here, too."

They sat silently for a moment, and Dennis felt a sense of peace, a connection to this land and its people, which went beyond his mission.

Naomi looked thoughtful. "You know, it's amazing," she said quietly. "The way they live—so in tune with the land, with the animals. It's something you don't see much anymore. These boys grow up knowing how fragile life can be and how strong they must be to protect it."

Dennis nodded, looking back at the young Maasai boy, now leading the cattle away from the village. "It takes a lot of courage," he said. "Not many people could do what they do."

Naomi smiled, a hint of admiration in her eyes. "No, not many people could. But for the Maasai, it's just part of life. It's who they are."

The villagers invited Dennis and Naomi to share a meal—a simple but hearty dish of grilled goat meat and fresh milk. They sat together under the shade of an acacia tree, the smoke from the fire rising lazily into the sky. The sense of community was palpable; everyone shared food, stories, and laughter. Dennis started to feel what Naomi had meant when she spoke of the importance of preserving the wildlife and the culture that had thrived here for centuries.

As they finished their meal, one of the elders approached Dennis and spoke, with Naomi translating. "He says you are always welcome here as a friend," Naomi said, smiling. "They appreciate what you're doing to protect the Mara."

Dennis nodded, touched by the words. Later, when Naomi dropped him at his tent, she reminded him to sleep early since the following morning, they were going to inspect a poacher camp.

Chapter 4: A Day with Naomi

The day was clear and bright as Dennis and Naomi shared a light breakfast of coffee and mandazi (Kenyan donuts). Naomi hesitated momentarily before telling Dennis, "I have something for you." Then, she reached into her bag and pulled out a second cell phone. It was in a similar condition to the one they had found at the poachers' camp—battered and partially burned, but not beyond hope.

Dennis raised an eyebrow. "Where did you get that?"

Naomi shrugged. "One of the rangers found it during another raid. It's in a similar condition as the first one. I figured you might be able to get something out of it."

Dennis took the phone, turning it over in his hand. "I'll see what I can do. With both phones, maybe we can start connecting some dots."

Naomi leaned back, her eyes wary. "Just be careful, Dennis. These people are more connected than we realize. We need to move smart, not just fast."

Samuel

Later that morning, Dennis spent hours analyzing the recovered phones. The first had already given him some

leads, but now the pieces started to come together with the second phone. Both devices had several numbers in common—contacts that seemed to point back to Kisumu. One of these contacts, listed simply as "Musa," appeared frequently in messages about meeting locations and supply routes.

Dennis knew he needed more context, so Kamau directed him to someone at the Wildlife Preservation Alliance who might help. His contact, Samuel, was born and raised in Nyawara but had been working with the NGO for years, building relationships with local communities to support conservation efforts. Samuel knew the area well and had connections that could prove invaluable.

Dennis called the WPA office. Samuel listened carefully as Dennis explained what he had found. Samuel stayed silent, considering the implications.

"You're saying these people are from Nyawara?" Samuel asked, his voice filled with concern.

Dennis nodded. "That's what it looks like. Too many connections are pointing back there for it to be a coincidence."

"OK," Samuel answered. "Let me investigate. But it just so happens that I'm supposed to go to Nyawara tomorrow for a couple of days for a wedding. I'm from a modest family, so don't expect luxury. It'll be like camping, but you're welcome to join me. It's a good way to get to know the village. I can pick you up in Narok—it's on the way."

Dennis didn't hesitate. It was a lucky opportunity. "That's very generous of you. I'd love to go with you. Where in Narok, and at what time?"

Lunch in the Savannah

Dennis and Naomi had found the perfect spot for a quiet lunch, perched under the shade of a lone acacia tree that cast a delicate, dappled pattern on the grass below.

As they settled under the shade of the umbrella acacia, Dennis gazed up at the sprawling canopy. "This tree is something else," he said, admiring its vast, flat-topped branches that spread like open arms across the sky.

Naomi glanced up, a fond smile on her face. "It's called an umbrella acacia," she began. "They're like guardians of the savannah, spreading out to create these perfect little havens of shade." She laughed. "They're the backbone of this ecosystem. Animals rely on them for shade in the heat of the day, and their seed pods are food for everything from elephants to baboons. Even giraffes can't resist their leaves, though they have to be careful of the thorns."

Naomi nodded, looking out over the plains where more umbrella acacias dotted the landscape. "They're tough, adaptable, and crucial for everyone out here. Without them, the Mara would be a very different place."

The midday sun blazed across the Maasai Mara, but the air was cooler here, under the sparse canopy, a soft breeze rustling the leaves above. Naomi spread a blanket over the warm earth, setting out a simple meal—grilled chicken, chapati, and fresh fruit. Their vibrant colors contrasted against the green and gold of the savannah. The scent of

spiced tea wafted from a thermos, mingling with the earthy aroma of the land around them.

The endless plains stretched out before them, bathed in the shimmering heat of the afternoon. Wildebeests and zebras grazed lazily, their rhythmic movements calming against the vast backdrop. In the distance, the silhouettes of a herd of elephants moved in unison, their massive bodies almost blending with the horizon, each step a slow, deliberate rhythm.

Dennis took a deep breath. The warm breeze brushing against his skin carried with it the faint sounds of wildlife—the low hum of insects, the distant call of a bird, and the occasional rustle of dry grass as the wind swept across the savannah. He savored the calmness, a rare, untouched moment in a place often teetering between serenity and violence.

"It's so peaceful," he said, breaking the stillness, his voice low as his eyes remained fixed on the horizon. "It's hard to imagine the chaos that sometimes unfolds here."

Dennis bit into the tender grilled chicken, savoring the smoky flavor as it mixed with the soft, chewy chapati. The tea, spiced with cardamom and cloves, warmed his chest with each sip, contrasting with the cool breeze on his face. He could taste the richness of the land in every bite, as if the Mara itself had offered up this meal.

Naomi nodded, her gaze soft as it followed his. "My father used to say the Mara has a spirit of its own— sometimes it welcomes you, and sometimes it reminds you just how small you are."

Dennis looked at her, curious. "You talk about your father a lot. He must have been quite a man."

Naomi smiled, a hint of sadness touching her eyes. "He was. He was a ranger, like me. He spent his whole life protecting these lands. I think that's why I do what I do. He passed away when I was eighteen, but everything I learned, I learned from him. He always taught us to respect the animals, to see them as part of us." She looked down, tracing her fingers along the rim of her cup. "He always dreamed that one day, people would understand that the wildlife here isn't separate from us and deserves our protection."

Dennis nodded, his voice soft. "I'm sure he'd be proud of what you're doing now. You carry on his dream every day."

Naomi's smile widened, the sadness giving way to warmth. "I hope so. My mother still lives near Narok. She never quite got over losing him, but she's tough—a true fighter. My sister's there too, helping her with the farm." She paused, her eyes distant for a moment. "Sometimes I feel guilty being here instead of helping them. But they understand why I do this. My sister always says that each of us has our own path, and this is mine."

Dennis hesitated before asking gently, "What happened to him? How did he pass?"

Naomi's smile faltered briefly, her gaze dropping. "He was killed on duty. Poachers ambushed his patrol one night, thinking the rangers had cornered them. It all happened so fast…" Her voice trailed off, and for a moment, the weight of those memories hung between them. Then she shook her head, her eyes regaining their strength. "It was a long time

ago, but that's part of why I do what I do now. To carry on his fight."

"What about your sister? Does she ever want to come out here?" Dennis asked, curious.

Naomi laughed softly, shaking her head. "No, she's happy where she is. She always said one ranger in the family was enough. Besides, someone has to take care of our mother." She took a bite of her chapati, chewing thoughtfully before speaking again. "My sister has her own dreams. She wants to start a small school to help the local kids near our village. She's always been the patient one— she loves teaching. I think she'll make it happen one day."

Dennis smiled. "Sounds like you both have big hearts, expressing them differently."

Naomi looked at him, her eyes exploring his face. "What about you, Dennis? Do you ever think about the future—what you want to do when all this is over? When you won't have to fight anymore?"

Dennis hesitated, the question catching him off guard. He looked out at the savannah, the distant shapes of antelope grazing peacefully. "I don't know. I guess I never really thought that far ahead. It's always been about the next mission, the next fight. It's hard to imagine a life that isn't... like this."

Naomi reached out, her hand resting gently on his. "Maybe it's time to start imagining it. Everyone deserves a dream, Dennis. Even you."

Dennis turned to look at her, her eyes filled with warmth and sincerity. He felt a lump in his throat, and for a moment,

the weight of all his past battles seemed to lift, just slightly. "Maybe you're right," he said quietly. "Maybe it's time."

Naomi smiled, squeezing his hand before letting it go. "For now, let's just enjoy this." She gestured toward the endless plains before them, the golden grass swaying gently in the breeze, the vast sky above them. "The Mara is enough for today. Tomorrow can wait."

Dennis nodded, a sense of peace washing over him as he took in the view, the gentle rhythm of the Mara wrapping around them. For the first time in a long time, he allowed himself to believe that maybe, just maybe, there could be a future beyond the fight—a future where he could find a place like this, a place to belong.

The Great Migration

It was late afternoon in the Maasai Mara, and the reserve was alive with traveling animals. Thousands upon thousands of wildebeest stretched across the savannah, dark silhouettes against the golden grass as they moved in an unending line. The low grunts and snorts of the wildebeest filled the air, a chorus that seemed to echo across the open plains. Zebras moved alongside them, their black and white stripes stark against the setting sun.

The Great Migration was a sight to behold. Every year, between July and November, driven by ancient instincts and the need for food and water, over two million wildebeest, accompanied by hundreds of thousands of zebras and gazelles, traveled in a vast loop between the Serengeti in Tanzania and the Maasai Mara in Kenya. They crossed rivers teeming with crocodiles, navigated treacherous terrain, and

faced predators at every turn. It was the largest terrestrial migration on Earth.

The migration followed the rains, and the herds moved in search of fresh grazing lands. Naomi pointed out the young calves, barely a few weeks old, struggling to keep up with their mothers, and the ever-watchful predators—lions, cheetahs, and hyenas—waiting for an opportunity to strike.

Naomi had told Dennis about it before, but nothing she said could have prepared him for the real thing. "It's hard to believe that all of this is happening right in front of us," Dennis said quietly, his eyes wide as he watched the great herd. He could see them as far as the horizon, a river of life, following the instinct that had driven their kind for millennia.

Naomi, sitting beside him in the open-top jeep, smiled. "This is the Mara. It's one of the last places on Earth where you can still witness something so raw, so untouched. The migration is about survival, life, and death—and it's all right here, in front of us."

She turned to Dennis, her eyes catching the light of the fading sun. It was a beautiful moment—the sky painted in hues of orange and pink, the acacia trees casting long shadows over the plains. Naomi watched him take it all in, and she felt a sense of pride in showing him her world, a world that meant everything to her.

They drove back slowly as the sun dipped below the horizon, bathing the Mara in a soft, warm glow. As the sun disappeared, the air grew cooler, and Dennis could hear the distant calls of lions as they woke to begin their nocturnal hunt. Naomi pointed out a small herd of elephants, their

massive forms almost ghostly in the twilight, moving with a grace that seemed impossible for creatures so large.

Dennis was captivated, and he found himself glancing at Naomi, seeing how her eyes shone as she spoke about the animals she so deeply loved.

Evening with Naomi

They returned to the ranger's station, where Naomi had a small bungalow. It was simple but cozy—a place she had made her own, decorated with colorful textiles and a few photographs of her family and the Mara itself. Naomi led Dennis inside, her smile playful. "I have a bottle of wine and one of gin," she said, opening a small cupboard and pulling out the bottles along with some snacks. "After a day like today, we've earned it."

Dennis laughed, nodding. "I won't argue with that."

Naomi excused herself. A few minutes later, she returned in a striking red African dress, a warm smile lighting up her beautiful face. At thirty, she was tall and lean, with a fit, muscular build honed by years of working in the Mara. The dress, vibrant against her skin, flowed around her like a second skin, hugging her body in all the right places and accentuating her graceful curves and toned arms.

Maasai beads adorned her neck and wrists, adding elegance to her athletic beauty. She moved with easy confidence, her dark eyes playful as she set the glasses down.

Naomi poured each of them a generous glass of wine, settling on the small couch beside Dennis. As she leaned back, her shoulder brushed his, her smile widening with a hint of mischief. "I hope I'm not making you miss the younger, prettier Leila," she teased, her eyes twinkling with a glint of humor.

Dennis laughed, shaking his head. "Leila has nothing on you," he replied warmly.

"Good answer," she chuckled, clinking her glass with his. "You're sharp, Dennis. But seriously, thank you for being here," she said, her voice softening as her eyes lingered on his. "For caring enough to come, for looking past the danger and seeing the people and animals here. It's rare to find someone who understands."

The night was quiet, and the sounds of the Mara drifted in through the open window—the distant roar of a lion, the chirping of crickets, and the rustle of the wind through the grass. Naomi leaned back, her shoulders relaxing as she sipped her drink.

"I don't think I've felt this relaxed in a long time," she said softly. She turned her head to look at Dennis, her eyes warm. "Thank you for coming here, Dennis. For caring about all of this—about the animals, the people. It means a lot."

Dennis met her gaze, his expression serious. "This place—it's incredible. It deserves to be protected." Naomi

smiled, a flush spreading across her cheeks, though she wasn't sure whether it was the wine or Dennis's words. She leaned closer, her eyes searching his. "You're different, Dennis. You're not like the others who come through here. You actually see what's happening and are willing to do something about it."

Dennis reached out, brushing a strand of hair from her face, his fingers lingering against her cheek. "I think I've found something worth fighting for," he said softly.

Their eyes met, and in that moment, the rest of the world seemed to fade away. Naomi leaned in, her lips brushing against his, tentative at first. Then, as Dennis responded, the kiss deepened, the intensity between them growing. She felt herself relax even further, the tension of the past days melting away as she let herself be vulnerable and let herself feel.

They pulled apart, both breathless, and Naomi looked at Dennis, her eyes filled with something beyond gratitude or admiration. There was a spark, a connection that had grown between them, forged in the fire of everything they had experienced together. She took his hand, standing up and leading him towards her bedroom, her heart pounding in her chest.

"Stay with me tonight," she whispered, her voice barely audible over the sounds of the Mara outside.

Dennis nodded, his gaze never leaving hers. He followed her, the door closing softly behind them.

She started undoing his shirt's buttons one by one, revealing more of his smooth skin underneath. As she

pushed the shirt off his shoulders, she ran her fingers across his chest and down to his stomach, feeling the hard muscles tighten beneath her touch.

With a moan, Dennis pulled Naomi closer to him. She could feel his heart beating rapidly against her chest as he trailed kisses down her neck and along her collarbone. Her breath hitched as he reached behind her to unclasp her bra, letting it fall to the ground.

Soon, they were lying down naked on the bed together, their bodies intertwined in a passionate embrace.

Dennis's lips moved slowly and deliberately across Naomi's skin—her neck, collarbone, breasts—and she returned each kiss with equal fervor, leaving a trail of goosebumps in their wake. His eyes were dark with desire, and his muscles tensed with every touch. Naomi's breasts were full and firm, the hard nipples with a peppery taste in Dennis's mouth.

Her hands moved eagerly across Dennis' toned body, tracing the curves and angles of his back, shoulders, stomach, and buttocks. Their skin glistened with a sheen of sweat, lit up by the soft glow of the moonlight coming through the window.

The scent of their skin mingled, a combination of sweat and desire filling the air around them, overpowering Naomi's perfume's subtle floral fragrance.

She felt herself grow more and more aroused with every touch.

With an almost primal instinct, Naomi's hips swayed as she climbed on top of Dennis and slowly impaled herself on

his erect virility. Her skin was glistening with a thin sheen of sweat under the moonlight. Her hair cascades down her back, framing her flushed face with wild tendrils.

They both gasped at the sensation—the intimate connection sending shivers through their bodies.

Naomi's hands rested on Dennis's chest, feeling his heart racing beneath her fingertips. As she moved her hips, she could feel every inch of him inside, igniting a fire within her.

Their bodies moved in a dance of desire, a symphony of curves and angles, a tangle of limbs and moans. At that moment, they were nothing but a carnal manifestation of love and lust. And as they gasped and moaned in unison, the room filled with the musky scent of passion and the sound of their hearts beating as one.

The night unfolded as the Mara fauna continued its endless dance just beyond the walls of the small bungalow.

Chapter 5: The Poachers' Village

Meeting Samuel

Dennis rose early, his mind already on the day ahead. He was bound for Samuel's village, Nyawara, where he would finally see the poachers in their natural environment.

He turned, glancing back toward the lodge where Naomi still slept—the night had been something different, something peaceful. They had talked until late, lying in the dark with nothing but the night sounds outside. It felt like the world had pulled them into a quiet pocket where time moved slower, softer. But now, the day was here, and there were things to do.

A safari vehicle was waiting for him just outside the Rangers Camp, ready to take him on the first leg of the journey: 90 minutes to Narok.

The safari vehicle rumbled to life, and Dennis settled in as the driver expertly navigated the dirt roads. The early light cast long shadows across the open plains, where herds of cattle grazed, accompanied by the occasional acacia tree dotting the horizon like nature's sentries. The vehicle moved along the dirt road, kicking up small clouds of dust that floated in the warm morning air. Slowly, the landscape began to transform from the arid, rugged expanses of the Mara to the more fertile lands near Narok.

They reached Narok by mid-morning, and Dennis stepped out, stretching his legs as he waited for Samuel. He found a small, bustling café along the main street where they

had agreed to meet. It was a modest place with a few tables and locals stopping by for their morning tea and mandazi. The scent of frying dough and fresh-brewed coffee filled the air.

Just after 10 a.m., Samuel appeared, greeting Dennis with a broad smile and a firm handshake. They ordered a light breakfast—steaming mugs of chai and plates of chapati with eggs. As they ate, they discussed the plan for the day, Samuel giving Dennis an outline of what he might expect in Nyawara.

With breakfast finished, they climbed into Samuel's truck, and prepared for the longer stretch of the journey. Samuel navigated the narrow, often bumpy road that led from Narok to Nyawara, his hands steady on the wheel as they passed expansive farmlands. Villages dotted the landscape, each a small hub of activity, with children playing near the roadside and farmers working in fields filled with maize and beans. Along the way, Samuel shared stories of his family and the local customs, helping Dennis feel more at ease with the unfamiliar surroundings.

Suddenly, Samuel slowed down, his eyes narrowing as a group of uniformed police officers appeared in the distance, standing next to their vehicle parked at the side of the road. A checkpoint.

"Here we go," Samuel muttered under his breath, his grip tightening on the steering wheel.

"What's going on?" Dennis asked, noticing Samuel's sudden shift in demeanor.

Samuel sighed. "Routine stop. Or what they call 'routine.'"

As they approached, one of the officers stepped forward, raising his hand to signal them to pull over. Samuel eased the car to a stop, keeping his expression neutral. The officer strolled over to Samuel's window, his face impassive but his eyes betraying a practiced calculation. Dennis could feel the tension thickening in the car.

The officer leaned down, his hands resting casually on the door. "Good afternoon. Everything in order today?" His voice carried a detached politeness, the kind that hinted at something more than just routine.

Samuel gave a tight smile. "Afternoon, officer. Yes, everything's fine."

The officer glanced at the windshield, eyeing the sticker with a raised eyebrow. He then walked around the car slowly, inspecting it with exaggerated care, as though he were looking for something specific. After a beat, he returned to Samuel's window.

"Your left rear light," the officer said, his voice taking on a more assertive tone. "Looks like it's... damaged. Might have to write you up for that."

Samuel didn't flinch. He knew the game. The light was perfectly fine—until it wasn't. He kept his tone calm, though Dennis could see the frustration lurking behind his eyes.

"Oh? It was working when we left Nairobi. I doubt it's broken now."

The officer shrugged, his expression blank. "Well, we'll have to see about that." He stepped back, motioning to one of his colleagues. "Check it."

Dennis turned slightly, watching as the second officer made his way to the back of the car. He crouched, giving the rear light a cursory glance, before standing up with a theatrical sigh.

"It's out," he called out, the verdict final.

Samuel sighed quietly. He knew what would come next. He could challenge it, refuse to pay, and they'd break the light themselves. That would mean a ticket, maybe even a trip to the police station, and hours wasted arguing over something trivial.

The officer at the window leaned in again, his tone softening. "Of course, we can handle this without too much trouble. You know how it is. Just something small to make it go away."

Samuel didn't respond right away. The request hung in the air, familiar but no less infuriating. Finally, he reached into his pocket and pulled out 200 shillings—a crisp note (around $1.60). He handed it over wordlessly.

The officer pocketed it with the same casualness he'd used when stopping them, as though this were simply part of the day's work. "Alright then," he said with a nod. "All sorted. Safe journey, and drive carefully."

Dennis watched in silence as the officers waved them on, the interaction over in less than five minutes. Samuel pulled the car back onto the road, his face set in a mask of resignation.

"That's it?" Dennis asked, the disbelief clear in his voice.

"That's it," Samuel replied, his voice low. "If I hadn't paid, they might've smashed the light themselves and written me a ticket for it. Then we'd be stuck dealing with the police for the rest of the day."

Dennis frowned, shaking his head. "Is this normal?"

Samuel chuckled, but there was no humor in it. "Unfortunately, yeah. It's part of the game out here. You either pay a small bribe and keep moving, or you fight it and lose more than just money. Going across the country, you might get stopped a dozen times."

Dennis looked out at the road ahead, the beauty of the landscape now tainted by the reality of what he'd just witnessed. The horizon stretched out before them, but the undercurrent of corruption lingered in the air, an unspoken part of the journey.

"I still don't quite understand why you're risking so much to help with this, Samuel. I know your role with the NGO is more about community work. It would be easy enough to stay out of all this," Dennis said.

Samuel smiled faintly. "It would. But 'staying out' doesn't really solve anything, does it? I've spent my whole life in this village, watching the land change, watching people change. Back then, the land could sustain us, and we respected wildlife. Now, the struggle just to get by is turning everything upside down."

"Still, putting yourself on the line—there's a lot at stake," Dennis commented.

Samuel paused, his expression serious. "This isn't just about me or the wildlife, Dennis. It's about the kids, the people here. I can't stand by and let them grow up thinking that helping poachers or turning a blind eye is just how we survive. They need to see that there's a choice. Even if it brings trouble, I'd rather show them it's worth doing what is right."

They drove for hours, occasionally passing small clusters of homes made from mud and sticks, with children playing in the dirt, waving excitedly as the Land Cruiser rumbled by.

In mid-afternoon, they arrived in Kisumu, along the shores of Lake Victoria. The city's colonial architecture mixed with modern buildings, and its streets pulsed with energy. Matatus weaved through traffic, and vendors called out from roadside stalls, selling everything from fresh tilapia to colorful kitenge fabrics. The air was thick with the scent of the lake, earthy and warm, mingling with the smoke of roasting maize and the distant hum of boda bodas zipping through the city.

The final segment, the road from Kisumu to Nyawara, was unpaved, dusty, and filled with potholes. Dennis had experienced rough terrain before, but these roads tested the vehicle's limits and his patience.

As they approached the village, the road led to a narrow dirt path bordered by dense scrub. Samuel turned the vehicle onto the path, and they bumped along until a cluster of simple homes appeared ahead. The houses were modest, their walls made of mud and cow dung, with thatched roofs made from reeds and grass. Some more prosperous families

had constructed homes from corrugated iron sheets, their rusted exteriors shining in the midday sun.

They parked near Samuel's family home, a modest mud-walled structure that looked like it had been standing for decades. His mother was the first to greet them, her face lighting up at the sight of her son. She hugged him tight and then turned to Dennis with a welcoming smile. She spoke in Swahili, her voice warm: "Karibu nyumbani kwetu. Wewe ni kama familia hapa!"

Samuel translated: "Welcome to our home. You are like family here."

Dennis nodded, returning the smile. "Asante. Ni heshima kuwa hapa." ("Thank you. It's an honor to be here.")

Samuel looked at Dennis, surprised. "Do you speak Swahili?"

Dennis gave an awkward smile. "Naongea kidogo tu." ("I speak just a few words.")

Inside, the house was divided into a few small rooms. The main living area was sparsely furnished, with a couple of wooden chairs and a low table. The walls were bare except for a few family photographs. Dennis noted the simplicity—the stark difference between life here and the chaos of Nairobi or Mombasa.

Figure 1 A Charcoal Jiko

Samuel's mother showed Dennis to the small kitchen, where she had prepared food over a charcoal jiko. These ever-present jikos all over Kenya are small barbecue-like ceramic contraptions on metal feet where the cook burns charcoal. The kitchen was separate from the main house, an open-sided shelter with a roof to keep out the rain. The scent of roasting maize filled the air, mixing with the smell of smoke from the charcoal. A few chickens wandered about, pecking at the ground for stray grains.

Samuel pointed out that the bathroom was a small outhouse a short distance from the main house. It was a simple pit latrine with no running water. Dennis wasn't fazed—he'd seen similar setups in other parts of the world. Still, he appreciated Samuel's warning to "watch for snakes at night."

The village was small, just a handful of homes clustered together, with larger homesteads spread across the countryside. Life here was slow and deliberate. It was clear that jobs were scarce and that other opportunities to make money were even scarcer. Most men worked on the farms or raised livestock, barely making enough to sustain their families. It was easy to see why some might be tempted by the promise of quick money, even if it meant stepping into the world of poaching.

The Wedding

That afternoon, Samuel took Dennis to the wedding, which had transformed the village of Nyawara into a vibrant celebration. The entire community seemed to have gathered for the event, and the air was thick with excitement and the scent of roasting meats. A large tent, made of bright fabric and supported by wooden poles, had been erected in the center of an open space, and everywhere Dennis looked, people were laughing, talking, and enjoying the occasion.

A group of musicians sat under a smaller tent, playing traditional songs on drums, kalimbas, and homemade string instruments. The rhythmic beats echoed through the village, a heartbeat of celebration that filled the air. Children, dressed in their best clothes, ran between the tables, laughing and playing, their feet kicking up small clouds of dust. Women moved gracefully between guests, balancing large trays piled high with steaming bowls of food—fragrant stews, roasted meats sizzling with spices, and golden-brown **chapati**, all set on long tables covered with vibrant kitenge cloths in swirling patterns of reds, blues, and yellows.

Samuel introduced Dennis to his extended family, explaining in the local dialect that Dennis was an old friend visiting from Nairobi. Dennis shook hands, smiling politely as he tried to blend into the crowd. The village elders greeted him warmly, their hands strong and calloused, and Dennis could feel their curiosity and their acceptance.

The ceremony began with a series of blessings from the village elders. The bride and groom stood beneath a canopy of woven banana leaves and flowers, both beaming with happiness. The bride wore a kanga wrapped around her in

vibrant oranges and reds, the fabric tied at her shoulder and flowing down to her feet. Her head was adorned with a delicate crown of beaded jewelry, and her wrists jingled with rows of colorful bracelets. The groom was equally striking, wearing a traditional shuka, a Maasai-inspired cloth in deep reds, draped over his shoulder, with intricate beadwork on his chest and arms, symbolizing his status and strength.

The families had agreed on the dowry weeks before the wedding—cattle, goats, and a small sum of money. The formal exchange had taken place in a gathering of elders, and now, with that behind them, the families were ready to celebrate the union of the bride and groom.

The ceremony was a mix of solemn tradition and joyous celebration. The elders, in deep and rhythmic voices, recited blessings for the couple, calling on the ancestors to protect them and ensure a fruitful marriage. At intervals, the crowd would break into applause or chant, the sound rising in unison as the community celebrated the union.

As the couple exchanged vows, Dennis couldn't help but admire the simplicity and beauty of the ritual. There were no grand speeches or complicated ceremonies—just the heartfelt blessings of the community, the laughter of children, and the warmth of family. The elders placed their hands on the couple's heads, a gesture of blessing and protection, while the crowd clapped and cheered.

After the formalities, the dancing began. Women in brightly colored kikoy wraps and beaded necklaces led the way, their bodies swaying gracefully to the beat of the drums. The men followed, clapping and chanting, their movements strong and rhythmic. The bride and groom

joined in, their faces alight with joy as they danced in the center of the circle, surrounded by the love of their families and friends.

Dennis stood to the side, watching the celebration unfold. He felt a warmth spreading through him—not just from the heat of the day, but from the sense of community, the closeness that tied everyone together. Even as an outsider, he could feel the power of the moment, the connection that came from shared traditions, from being part of something greater than oneself.

The feast began in earnest as the sun began to set, casting a golden light over the village. Guests filled their plates with rich stews, tender meat, and soft chapati while children ran around with sticky hands, sneaking extra treats from the dessert table. Laughter echoed through the evening air, and the drums continued to beat, the heart of the celebration carrying on into the night.

Dennis sat with Samuel's family, enjoying the meal and the conversation. He looked around at the faces of the villagers— some old and weathered, others young and full of life—and felt grateful to have witnessed something so real, so deeply rooted in tradition and community.

Later, Samuel pulled Dennis aside, pointing to a group of men standing near the edge of the tent, drinks in hand. "Those two," Samuel said quietly, nodding towards a couple of men in worn clothes, their faces weathered from the sun. "Their names were in the list of contacts from the phones. Locals. They don't have steady jobs; they just do odd work here and there. Sometimes, they disappear for a few days—

always come back with money. Too much money for farm labor."

Dennis studied the men, noting their uneasy expressions and how they kept glancing around as if checking to see who was watching. Samuel continued, his voice low. "I'll introduce you, but be careful. They're suspicious of strangers, and they know me too well. I'll try to get them talking, but it's better if you stay in the background."

Dennis nodded. "I understand. Just see what you can find out."

They approached the men, Samuel greeting them warmly. There was a brief moment of tension as they eyed Dennis, but Samuel quickly explained that he was family, here for the wedding. The men relaxed slightly, and they exchanged pleasantries. Dennis hung back, listening as Samuel steered the conversation towards work, asking how they managed and if they had found any new opportunities.

One of the men, a tall, wiry fellow named Juma, shrugged, his expression hardening. "No work here, you know that, Samuel. Just the same old struggles. We have to do what we can to get by."

Samuel nodded sympathetically. "I heard some of the guys were making good money recently. Maybe doing some work outside the village?"

Juma glanced at his companion, then back at Samuel, his eyes narrowing. "Who told you that? No work around here pays well—unless you're willing to take risks."

Samuel smiled, trying to keep the mood light. "Just curious, that's all. You know me—I always keep my ears open."

Juma snorted, taking a sip of his drink. "Well, some risks are worth it. If you have the guts."

The music grew louder as the night wore on, and the dancing became more animated. Laughter and chatter filled the air, and Dennis found himself drawn into the energy of the celebration. Several young women dressed in brightly colored dresses approached him, their eyes sparkling with curiosity and mischief. They gathered around him, their laughter echoing as they flirted and teased.

"You are not from here, are you?" one of the girls asked, her voice laced with curiosity. She was petite, her hair tied back in braids, her smile infectious.

Dennis chuckled, shaking his head. "No, just visiting with Samuel. I'm here for the wedding."

One of the girls, a beautiful young woman named Amina, stepped forward, her smile wide. "Hello, Dennis, right? Samuel's friend from Nairobi? I am Amina."

Dennis smiled, nodding. "That's right. It's nice to meet you, Amina."

Amina laughed, her friends nudging her forward as if daring her to keep the conversation going. "You must think our village is very small compared to Nairobi. Do you like it here?"

Dennis could see the curiosity in their eyes. He chuckled, keeping his tone light. "It's different, yes, but in a good way. Being here is something very special—everyone is so welcoming."

The others giggled, and Dennis relaxed. The warmth of their company made him forget, if only for a moment, the reason he was really here. Another girl, bolder than Amina, stepped up and leaned closer to Dennis. "You should stay longer. We can show you around and make sure you have a good time."

The flirtation was evident, and Dennis felt a mix of amusement and awkwardness. He had been in situations like this before—though rarely in the middle of a remote village wedding. He smiled politely, trying to navigate the attention without offending anyone. "I appreciate that. Samuel's

already been a great guide, but I'm sure there's much more to see."

The girls laughed, and one of them playfully touched Dennis's arm. "Samuel might know the village, but we know all the secrets. You should let us show you."

One of the younger girls leaned closer, her voice barely above a whisper. "So, will you dance with us, mzungu?" She used the Swahili word for "foreigner," but her tone was playful.

Dennis laughed, raising his hands in mock surrender. "All right, all right. But I'll warn you, I'm not the best dancer."

The girls pulled him towards the makeshift dance floor, the crowd parting slightly to let them through. Watching from the sidelines, Samuel gave him a knowing smile and a thumbs-up. The music picked up, the rhythm pulsing, and Dennis started moving to the beat, the girls surrounding him, their laughter infectious. For a brief moment, he was just a guest at a wedding, caught up in the joy of the celebration.

As the night wore on, the girls continued to flirt, their teasing becoming more direct. One of them, the tall girl with striking features, stayed close to Dennis, her hand occasionally brushing his arm. She smiled up at him, her eyes filled with curiosity. "You know, it's not often we get someone like you here," she said, her voice soft. "Maybe you should stay a little longer."

Dennis met her gaze, her meaning clear. He hesitated for a moment, the warmth of her presence tempting him. But he knew why he was here and the dangers ahead. He gave

her a gentle smile, shaking his head. "I'd love to, but I have to leave soon. Maybe another time."

"Haha, Faith, he is not interested..." exclaimed Amina. This was when Dennis remembered the sweet Amina and the explicit pictures of Faith that were in the messages of the phone he had recovered from the poacher camp.

Faith pouted playfully but then smiled, nodding. "Another time, then. But you should know, we don't forget easily here."

Samuel, who had been watching from a few steps away, walked over, grinning. He put an arm around Dennis's shoulders, his voice teasing. "Be careful, Dennis. These girls will have you married off before you even know what's happening."

The girls burst into laughter, and Amina blushed, swatting at Samuel playfully. "We're just being friendly, Samuel!"

Dennis laughed along with them, shaking his head. The attention was flattering, but he knew he had to keep his focus on why he was really there. The girls eventually drifted away as the night wore on, leaving Dennis with Samuel.

Samuel gave him a knowing look. "You handled that well. I thought you might take one of them up on their offer."

"It looks like you've made quite an impression," Samuel said, his eyes twinkling.

Dennis shrugged, a grin tugging at his lips. "They're charming, I'll give them that. But I've got enough complications as it is."

Samuel laughed, clapping Dennis on the shoulder. "Wise choice, my friend, in general... But for tonight, enjoy yourself. These moments are rare."

Dennis nodded, looking out at the crowd, the music, the laughter. It was a fleeting moment of peace in a world filled with danger and uncertainty, and he intended to make the most of it. The work would still be there in the morning, but for now, he allowed himself to relax, if only just a little.

Dennis could feel the tension in the air, the unspoken understanding that Juma was talking about more than just farm work. He watched Samuel nod, his expression unreadable, before changing the subject to something lighter. The conversation drifted back to the wedding, and the men seemed to relax again, their guard lowering slightly.

Later that evening, as they walked back to Samuel's family home, Dennis turned to him. "You did well, Samuel. It's clear they're involved in something—they didn't deny it. We'll need to keep digging, but this was a good start."

Samuel nodded, his face troubled. "It's hard, Dennis. These are my people. They're good men, but they're desperate. There's no work, no way out of poverty. When someone offers money, even if it means breaking the law, they take it. They have families to feed."

Dennis placed a hand on Samuel's shoulder, understanding the weight of what he was saying. "We'll find a way to help them. But first, we need to stop the people exploiting them—the ones at the top."

Samuel nodded, his eyes reflecting a mix of determination and sadness. They continued walking in

silence, the sounds of the village quieting as night fell, the stars beginning to emerge in the darkening sky. This place, so far removed from the power struggles of the city, was where the real victims of poaching lived—people with no choices, caught in the crossfire of greed and survival.

The Shopkeeper

The general store in the village was a modest affair, a small rectangular building with wooden walls that had endured years of harsh weather. Its tin roof gleamed dully under the sun, and the only sign it was a shop was a faded hand-painted board above the entrance, reading *"Kijiji Market."* The store was the village's lifeblood, a place where people gathered not just to buy essentials but also to catch up on the latest news and gossip.

Inside, the store was dimly lit, with shelves of roughly cut wood sagging under the weight of goods. There was a little bit of everything—bags of maize flour, sugar, salt, cooking oil, and tins of sardines. A few bars of soap, some matches, and small bags of washing powder lined another shelf. At the back of the shop, a glass counter displayed a collection of colorful sweets, phone credit cards, and packets of cheap cigarettes. On a nearby shelf, containers filled with dried beans, lentils, and rice stood next to dusty bottles of Coca-Cola. The shop also carried basic medical supplies, second-hand clothing, and a collection of plastic sandals that hung from a nail on the wall.

Dennis stood near the counter, chatting with the shopkeeper, a middle-aged man named Kassim. Kassim had a kind face with deep lines that spoke of a lifetime of laughter and struggle. Always ready with a smile, he had a

sharp wit and a balanced perspective on the community, which Dennis valued.

"These men who go south to poach—they are not all bad people," Kassim said, his eyes meeting Dennis's as he handed over a packet of tea leaves. "Some are just desperate. They have families and children to feed. The farms don't give much, there are hardly any jobs here, and there is no money. So, when someone comes along and offers them many shillings, they take it. What else can they do?"

Dennis nodded, listening carefully. He understood the hardships these people faced, but hearing them from Kassim made it all the more real. "But not all of them are the same," Dennis said, prompting Kassim to elaborate.

Kassim sighed, leaning back against the counter. "No, they're not. Some of them are rough, dangerous men. They enjoy the thrill, the money, the power it gives them. They come back to the village and act like kings. But others hate what they do. They go because they have no choice. And then there are the women—the wives and girlfriends who wait for them to return. You see them, hoping that this time their men will return with money, that maybe this will be the last time they have to go."

He shook his head slowly, a sad look crossing his face. "The worst part is the waiting. You can see it in their eyes—the worry, the fear that their husbands or sons won't return one day. Some of these men go south and disappear. Maybe they've been killed by rangers or by other poachers. And the women are left here with nothing but questions."

Dennis could hear the weariness in Kassim's voice. The village was a place caught between desperation and survival,

where every decision was a gamble. Kassim's words painted a vivid picture of the complexities these families faced—not a world of simple right and wrong, but one filled with shades of gray.

"I suppose it's hard to judge when you're not in their shoes," Dennis said quietly, glancing around the shop. The shelves filled with basic goods were a testament to how little these people had and how much they were willing to risk for a chance at a better life.

Kassim nodded. "That's right, my friend. It's easy to say it's wrong, but when you have mouths to feed and no way to do it, right and wrong start to look very different." He gave Dennis a small, sad smile. "But you—you are different. You are trying to help, and you have my respect. Just remember, these men are not all your enemies. Some of them are just fathers and brothers trying to survive."

Dennis left the store with a heavy heart, the weight of Kassim's words lingering in his mind. He knew his mission was important—stopping poaching would help protect the wildlife and the people who depended on it. But it was also clear that the story was more complicated than he had imagined. Behind every poacher was a family, a village, a story of desperation and survival. And that made the fight all the more difficult—and all the more necessary.

Questioning the poachers

The morning after the wedding, Dennis and Samuel sat on wooden stools in the shade of a tree behind Samuel's family home. The air was cool, the early sun still low in the sky, casting a golden light over the village. Dennis leaned forward, his voice low. "Do you think you can talk to Juma

and his friend again? Ask them where someone could find work like theirs?"

Samuel nodded thoughtfully, his expression tense. "I can try. But they are not going to be eager to share that kind of information. They know it's risky, especially with a stranger around."

Dennis gave a small smile, his voice filled with encouragement. "If anyone can get them talking, it's you, Samuel. Just tell them I'm here to help your family, nothing more. We need to know who's running this operation. It could give us our next lead."

Samuel sighed, rubbing his forehead as he considered the request. Finally, he nodded. "I'll see what I can do. Just keep out of sight. They still don't trust you."

Two hours later, Samuel spotted Juma and his companion sitting near the village's communal water point, talking in low voices. He approached them slowly, greeting them with a warm smile. The men seemed more relaxed than they had the previous evening; their guards lowered slightly in the comfort of familiar surroundings.

"Juma, I need to ask you something," Samuel began, keeping his tone casual. "You mentioned yesterday that some people were making good money. I need to know—where can someone go if they want to find work like that? Times are tough, and I could use the extra cash."

Juma looked up, his eyes narrowing suspiciously. "Samuel, why are you asking this? You know it's dangerous. It's not the kind of work you should get involved in."

Samuel forced a smile, shrugging. "I know, but you said it yourself—sometimes the risks are worth it. I have a family to care for, and the farm alone isn't enough. If you know someone, tell me how to reach them."

Juma exchanged a long look with his companion, who shifted uncomfortably, glancing around to ensure no one else was listening. Finally, Juma leaned closer, his voice barely a whisper. "We don't give out names just like that. But maybe someone will reach out to you if they need people. It doesn't work the other way around. You just have to be ready."

Samuel frowned, pressing gently. "But there must be someone running things to talk to if you want in. How do they know who to call?"

Juma hesitated, then sighed, his voice resigned. "All right, all right. The one who makes the calls—his name's Mrefu. But don't say I told you. He decides who gets in and who stays out. If he wants you, he'll find you."

Samuel nodded, trying to hide his surprise. He recognized the name instantly—it was in the half-burnt contact list from the phone Dennis had recovered. He forced himself to stay calm, giving Juma a grateful nod. "Thanks, Juma. I owe you one."

Juma shook his head, his face serious. "Just be careful, Samuel. It's been getting much worse in the last few years. This isn't something you can back out of once you're in."

Samuel patted his shoulder, giving a reassuring smile. "I know what I'm doing. Thanks, my friend."

As Samuel walked back to the family home, his heart pounded with a mix of excitement and fear. He had gotten

the name—Mrefu, the man who held the key to the poaching network. He glanced toward Dennis, who was waiting in the shade, and he knew this was the lead they had been hoping for. Now, it was up to Dennis to decide the next move.

Mrefu

Dennis sat on the edge of Samuel's cot, the early morning sunlight filtering through the modest room's small window. The air was filled with anticipation as Samuel closed the door behind him, his expression a mixture of pride and concern. He had just returned from meeting Juma, and Dennis could tell by the look on his face that he had news.

"I got a name," Samuel said, his voice low. "Mrefu. He's the one who makes the calls—decides who gets in, and who stays out. But they didn't give me a way to contact him. If he wants to talk to you, he'll find you."

Dennis's eyes narrowed as he leaned forward, the name sparking recognition. It matched one of the contacts they had recovered from the half-burned phone, but without any details. He nodded slowly, processing the information. "Good work, Samuel. This is exactly what we needed."

Samuel pulled out his phone and showed Dennis the number from the list. "This is what we have on him. It's not much, but it's a start."

Dennis took a deep breath, his mind already working through their next steps. "There are two ways we can go about this," he began, his tone measured. "We can either use the phone company to trace his details or use IRIS's connections to get a deeper look into his network. We need

to know where he is, what name he's using, and anything else that can give us an edge."

Samuel nodded, understanding the complexity of the task ahead. "What do you need me to do?"

Dennis smiled faintly. "For now, just keep your ears open. The fewer people who know we're looking into this, the better. I'll handle the rest."

Samuel hesitated, his voice soft. "My family worries about me. My wife especially. She doesn't understand why I keep at it. To her, this is all unnecessary."

Dennis studied Samuel's face. "Maybe she's just worried about what could happen if you get pulled in too far. Have you thought about stepping back?"

Samuel sighed, gazing out the window. "Every day, actually. But then I remember the young boys who see the poachers as heroes. Or my own son, watching me, wondering if his father is doing enough to protect what's here. If I walk away now, I'd be teaching him to take the easy path, and I can't do that."

Dennis nodded thoughtfully. "Sounds like you're trying to be more than a father. You're trying to be an example."

Samuel smiled softly. "That's the hardest thing to be in this line of work. The world keeps testing you."

Amina and Dennis

Later that day, Amina found Dennis sitting on a log near the edge of the village, taking a break from the afternoon heat. She approached quietly, her smile warm as she called out, "Dennis, uko sawa? Are you doing all right?"

Dennis looked up, returning her smile. "Niko sawa, Amina. Just taking in the sights." He patted the log beside him, inviting her to sit down.

She sat, smoothing her dress and glancing at him with a shy smile. "You know, the way you handled yourself last night, you seemed to fit right in. Not many outsiders would look so comfortable here."

Dennis chuckled, shrugging. "I think it's mostly thanks to Samuel and his family. They make it easy to feel at home. Besides, everyone has been so welcoming." He paused, his gaze shifting to her. "Especially you."

Amina's smile widened, and she leaned closer, her eyes locking with his. "Maybe it's because we like having you here. Maybe I like having you here."

Dennis could feel the flirtation in her tone, and there was no mistaking the glint in her eyes. He hesitated for a moment, then smiled. "Is that so? Well, having you around has been a lot more enjoyable, too."

Amina laughed softly, reaching out to touch his arm. "You should let me show you a place I like to go. Somewhere quiet, away from all the noise."

Dennis raised an eyebrow, curious. "Lead the way."

She took his hand, pulling him to his feet, and led him away from the village. They walked for a few minutes until they reached a small grove of trees, the branches heavy with green leaves that provided a natural canopy, shielding them from the sun. The grove was quiet, save for the sound of birds and the rustle of leaves in the breeze.

Amina turned to face Dennis, her eyes searching for his. "This is my favorite spot," she said softly. "I come here when I want to be alone... or when I want to be with someone special."

Dennis felt his heart beat faster as she stepped closer, her hand resting on his chest. He could see the mix of shyness and boldness in her expression, and he smiled, brushing a strand of hair away from her face. "I'm honored you brought me here, Amina."

She looked up at him, her lips parting as she whispered, "Dennis... nataka uwe karibu." *I want you to be close.*

Without hesitation, Dennis leaned down, their lips meeting in a slow, gentle kiss. Amina responded eagerly, her arms wrapping around his neck as she pressed herself against him. The world around them seemed to fade away, leaving just the two of them alone in the quiet grove. Dennis could feel her warmth, her breath against his skin, and he let himself get lost in the moment.

They pulled back, both breathless, and Amina smiled, her fingers tracing the line of his jaw. "You're different, Dennis. I can tell."

Dennis smiled, his voice low. "Different in a good way, I hope."

She laughed, her eyes twinkling. "Very good."

They stayed in the grove longer, talking, laughing, and stealing kisses, enjoying the privacy of the quiet place away from the rest of the village.

Dennis wasn't forgetting his mission. "Amina," Dennis began gently, his voice barely above a whisper, "I need to know about the poachers. Anything you can tell me—it could help."

"What are your relations with Juma?" Amina looked at him, surprised. "He is an old friend. He was a friend of someone who was important in my life, and whom I lost. He helped me with that."

There was sorrow in her face. "What happened?" asked Dennis.

Amina's expression tightened, her fingers playing nervously with the edge of her dress. She looked away, her eyes focusing on the horizon. "Dennis, it's not that simple. I cannot talk about it. It's... it's a painful story."

Dennis reached out, taking her hand in his, his touch reassuring. "I understand. You don't have to tell me if it's too much. But if there's anything that could help, anything at all, I need to know."

Amina took a deep breath, her eyes filling with tears that she tried to blink away. "I was young—barely out of school. I had a fiancé. His name was Faraji. I loved him so much, Dennis. He wanted to make something of himself and earn enough money to give my family a dowry—cows, goats, something to show he could care for me. He wanted to go south to hunt ivory to earn the money we needed; poaching bushmeat was not enough. He went with a syndicate."

Her voice broke, and she paused, swallowing hard. "He never came back. I waited and waited, but there was no word. One of his best friends went with him, and he went

missing too. Later, I heard... They were both buried in an unmarked plot in the Maasai Mara. Just left there, with the great migration walking over their graves."

She looked at Dennis, her eyes filled with sorrow and anger. "So many men do this when they need money. They think they can make a quick fortune, but sometimes they don't come back. Some who do come back are not the same. They're crippled, or they're haunted by what they've seen. I've heard men screaming in the middle of the night, looking at people with those crazy eyes, or forever sad about someone they killed, or some friend killed next to them."

Dennis's heart ached at the pain in her voice. He squeezed her hand gently, his eyes searching hers. "I'm so sorry, Amina. I can't imagine what that must have been like for you."

Amina shook her head, tears spilling down her cheeks. "It wasn't just me, Dennis. It was their families, their mothers, their children. So many lives were destroyed for the sake of money. And the worst part is, it keeps happening. No one seems to learn."

Dennis pulled her closer, wrapping his arm around her shoulders as she cried softly. He knew that her story was just one of many—each man who went south carried with him the hopes and dreams of those who loved him, and each loss left behind a void that could never be filled. He held Amina, his resolve hardening. This wasn't just about poaching or protecting wildlife. It was about the people being crushed under the greed and desperation of a few corrupt individuals. And he wouldn't let it continue—not if he could help it.

The Drive Back to Nairobi

The drive back to Nairobi was long and uneventful. The dusty roads stretched endlessly ahead as the Land Cruiser rumbled along, stopping only at the occasional roadblock. Samuel was driving while Dennis leaned back, his mind racing with everything they had learned. The village slowly faded into the distance, replaced by the open plains and acacia trees that dotted the landscape. They drove in relative silence, the weight of their discovery hanging heavily in the air.

Dennis glanced over at Samuel, noting the tension in his friend's expression.

"You did well, Samuel. Getting that name—it was more than I expected." He mentioned his chats with Amina and with Kassim, the shopkeeper.

Samuel nodded, his eyes focused on the road ahead. "I just hope it helps. The situation seems to have become worse. Even the occasional poachers are afraid of the syndicates, Dennis. These people... they're my people, my family. If we can stop this, maybe we can improve things for them."

Dennis reached over, patting Samuel on the shoulder. "We will. One step at a time. We have the name now. We'll use it, find out who Mrefu is, and take it from there."

Dennis hesitated before speaking again. "I remember you mentioning your brother once... he got involved with poachers, didn't he?"

Samuel sighed, looking down.

"He did, yes. An older brother. It broke our family. He joined young, drawn in by the quick money. I couldn't understand it then, but it's like you said earlier—people make choices in desperate times."

Dennis nodded sympathetically.

"That must have been hard. How did that affect you?"

"It left scars, Dennis. The shame brought to my family, the way the village looked at us… it was heavy. I saw firsthand how easily he got swept into it. And when he disappeared, I knew I had to make sure no one else in our family—or the community—fell into that same darkness. It's… It's why I work for the NGO and am now with you."

"You're trying to protect others from making the same choices?" Dennis asked gently.

"Yes. I lost a brother to this, Dennis. I can't watch anyone else fall into it." Samuel nodded, his voice filled with quiet resolve.

The sun was beginning to set as they approached Nairobi, the sky turning shades of orange and pink, and the city skyline coming into view in the distance. Dennis felt a sense of urgency, knowing that their work was far from over. Even though they had made progress—small but meaningful—it was enough to keep them going.

Nairobi

Soon, they reached Dennis's boarding house, the same quiet, unassuming place tucked away in Kilimani. The streets here were lined with jacaranda trees, their purplish-blue blossoms carpeting the ground. Dennis stepped out of

the car, slinging his bag over his shoulder, and headed inside to his familiar room.

He dropped his bag on the floor and sat on the edge of the bed, the weight of the day settling in. Tomorrow, there'd be the gala. Speeches. Small talk. The usual crowd dressed up and pretending the world outside didn't exist. He'd be there, smiling, shaking hands, but his mind would still be on the Mara, remembering how the sky had stretched out forever in Naomi's smile.

For now, though, he lay back, staring up at the ceiling, letting the hum of the city fade away. Tomorrow, he will meet with Kamau for lunch.

Chapter 6: Political Corruption in Nairobi

Kenyan Politics

Since the turn of the century, Kenya has experienced considerable political transformation, marked by both progress and setbacks.

The political landscape has been shaped by cycles of hope, disillusionment, and a gradual march toward democratic consolidation. Key events, including contentious elections, constitutional reforms, corruption scandals, and shifts in leadership, have deeply influenced the nation's trajectory.

Kenya entered the 21st century under the firm grip of President Daniel Arap Moi, who had ruled since 1978. His government was characterized by allegations of corruption, repression, and economic mismanagement. In 2002, Moi stepped down in compliance with constitutional term limits, marking the end of the Kenya African National Union (KANU)'s 39-year rule since independence.

The 2002 general elections were pivotal. A coalition of opposition parties, the National Rainbow Coalition (NARC), led by Mwai Kibaki, successfully challenged KANU's candidate, Uhuru Kenyatta. This election was celebrated as a triumph for democracy in Kenya, as it signified the first peaceful transition of power since independence. Kibaki's victory was greeted with widespread optimism, with

promises to tackle endemic corruption and revive the economy.

Mwai Kibaki's early years in office were marked by efforts to fight corruption and deliver on his promises of economic revitalization. His government introduced the Free Primary Education program in 2003, significantly boosting enrollment numbers and providing opportunities for many underprivileged children. However, internal disagreements and unfulfilled promises of political inclusivity began to erode the optimism of the NARC coalition.

The quest for a new constitution, which had been a central campaign promise, became a source of political tension. Disagreements within the ruling coalition about the draft constitution led to divisions, and in 2005, a national referendum was held. Voters rejected the proposed draft, revealing fractures within the political elite and foreshadowing future instability.

The 2007 general election marked one of Kenya's darkest political chapters. The election pitted the incumbent President Kibaki, representing the Party of National Unity (PNU), against Raila Odinga of the Orange Democratic Movement (ODM). Allegations of vote rigging led to widespread protests and violence, which quickly escalated along ethnic lines, resulting in over 1,100 deaths and more than 600,000 people displaced.

To resolve the crisis, international mediation led by former UN Secretary-General Kofi Annan resulted in a power-sharing agreement in February 2008. The accord established a coalition government, with Kibaki remaining as President and Odinga taking up the newly created position

of Prime Minister. This uneasy alliance provided a temporary respite from violence, though tensions simmered beneath the surface.

One of the most significant achievements of the post-crisis period was the adoption of a new constitution in 2010. The new constitution, approved through a national referendum, represented a critical step forward in addressing governance issues. It introduced a devolved system of government, reducing the power of the presidency and giving greater autonomy to the counties. It also established a Bill of Rights, reformed the judiciary, and created independent commissions to enhance accountability and transparency.

The 2013 general election was the first to be held under the new constitution. Uhuru Kenyatta won the presidency alongside his running mate, William Ruto, despite both facing charges at the International Criminal Court (ICC) for their alleged roles in the 2007-2008 post-election violence. They campaigned on a platform of unity and sovereignty, framing the ICC cases as an infringement on Kenya's independence.

The election was relatively peaceful compared to 2007, although Raila Odinga, Kenyatta's main opponent, challenged the results in court, citing irregularities. The Supreme Court upheld Kenyatta's victory, and he was sworn in as president. Kenyatta's tenure was marked by ambitious infrastructure projects, including the construction of the Standard Gauge Railway (SGR), financed largely through Chinese loans. The increasing influence of China in Kenya's

economic affairs became a point of contention, with concerns about rising debt levels and economic sovereignty.

The 2017 general elections were once again fiercely contested between Uhuru Kenyatta and Raila Odinga. Allegations of irregularities led the Supreme Court to annul Kenyatta's victory, citing procedural flaws and illegalities. A fresh election was ordered, which Odinga boycotted, effectively handing Kenyatta a second term.

In March 2018, Kenyatta and Odinga publicly shook hands, symbolizing a commitment to work together for the nation's stability. This "Handshake" led to the Building Bridges Initiative (BBI), which sought to address issues like ethnic division, exclusion, and governance reform. While the initiative aimed to bring political unity, it also faced criticism as an attempt by the political elite to consolidate power.

The COVID-19 pandemic strained Kenya's healthcare system and slowed economic growth. Lockdowns and restrictions affected livelihoods, particularly in the informal sector. The government's response was criticized for corruption in the procurement of medical supplies, highlighting systemic graft.

The BBI initiative faced legal challenges, and in 2021, the High Court and Court of Appeal ruled the process unconstitutional, halting the proposed amendments. As the 2022 elections approached, political alignments shifted, with William Ruto positioning himself as the "hustler" candidate, representing marginalized Kenyans. His campaign slogan, the "hustler nation," resonated with many young Kenyans facing unemployment and economic hardship.

The 2022 elections were a test of Kenya's democracy. William Ruto emerged victorious, defeating Raila Odinga in a hotly contested race. The elections were largely peaceful, though Odinga once again challenged the results in court. The Supreme Court upheld Ruto's victory, and he was inaugurated as the fifth President of Kenya in September 2022.

Ruto's presidency began with promises to tackle corruption, reduce the cost of living, and support economic empowerment for ordinary Kenyans. However, his administration faced challenges, including managing the country's high debt burden and addressing the economic fallout from the pandemic.

Lunch with Kamau

Dennis and Kamau sat at a small outdoor café shaded by jacaranda trees, the hum of Nairobi's city life providing a lively backdrop. Their food arrived—steaming plates of pilau rice spiced with cloves and cinnamon, accompanied by a fresh kachumbari salad. Kamau leaned back, watching Dennis with a reflective expression.

"So, Dennis, how was the Maasai Mara?" Kamau asked, lifting his glass with a grin. "I hear it has a way of getting under your skin." He raised an eyebrow, his gaze knowing.

Dennis took a sip of his drink, playing it cool. "It's… breathtaking, really. Nothing quite like it." He could see Kamau's smirk widening and decided to give him a little more. "I met a few locals, saw the landscape—and, yes, Naomi and I got along well."

Kamau chuckled, clearly enjoying the hint of mystery. "Got along, huh? You know, she's a tough one, but she's got a soft spot for anyone who genuinely cares about what we're trying to do out there. It's not an easy life."

Dennis nodded, leaning forward. "No, it's not. She's dedicated, you can see that. The work is dangerous and exhausting. But she handles it all with this... steady resolve." He chose his words carefully, but Kamau picked up on the undertone.

"Well, if Naomi's letting you in, then you're doing something right," Kamau said, giving him an approving nod. "The Maasai Mara has that effect, too. It makes people realize what really matters. Did you make it out to any of the villages?"

Dennis smiled, recalling the warmth of the community and their reverence for the land. "Yes, I spent some time with a few of the Maasai. They know the Mara better than anyone. And the poaching camp we came across—it's something you can't shake off."

Kamau's expression shifted to one of respect and concern. "I get it. But be careful, Dennis. There's a lot at stake here. And Naomi, she's... well, she doesn't let people in easily. Keep her trust."

Dennis nodded. "Thanks, Kamau. I will."

Lunch was a brief pause from the tension of their work, but Kamau was never one to avoid harder conversations.

"Look around, Dennis," Kamau gestured with his fork toward the skyline, dotted with cranes and half-built skyscrapers. "All these new buildings, the expressway—

Chinese investments. It's not all bad, of course; it's helped with infrastructure. But the flip side, my friend, is our debt, and then... corruption." He paused, almost with a sigh. "Corruption here is like an infection. Every administration says they'll clean it up, but the scandals just keep rolling out."

Dennis took a bite of pilau, savoring the spices, but his attention was on Kamau's words. "I've seen it mentioned in reports," he said, "but not the full scale of it."

Kamau shook his head, his eyes hardening. "Take the National Youth Service. It was supposed to help young people learn trades and build futures. Instead, billions of shillings have vanished. Ministries, departments—they're all tainted." He leaned in, lowering his voice. "And who funds many of these projects? The Chinese. They're here with money, and their contracts are often opaque, with no transparency. Beijing hands over the funds, Kenya hands back the debt, and the details are murky."

Dennis nodded, absorbing the implications. "Does it ever stop?"

Kamau smirked, shaking his head. "Our leaders play the 'politics of the big man,' rallying by tribe, promising change. But at the end of the day, ethnic allegiances, money, and power drive it all. And Kenya's debt just keeps piling higher."

"So, what happens next?" Dennis asked, his tone probing but careful.

Kamau sighed, glancing down at his plate before looking back at Dennis. "It's complex. The 2010 constitution

brought some hope with devolution—about equitable development and giving people a voice. But corruption and this cycle of debt keep things… unbalanced. To make real progress, we have to break free from this grip. Until then, the promises are just… words."

The two continued their meal, the fragrant rice and fresh kachumbari providing a brief reprieve in a city striving forward but still tethered to deep-rooted challenges.

The Gala

As the sedan rolled through Nairobi's chaotic traffic, Dennis turned to Dr. Mugo beside him, adjusting his bow tie with a nervous chuckle.

"I have to admit, Doctor, I never thought I'd be suiting up for a gala like this one."

Dr. Mugo smirked, glancing out the window as they neared The Windsor Golf Hotel and Country Club, where the golden glow of chandeliers spilled out from the arched windows onto the perfectly manicured lawns.

"It's a world apart from the Mara, that's certain. But tonight, this is where the power lies. Business tycoons, government officials, foreign investors—this crowd has the resources and the influence."

"And we're here because…" Dennis trailed off, prompting.

Dr. Mugo leaned back, lowering his voice. "Tonight, we're not just networking. People like **Ziad Haddad**—a Lebanese businessman, influential but shadowy—will be here. I'd wager others with interests in… well, let's call it

'alternative trade routes,' will be lurking, too." He gave Dennis a knowing look.

Dennis nodded, glancing down at the invitation in his hand. "So, we're here to listen?"

"Listen, observe, and catch them off guard if we're lucky," Dr. Mugo said, smiling as the sedan pulled to a stop at the hotel's entrance. "And don't underestimate the power of these gatherings. Kenya's elite and its expatriate network can move mountains—or bury them."

They stepped out of the car to the soft murmur of conversations and the hum of luxury engines idling in line. High-end vehicles dotted the drive, their drivers watching with cool precision as Nairobi's elite made their entrances. The sprawling Windsor grounds stretched out under the evening sky, lined with flowering hedges, the faint scent of jasmine mingling with the cool breeze.

Dennis handed his invitation to the valet, and he and Dr. Mugo strode toward the entrance, taking in the venue's opulence. Inside, the ballroom was filled with polished marble floors reflecting the light of grand crystal chandeliers. The high ceilings were adorned with intricate carvings, and the walls, draped in crimson velvet, lent an air of regal secrecy.

Dr. Mugo leaned in as they took their first step inside. "See that group by the far wall?" He nodded toward a cluster of men in tailored suits. "Government officials, powerful investors. They look unassuming, but they're some of the most influential people in the country. Some of them are rumored to have strong ties to… unconventional trading practices."

"And Ziad?" Dennis asked, keeping his voice low as they navigated the room.

"Likely at the bar," Dr. Mugo replied, scanning the crowd. "He's usually close to his allies, close to his sources. He'll show up, but he won't come without an agenda. There's always a deeper game with men like him."

They moved into the thick of the crowd, each step drawing them further into the hum of conversations on politics, investments, and international trade. Waiters in crisp white jackets wove through the crowd with trays of champagne flutes and hors d'oeuvres, and a live orchestra played softly in the background. Dennis caught snatches of conversations, some light, others hinting at power plays and negotiations hidden beneath polite laughter.

As they neared the bar, Dr. Mugo placed a hand on Dennis's shoulder.

"Remember, blend in. Let's be the invisible ones tonight."

Dennis smiled, raising a glass offered by a passing waiter, and let his eyes sweep the room. Tonight, they would be part of Nairobi's glittering society—but only to watch, listen, and wait for the secrets that would, sooner or later, spill over the crystal glasses and whispered words.

He spotted **Ziad Haddad** almost immediately, standing by the grand marble bar. The Lebanese businessman had a drink in hand, his sharp eyes scanning the room in between his hushed conversation with **Charles Otieno**, the Governor of Nairobi County.

Otieno was smiling, his signature charm on display. Dressed in a tailored tuxedo, he looked every bit the ambitious politician, always positioning himself as a man of the people while courting the powerful. But Dennis knew better. The way Otieno stood close to Ziad, nodding at his every word, the small but knowing smile playing on his lips—it all told a story of complicity.

Dennis approached the bar slowly, not too close but enough to catch snippets of their conversation. Ziad spoke in low, measured tones, his thick accent curling around words that sent alarms ringing in Dennis's head: **"shipments"** and **"funding."** Otieno responded in short, clipped sentences, his body language suggesting a man accustomed to operating in the shadows. Their conversation was casual to an outsider, but Dennis could sense the undercurrent of something more. **Something dangerous.**

The bar itself was a marvel of design—gleaming black marble with gold accents, bottles of rare whiskey and champagne lined up like trophies on glass shelves. The bartender moved swiftly, mixing cocktails for the crowd, but Dennis barely noticed. He was focused on the interaction unfolding a few feet away, the subtle exchange between Ziad and Otieno, the glances around the room that hinted they were discussing more than just business deals. This was the heart of what he was looking for—a connection between the powerful men behind the poaching and smuggling operations that had plagued Kenya.

Dennis ordered a drink, using the moment to assess the crowd more thoroughly. The guests were a who's who of the city's elite—senior government officials, CEOs of

multinational companies, and NGO leaders. Each was there for a reason, and in their midst, Dennis moved like a shadow, blending into the opulence while his mind worked through the pieces of the puzzle.

Dennis moved smoothly through the crowd, his eyes flickering over each face, each handshake an opportunity. He'd mastered the art of mingling, slipping into conversation as if he belonged to Nairobi's high society. He nodded, smiled, and even laughed when appropriate, all while keeping Ziad and Otieno in his periphery. But he needed more than just proximity—he needed people who might offer information, intentionally or not.

His first encounter was with a man in his mid-fifties, impeccably dressed in a deep blue suit with an air of authority that suggested he was more than just another businessman. This was **Andrew Mburu**, a logistics tycoon whom Dennis knew handled several shipping routes across East Africa. Dennis extended his hand.

"Andrew, it's a pleasure to meet you," Dennis began. "I've heard about your work—quite the operation you're running on the coast."

Andrew's eyes sparkled with pride. "We aim to make East Africa a strong player in global trade. Logistics is the backbone of any market, you know."

Dennis nodded, steering the conversation toward more discreet subjects. "I imagine it's a challenge to keep operations smooth, given the, let's say, complexities of local governance."

Andrew laughed dryly, a flash of resignation in his eyes. "Complexities, indeed. I won't pretend corruption doesn't factor into our... operations. Everything slows down in a system where you have to grease the wheels to keep things moving. Licensing delays, customs backlogs—some palms just expect to be lined."

Dennis raised an eyebrow, maintaining an air of understanding. "That must be a challenge. How much does it affect your bottom line?"

Andrew glanced around, his voice dropping slightly. "It's the cost of doing business, really. Kenya's a beautiful country, but it's a hard place to operate without paying dues to people who think they deserve a cut. It's not like in Europe." He shook his head, his expression a mixture of frustration and acceptance. "Here, you've got to navigate the politics as much as the logistics. If you want to make deadlines, keep clients happy—you adapt."

Dennis nodded thoughtfully, filing away the information. Andrew wasn't the first to mention this problem, and he likely wouldn't be the last. But it confirmed what Dennis suspected: corruption wasn't just a side effect here; it was a deeply embedded part of the business landscape, fueling illicit activities in ways he hadn't fully seen before.

The conversation shifted to lighter topics, but Dennis could tell that Andrew's frustration ran deep, laced with hints of resentment and wariness. It was clear that he'd paid his dues to stay competitive but felt growing pressure from those expecting to profit from his success. Dennis thanked him, noting that Andrew's "complexities" would be worth

investigating further. The man was close enough to smuggling routes to either supply valuable intel or, perhaps, indicate those deeply entrenched in Nairobi's web of power.

Moving on, Dennis found himself face to face with a younger man, sharply dressed and visibly keen to network. Lucas Kendi was his name—a rising politician whose ambitions were matched only by his tendency to skirt the law. Kendi was eager to please and quick to speak of his plans for reforming the country's infrastructure.

"Dennis Bellamy, a pleasure," Dennis introduced himself, allowing Lucas's enthusiasm to lead the conversation.

"Ah, Mr. Bellamy! I've heard your name mentioned— wildlife conservation, correct? Kenya needs more allies like you." Lucas gave a broad, easy smile, though his eyes held a restless energy.

Dennis smiled, noting the eagerness. "I'm here to support Kenya in any way I can. Tell me, Lucas, what's your stance on border trade? I imagine that's quite an operation to keep in line."

Lucas chuckled, shrugging lightly. "A country like ours is always balancing priorities, Dennis. What's vital to one party may not be to another. But I believe in leveraging every asset we have." He paused, his gaze shifting over Dennis's shoulder. "Sometimes, opportunities find those willing to… bend a little."

Dennis offered a noncommittal nod. Lucas's words hinted at a flexibility that could suggest he'd looked the other

way once or twice. Dennis filed the conversation away, a thread he could pull if he needed it.

As he moved along, Dennis spotted a tall, lean man by the window, his salt-and-pepper hair swept back and his dark eyes alert, observing the room with quiet authority. Dennis realized this was Babu Ismail, a lawyer known for his connections to high-profile clients and delicate international dealings. He was the type people called when they needed something hidden or washed clean. Dennis approached him, slipping easily into polite conversation.

"Mr. Ismail, I presume?" Dennis greeted, extending a hand.

Ismail took it, his grip firm, his gaze sharp. "Ah, yes. And you are?"

"Dennis Bellamy. I've heard you're a trusted figure in matters of... well, discretion."

Ismail's mouth curled into a hint of a smile. "Discretion is valuable, Mr. Bellamy, as is trust. People here value both immensely." He raised an eyebrow. "Do you?"

Dennis leaned in slightly, keeping his voice low. "I wouldn't be here otherwise."

Ismail's eyes flickered with interest, though he kept his expression guarded. Dennis sensed that Ismail wasn't just another guest; he was someone who facilitated the less visible affairs of the elite. It was tempting to press further, but Dennis knew better than to push.

Ziad and Otieno

An opportunity finally presented itself. Otieno and Ziad moved toward a quieter corner of the ballroom, stepping onto a balcony. Dennis followed at a distance, slipping onto the balcony just in time to hear Otieno speak. He had already inserted the directional voice amplifier into his ear and could hear the discussion distinctly. This Bluetooth device also recorded the conversation and stored it on Dennis's phone.

"Everything is set for the next phase," Otieno said, his voice low but confident. "The funds will be in place, and you know how much we need them for our campaign." He paused, glancing at Ziad. "Just make sure your people handle the shipments without any issues. The last thing we need is more attention from the authorities."

Ziad nodded, a smirk on his face. "Don't worry, Charles. My people are professionals. No mistakes." He took a sip of his drink. "And once you're in office, we can expand our operations without interference. It's in both our interests, after all."

Dennis lingered near the balcony, straining to catch more of their conversation.

"…we'll have the shipment coming in next week. Chinese weapons on their way north, about five tons' worth—enough to equip the entire region. The value alone should be enough to cover our campaign expenses twice over," Otieno said, a satisfied edge to his tone.

Dennis felt a surge of adrenaline. This was proof that Otieno was not only aware of the smuggling operation but was actively involved, using it to fund his political

ambitions. The implications were staggering. A man who could soon be running the country was in league with criminals.

Dennis barely processed the enormity of what he was hearing when a shadow loomed near him. He turned to see one of Otieno's bodyguards, his expression hard and suspicious, eyes narrowing as he looked Dennis up and down.

"You lost, sir?" The bodyguard's voice was firm, the underlying warning clear.

Dennis glanced down, catching the glint of the man's name tag: Mutua. "Just enjoying the view, Mutua," Dennis said with a nod, trying to keep his tone light and casual.

Mutua's gaze stayed steady, his eyes scanning Dennis's face, assessing him. "Well, the view's for invited guests only."

"Of course," Dennis replied, nodding courteously before easing away from the balcony. He could feel Mutua's eyes on him as he walked back into the ballroom, his mind racing.

He had to be careful now. Otieno's men were clearly keeping a close watch, and any misstep could blow his cover. He returned to the heart of the gathering, blending quickly into the crowd. Spotting a group of American NGO workers, he slipped into their circle, an easy-going mix of three men and two women, each with a friendly, open presence.

The group welcomed him into their conversation, and Dennis listened as a tall, wiry man with a Southern accent animatedly recounted his outreach work in rural Kenya.

Beside him, a bespectacled man with a quiet demeanor nodded along, adding statistics on water conservation efforts.

In contrast, the third man—a broad-shouldered rugby type—shared tales from Amboseli, where he'd once driven into a mud trap to rescue a stranded elephant calf. His enthusiasm drew laughter from the group, lightening the mood.

Across from Dennis sat the two women, both seasoned fieldworkers whose experience gave them an edge in navigating tough Kenyan landscapes. The first, a petite woman with close-cropped blonde hair, spoke with a New England lilt as she described their training programs for local rangers. The second, a redhead with freckles and a sharp sense of humor, had everyone laughing with stories of adapting to Kenya's bureaucracy.

Dennis stayed with the group, feeling the adrenaline still coursing through him. He had the evidence. Now, he just needed to get out safely.

As Dennis chatted with the NGO workers, he kept a casual eye on the room, observing the strategic mingling of Ziad and Otieno. He noticed Ziad talking to a few other men, each exuding the polish and gravitas of seasoned politicians or influential business leaders. Their exchanges were brief—almost too businesslike for a social gathering—with curt nods and handshakes suggesting more to be said behind closed doors.

Dennis casually raised his phone, angling it to snap discreet photos of Ziad's brief meetings. Each exchange hinted at something Dennis couldn't ignore: men from

different political parties and sectors, perhaps, but united in purpose.

Otieno, meanwhile, was also making his rounds. The Kenyan politician moved fluidly through the crowd with an air of practiced charisma, his easy charm disarming those around him. Dennis watched as Otieno stopped to chat with several government officials and high-ranking businesspeople, lingering just long enough to show interest before moving on.

Dennis photographed these encounters, too, carefully tagging each face for later reference. Who were these men? He wondered how many were part of the shadow network that fueled Kenya's smuggling operations.

By the time the speeches began, Dennis had observed enough. He made a quiet exit, slipping unnoticed and returning to his hotel room, his thoughts racing with the night's findings. Settling in at his desk, he reviewed the photos he'd taken, matching faces with the mental notes he'd made. It was clear that Ziad and Otieno were more than familiar with the political elite, and their connections painted a network that extended well beyond smuggling.

Dennis quickly messaged Kamau: "I got photos of *Ziad, Otieno, and their allies. We need to strategize tomorrow.*

But as he reviewed his notes and recordings, he felt the weight of it all—the potential consequences of exposing men like Otieno and Ziad. This wasn't just a fight against poachers or smugglers anymore. It was a fight against the system that enabled them.

Chapter 7: Corruption

Breakfast at the Westgate Mall

Dennis sat across from Kamau in Artcaffe, a fancy breakfast spot at Westgate Mall in Nairobi. The place was bustling with people—professionals on their way to work, tourists enjoying their morning coffee, and the soft jazz playing in the background. The scent of freshly brewed coffee and baked pastries filled the air, providing a comforting contrast to the tension of their conversation.

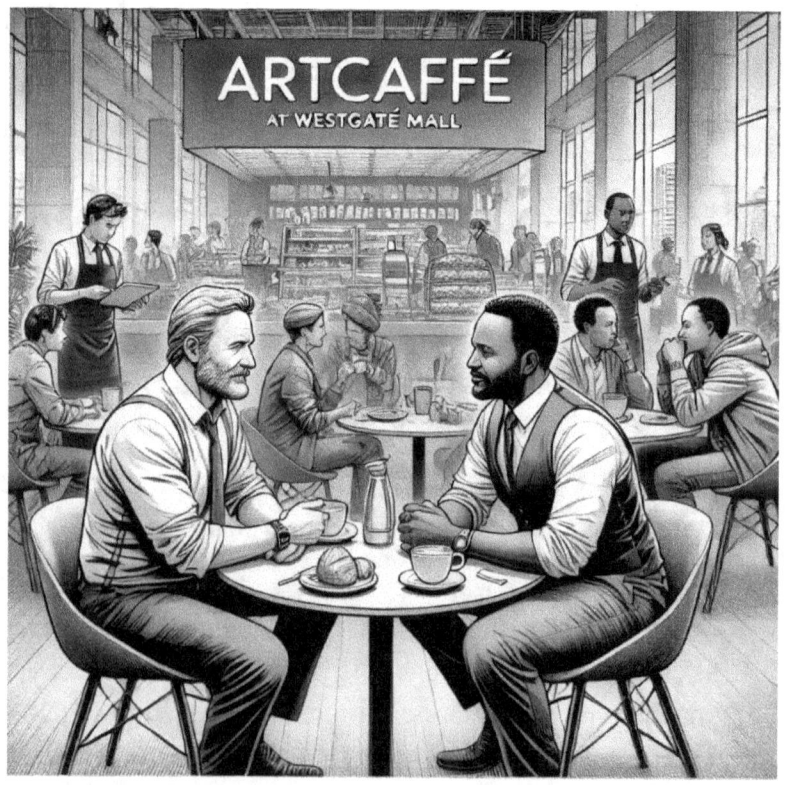

Kamau took a sip of his cappuccino, his eyes focused on

Dennis. "You really think this is the best way to do it?" he asked, his voice low to avoid drawing attention. "You want to pose as an ivory buyer? Do you realize how dangerous these people are? The other disadvantage is that they will know what you look like."

Dennis nodded, his expression resolute. "I know. But it's the only way we can get inside. We need to figure out who's running this, and the only way to do that is to make contact. We must show them we're serious—someone with the kind of money they can't resist."

Kamau sighed, his eyes dropping to the table. "This isn't just about money, Dennis. These people—they're killers. If they think you're a threat, they won't hesitate. Are you sure about this?"

Dennis leaned forward. "Kamau, we're running out of options. Otieno is involved, Ziad is pulling strings, and there's someone else above them—a figure they call The Broker. This person is orchestrating everything, from poaching to weapons trafficking. If we want to bring this network down, we must get close enough to gather evidence."

Kamau studied him for a long moment, then nodded slowly. "Fine. But we do this my way. You'll need backup, and we'll have eyes on you the entire time. The second things go sideways, we're pulling you out."

Dennis gave him a small smile. "Agreed. We'll play it safe."

Corruption marches

After their conversation, Dennis leaned against the office window, the late morning sun slanting through the blinds. He hadn't slept much the night before, his mind restless, turning over the puzzle pieces—Mrefu, the ivory trade, the corruption that oiled the wheels. Nairobi was a city of shadows, and today, he and Daniel would dig a little deeper into one of its darkest corners.

A knock at the door broke his thoughts. He turned to see Daniel standing there, a casual smile on his face, hands tucked into his pockets.

"Ready to go?" Daniel asked, his voice easy, as though they weren't about to dive into the thick of Gikomba Market—partly to see where illegal goods traded hands, partly to connect with Kenyan culture.

Dennis grabbed his jacket, giving Daniel a nod. "Let's do it."

As they drove, Dennis leaned back in his seat, watching as Daniel expertly navigated the chaotic streets of Nairobi. The city was always bustling, but the traffic seemed worse than usual. Horns blared in frustration as cars crawled along and pedestrians spilled out onto the streets, some waving banners and placards. The usual hum of the city was overlaid with the sounds of protest, the air thick with tension.

"What's going on here?" Dennis asked, glancing out the window at the mass of people moving through the streets, some chanting slogans he couldn't quite make out.

Daniel sighed, shaking his head as he maneuvered the car onto a side street to avoid the blocked roads. "It's the protests again. People are fed up, Dennis. They've had

enough of the government, the corruption. You know about the tax bill, right?"

Dennis raised an eyebrow. "Tax bill?"

"Yeah, the government proposed raising taxes to pay off the debt we owe, especially to China. But people are angry because they know a lot of that debt is due to corruption. They don't want to pay for the crimes of politicians who took bribes and wasted the money on projects that failed because the politicians chose contractors based on the amount of kickbacks they received."

Dennis watched the crowd as they passed. Many were young, their faces determined, frustration evident in their expressions. "I didn't realize it was this bad."

Daniel let out a bitter laugh. "It's always been bad. It's just that now, with the economy struggling, people are starting to fight back more. Especially the youth. They're the ones who feel it the most—they don't see a future here if things don't change."

They slowed to a near stop as the crowd thickened, forcing them to take another detour. Dennis could feel the tension in the air, a simmering anger that reminded him of how fragile stability here could be.

"You ever had trouble with the police?" Dennis asked, more out of curiosity than anything else. He knew that in many places, law enforcement could be just as corrupt as the politicians they served.

Daniel scoffed. "All the time, my friend. Hasn't Samuel explained it to you already? Everyone with a car has been stopped many times. You get stopped for anything—a

broken taillight, a wrong turn, even if you've done nothing wrong. It's always the same: hand over some money, and you can go. If you don't pay, they can make your life miserable. It's just part of the system."

Dennis nodded, his mind turning over what Daniel was saying. "So, this tax bill—people are angry because they're being asked to pay for corruption?"

Daniel shot him a glance before returning his eyes to the road. "Exactly. The government keeps taking loans from China and the World Bank, but they're not using the money as they should. They pay off the officials, build half-finished projects, and then ask us—the regular people—to foot the bill. It's no wonder people are out in the streets."

Dennis absorbed the information, watching as the protestors continued to move through the streets. He could hear snippets of their chants now—calls for justice, an end to corruption, and a future they felt had been stolen.

"Has it always been this bad?" Dennis asked.

Daniel shrugged. "In some ways, yes. Corruption has been here for as long as I can remember. But it's gotten worse over the years. Politicians don't even try to hide it anymore. They take the bribes, sign the bad deals, retire in the Caribbean, and expect us to live with it. But now? People are waking up. They're realizing this country has so much potential, but it's being held back by a few people at the top, lining their own pockets."

Dennis thought back to the conversations he'd had with Naomi about Kenya's future. She'd always been hopeful, believing the country could rise above its challenges with the

right leadership. But it was clear that corruption had dug its claws deep into the fabric of society, making it hard for people like Naomi—and Daniel—to see a way forward.

"It's tough," Daniel continued, his voice dropping slightly. "You want to believe that things will get better, but it's hard when someone's stealing from the country every time you turn around. And now, with the debt we owe to China… it's like we're trapped."

Dennis said nothing for a while, letting Daniel's words sink in. Corruption, debt, and simmering anger were all connected. And while he was here for other reasons, the corruption they discussed was tied to everything—even the fight against poaching. The poachers, syndicates, and brokers all operated in the same system, exploiting the same weaknesses.

As they finally pulled free of the crowded streets and back onto the main road, Dennis glanced at Daniel. "How do people keep going, knowing all of this?"

Daniel smiled faintly, but there was no joy in it. "We keep going because we have to. For our families, for our future. And maybe because we still have some hope left, even if it's just a little."

Dennis nodded, gazing out the car's window as Nairobi blurred past. He understood that hope. It was the same thing that kept him fighting. Even in the face of overwhelming odds, sometimes hope was all you had. And it was enough to keep you moving forward, one step at a time.

The Gikomba Market

Arriving near Gikomba Market, Daniel maneuvered the car into a tight parking spot, skillfully avoiding the chaos of carts and vendors spilling into the road. They stepped out into the humid air, the streets alive with the sounds of bargaining, laughter, and the constant buzz of activity.

The market was a labyrinth of narrow paths and tightly packed stalls. Vendors called out to passersby, advertising their wares—clothes, household goods, electronics, and fresh produce. The scents of roasted maize, frying samosas, and wood smoke mingled with the less pleasant odors of sewage and refuse.

Dennis followed Daniel closely, their movements purposeful but unremarkable to blend in. "Keep your eyes open," Daniel muttered as they weaved through the crowd. He didn't need to say more—Dennis knew what they were looking for.

They passed rows of secondhand clothes piled high, hawkers shouting their prices in Swahili. The market was overwhelming, an assault on the senses, but Dennis's focus remained sharp. Gikomba was known for its legal goods, but it was also a haven for the illegal—ivory, bushmeat, and items that thrived in the cracks of enforcement.

"Before we get to work, let's grab something to eat," Daniel said, nudging Dennis toward a small restaurant tucked between two stalls selling secondhand clothes.

Dennis didn't argue. His stomach had been empty since morning, and the heat of Nairobi made his hunger sharper. They slipped through the crowd into a small, nondescript restaurant nestled between two stalls selling secondhand clothes. A faded sign above the door read *Mama Njeri's*

Café, though the letters were peeling from exposure to the weather. Inside, the space was tight, the air thick with the smell of frying meat, oil, and spices.

A few rickety wooden tables were crammed into the small room, leaving barely enough space to walk sideways between them. The walls were painted a fading sage green, and a simple counter at the back displayed an assortment of food—grilled meat, fried samosas, and steaming plates of ugali stacked high. It wasn't fancy, but it was the kind of place where the food hit the spot.

They found a table near a window that opened onto a crowded alley, the chatter from the market filtering in through the open door. A young woman came over, wiping her hands on her apron, and Daniel ordered quickly in Swahili—a couple of plates of nyama choma, the Kenyan grilled meat, with ugali to go with it.

As they waited, Dennis looked around. The other customers were locals, some finishing their lunch, others deep in conversation. This wasn't a place tourists usually found, but that was precisely why Dennis liked it. There was no pretense here, just honest food and the steady pulse of the city outside.

The food arrived quickly. The meat was charred and fragrant, and the ugali was a dense slab of maize flour cooked to perfection. Dennis tore into it with his hands, savoring the smoky flavor of the nyama choma cooked over a charcoal grill. The meal was rich and satisfying.

They ate in silence for a while, the simple act of eating grounding them for the work ahead.

"This place hasn't changed much," Daniel said between bites, grinning. "I used to come here when I was a kid. Same tables, same smell. Food's still good, though."

Dennis nodded, chewing thoughtfully. "It's perfect."

Daniel wiped his hands on a napkin and leaned back in his chair. "We'll head deeper into the market after this. There's a stall I've heard about—sells curios, but sometimes they slip a little ivory in with the rest."

Dennis nodded. He knew what that meant: a merchant who played both sides, blending the legal with the illegal. The kind of person who could tell you everything about the black market, if you knew how to ask.

They finished their meal, paid quickly, and stepped back into the market. The noise hit them again like a wave, the vibrant energy of the place buzzing around them. It was time to get to work.

Daniel stopped by a stall selling wooden carvings, glancing at Dennis. The vendor, a man in his late fifties with a toothy smile, nodded at them. The small trinkets on display seemed innocent enough—wooden animals, bowls, and beaded bracelets. But Dennis's eyes were trained. He spotted it right away, tucked in the back behind the more apparent goods—a small piece of ivory carved into the shape of an elephant.

Dennis picked it up casually, turning it over in his hand. The carving was delicate, the ivory smooth under his fingers. It was a beautiful piece, but it was also illegal. "This is a rare antique. Ivory is now illegal. You won't find much of it in this market," added the merchant.

"Nice work," Dennis said, keeping his tone light. "But isn't this a problem at customs?"

The merchant smiled, shaking his head. "No problem, boss. Customs don't care. You go through it, and no one will check it. It's all good."

Dennis frowned, pretending to think it over. The merchant's tone was easy, practiced. He had told this lie before. But Dennis knew better. He'd seen enough of this trade to know how serious the consequences could be.

"How much for this one?" Dennis asked, playing along.

"Special price for you," the merchant said, leaning in. "Five thousand shillings."

That was around 40 US dollars. Dennis set the trinket back down. "Seems risky," he said, meeting the man's eyes. "You sure no one will stop me when I land in the US?"

The merchant waved his hand dismissively. "No one cares, my friend. People bring these things all the time. Just keep it in your bag. No one checks. Easy."

Dennis nodded, but the lie hung heavy in the air. He knew better. Customs officials in the US were cracking down harder than ever on smuggled wildlife products. Ivory was high on their list. If someone got caught with this at the airport, there would be hell to pay.

Daniel stepped forward, picking up a small wooden carving. "What about these?" he asked, keeping the merchant's attention off Dennis.

Dennis glanced around, scanning the market. The illegal goods weren't everywhere, but you could see some. They

were hidden in plain sight. Most people wouldn't even notice—just tourists buying, curious, not thinking about where the items came from or what laws they were breaking by taking them out of the country.

The merchant bagged the ivory carving for Daniel, still smiling, still acting like they were just two regular buyers looking for souvenirs. But Dennis knew this went deeper. There were men like this all over—small-time sellers moving pieces of illegal ivory or animal parts. They weren't at the top of the chain but part of the system. A system that killed elephants and rhinos for trinkets like the one he had just held.

"Thanks," Dennis said, stepping back from the stall. He didn't buy anything. There was nothing more to gain from this man. He had heard what he needed to hear.

As they moved away from the stall, Dennis turned to Daniel. "You think he believes his own lie?"

Daniel shrugged. "Maybe. Maybe not. Either way, he knows people don't ask questions. As long as the money flows, that's all that matters here."

Dennis nodded, but his mind was already working. The ivory trade was still alive, significantly diminished, hiding in markets like this, creeping through cracks in the law, but ready to start at any time if given a chance. And people like that merchant were fueling it, one trinket at a time.

As they left Gikomba, the noise and heat fading behind them, Dennis knew the fight was far from over. There was still work to do. But for now, he had seen enough. Enough to know the problem wasn't going away anytime soon.

Morah vs. Corruption

Dennis leaned against the counter at the WPA office, waiting for a call to come through. Morah, the receptionist, was typing something on her computer, her face tight with concentration. The office was quiet, and the hum of Nairobi was just a faint backdrop. Dennis glanced at her, sensing something off.

"You all right, Morah?" he asked.

She sighed, pausing her work and looking up. "You know how it is, Dennis. Kenya can really wear you down sometimes."

He raised an eyebrow. "What's on your mind?"

She hesitated, then leaned back in her chair, folding her arms. "Something happened a couple of weeks ago—Friday night. I was stressed and couldn't sleep, so I left the house just before midnight. I thought it would be okay. Blow off some steam, grab a couple of beers."

Dennis nodded. "And?"

She shook her head. "I went to this small club; it was nothing fancy. I had my two beers and danced a bit. Everything was fine until about 1 a.m. Then the cops showed up—four of them—two men, two women. The women were especially arrogant. Just stormed in like they owned the place."

"What did they want?" Dennis asked, though he could already guess.

"Mututho Laws," Morah said, rolling her eyes. "The law says bars are supposed to stop serving alcohol by 11 p.m.

and close by midnight, but clubs often stay open later. We all knew we were pushing it, but honestly, no one expected them to show up like that."

Dennis leaned forward. "So, what happened?"

"Some people ran, but I couldn't. My sister was with me, and we were both caught. They rounded up everyone in the club—customers, bartenders, even the DJ. It was a mess. The cops didn't care. They just loaded us into their lorry and kept driving from club to club, arresting more people. By the end of it, we were almost fifty crammed in there."

Dennis frowned. "Fifty people?"

"Yeah," she said, shaking her head in disbelief. "It was around 4 a.m. when we finally got to the station. The whole thing was to squeeze money out of us. They were harsh, Dennis, really harsh. One slapped me. I told them I knew my rights at one point, but you know how it is here. Kenya is just Kenya."

"Let me guess. They wanted a bribe."

"Exactly. They wanted 10,000 shillings—80 US dollars—from each of us. Fifty people, that's half a million shillings. Corruption, plain and simple."

Dennis frowned. "That's so much money."

Morah leaned forward, her voice dropping slightly. "It's how they get you. If you wait two days until Monday and see a judge, the judge might be in cahoots with them, and the real fine might be higher—30,000 to 50,000 shillings, with up to six months in jail if they want to make an example of you. Who can afford that? So, they know that you'll pay the

bribe. No one wants to sit in jail for two days waiting for a hearing. The jails are filthy, Dennis. You could get sick just being in there."

Dennis clenched his jaw. "So, it's like you're trapped."

Morah nodded, her face darkening. "I only make about 25,000 shillings a month, Dennis. Eight thousand is nearly a third of my salary, but what choice did I have? I couldn't afford to pay the official fine. If I hadn't paid up today, I'd still be rotting in that cell, waiting to see a judge."

Dennis shook his head. "They're counting on that fear. Knowing you can't fight back."

"Exactly," Morah said bitterly. "It's a game they've perfected. They don't strike fancy clubs where they might annoy powerful people. They prey on people like us. They know most of us can't risk waiting to go to court. You try, and by the time you see the judge, you've already spent at least two days in a cell, lost your job maybe, and you still must pay an insane fine. So, they take what they can get, and we pay because we have no choice."

Dennis rubbed his temples, the weight of it settling in. "And this just keeps happening?"

Morah nodded. "Over and over. People are just trying to live, and the cops are out there hunting for bribes. They don't care about enforcing the law but about lining their pockets. It's survival for them, too, in a way."

"It's not right," Dennis said quietly, his frustration simmering.

"No," Morah agreed, her eyes flashing with anger. "But it's how things are. When you live here long enough, you get used to it. That doesn't mean you stop hating it, though."

Dennis nodded, feeling the familiar anger rise in his chest. "And it won't change until the system changes."

Morah gave him a sad smile. "Exactly. But until then, we survive. What else can we do?"

Human Trafficking

Dennis was sitting at his temporary desk in the WPA office, the late afternoon sun casting long shadows across the room. The weight of what he'd uncovered hung in the air, thicker than the heat. He had just returned from the field, where he'd pieced together more evidence—receipts, schedules, documents linking the poachers to something far bigger. Names like Otieno and Ziad weren't just whispers anymore. They were part of a sprawling syndicate.

Kamau entered the room, his usual easy demeanor replaced by something more serious. He slid Dennis a bottle of water across the table before sitting down. The room was quiet except for the faint hum of the ceiling fan. Dennis took a long drink, the cool water doing little to cut through the tension.

Dennis and Kamau sat across from each other, reviewing the documents that unraveled a grim picture. Dennis pointed to a list of names and destinations tied to trafficking in people, drugs, and arms. "It's a full-scale network. They're moving people alongside ivory and drugs."

Kamau nodded, his face shadowed. "Yes, human trafficking runs alongside everything else. Migrants from Ethiopia, Somalia, or Sudan—up to 5,000 yearly—are promised work abroad or safety in Kenya, only to be forced into labor or sex trafficking rings. They're funneled south, and many end up shipped out of Mombasa, scattered into slavery and exploitation, never seen again."

Dennis's jaw tightened. "Weapons and migrants cross the Ethiopian-Kenyan border at Moyale and are smuggled down the A2 highway. Bribes paid at checkpoints keep police quiet, adding protection for people like Otieno and Ziad."

Kamau replied grimly, "Otieno keeps everything running with his connections, greasing palms to silence officials."

"And then there's The Broker," Dennis added, his voice low. "The one linking these Kenyan channels to buyers in the Gulf and China. He's the one orchestrating it all."

Kamau leaned in, his voice hard. "Yes. Every shipment out of Mombasa strengthens his network. That port is their lifeline, and Ziad has eyes all over it."

Dennis stood, his mind made up. "I'll go to Mombasa. I need to find the proof."

Kamau's gaze was stern. "Just remember, the closer you get, the deadlier this becomes. They won't hesitate to eliminate you—Otieno, Ziad, The Broker. They have too much to lose."

Dennis took a breath, feeling the weight of their mission. This wasn't just about wildlife anymore.

A Night on the Town

That evening, after spending his afternoon at the WPA comparing his notes to their archives, Dennis sat in the plush leather booth of Leopard Lounge, one of Nairobi's upscale night spots, where the hum of low jazz drifted through the air. The bar was dimly lit, with flickering candles on the tables casting soft shadows on the polished wood. The walls were lined with dark mahogany, and the crowd around them was a mix of Nairobi's wealthy locals and tourists looking for a taste of luxury. Expensive cocktails sat on marble countertops, and now and then, the pop of a champagne bottle rang out, followed by laughter and applause.

Morah looked perfectly at ease here, though Dennis knew she didn't live in this world. She had put on a nice dress—a sleek black number that hugged her curves. Her face was striking, her hair done up like she was one of them. But the truth was, her life was far from this. Dennis sipped his drink and let her talk, the rhythm of her voice cutting through the bar's background noise.

"They say this place is fancy," Morah said, waving a hand around the room. "But it's all the same once you know what's happening behind the scenes. You can pick out the girls, can't you?"

Dennis raised an eyebrow. "Girls?"

Morah chuckled softly, glancing around the room. "Prostitutes. Pay-as-you-go girlfriends. They're everywhere. Nairobi nightlife is full of them, even in places like this. The girls dress up; they look like they belong, but they're not here only for the drinks. They're here for business."

Dennis followed her gaze as she nodded toward the bar, where a few young women stood, laughing and chatting with a group of men in sharp suits. The women were beautiful, dressed to the nines, but there was something detached about the way they held themselves. They weren't here for fun.

"They look like any other girl out for a good time," Morah continued, "but they're working. The men know it. The girls know it. Everyone knows the score."

Dennis glanced back at Morah. "How does it work?"

Morah leaned forward, lowering her voice, though there was no need—no one was paying attention to them. "The girls wait. Sometimes, they approach the men, but usually, the men approach them. They'll chat for a while, maybe buy a drink. Then, they'll take the conversation somewhere else. A lot of the clubs have deals with the hotels nearby—it makes it easy. The price? It depends on the girl. Some charge as low as 2,000 Kenyan shillings for the night. But in a place like this?" She tilted her head toward one of the women at the bar. "Those girls charge more. Five thousand, maybe even ten thousand shillings."

Dennis did the math in his head. Not much in dollars— $20 to $80 for the night, depending on the girl. It was cheap, he thought, cheap for something so dangerous.

Morah caught his look and gave a knowing smile. "They say prostitution is illegal, but everyone knows where to find the girls. Some pick them up at fancy clubs like this one. But if you really want to see it, all you have to do is head down to Koinange Street. That's where they're out in the open. You can drive down there at night, and the girls line the street

like they're waiting for a bus. Some of them are barely teenagers."

Dennis frowned. "And the police?"

Morah laughed, a bitter sound. "The police? Please. They take their cut. They always do. They'll raid a club once in a while and make a show of it, but it's mostly for bribes. No one cares about the girls. They're just business."

Dennis nodded, his eyes drifting back to the crowd. He could see it now—the way some of the men leaned in too close, the way the women touched their arms just a little too casually. Deals were being made here, all under the guise of a good time.

"You'd never do it?" Dennis asked, though he already knew the answer.

Morah shook her head, her expression firm. "No. I won't. It's tempting, don't get me wrong. It crosses your mind when you're struggling to pay rent or your kid needs school fees and uniforms. But I can't. I won't go down that road."

Her words hung in the air for a moment, and Dennis felt their weight. He admired her resolve but could see the strain in her eyes—the cost of staying clean in a city where survival was almost out of reach for someone without an above-average salary.

The night wore on, and the bar began to thin out. The crowd shifted, some moving to the dance floor, others disappearing with their new "friends." Morah's hand brushed his on the table, and Dennis glanced at her, seeing the softness in her eyes and the subtle shift in her body

language. She was cute, no doubt about that. Her laugh, her humor—they'd kept the night light. But he could see something else now. Something in the way she was leaning toward him, her smile lingering just a little longer.

"You know," she said quietly, "we don't have to end the night now. You could invite me back to your hotel."

Dennis looked at her for a long moment. She was interested in him. And under different circumstances, he might've been interested in her, too. But his mind was somewhere else. Back in the Mara, with Naomi. He missed her, missed the way she made him feel whole. And as much as Morah was charming, this wasn't what he wanted.

"I've got an early morning," Dennis said, his voice soft but firm. "You are very attractive, but honestly, my head's somewhere else tonight."

Morah watched him, her smile fading slightly, but she didn't push. She was smart enough to know when to back off. "Naomi, huh?"

Dennis nodded, letting out a small sigh. "Yeah. Naomi."

Morah smiled gently, though there was a trace of sadness in it. "She's lucky to have you."

Dennis chuckled, shaking his head. "Maybe I'm the lucky one."

Morah stood, smoothing out her dress as she looked around the bar. "Come on, let's get you back to your hotel before it gets too late."

Dennis dropped some bills on the table and followed her into the cool Nairobi night. The city was quieter now, the

streets dimly lit. They stood on the sidewalk, waiting for a taxi to pass. Morah glanced up at him, her face soft in the streetlight's glow.

"You take care of yourself, Dennis."

"You too, Morah," he said warmly. "And thanks for tonight."

She winked at him before slipping into the taxi, leaving Dennis alone on the sidewalk. As the car pulled away, he watched the city lights blur into the night, his thoughts drifting back to Naomi. It had been a good night, but as he took the next taxi to his boarding house, he knew where his heart was: the Mara, Naomi, and whatever came next.

Meeting The Enemy

Kamau had finally made the call, passing the word to the right channels: he had a buyer interested in high-end ivory, supposedly representing an auction house seeking to move large quantities overseas. It was a risky lead, and they both knew it. Dennis's cover was thin, but there wasn't time to craft a flawless backstory. If they could get him in, it might open the doors they needed—an inroad to the traffickers' network and, if they were lucky, a connection to The Broker.

The rendezvous was set for that afternoon in an abandoned warehouse near Narok—a place where forgotten deals and clandestine meetings thrived in the shadows. In the dim light, Kamau handed Dennis a small earpiece, his tone severe, almost parental. "Listen. I'll be on the line. If you sense anything's off, don't hesitate. Get out. No playing the hero."

Dennis slipped the earpiece in, feeling the familiar weight of Kamau's gaze. "I got it," he replied, confident but acutely aware of the risks. They exchanged a final nod before Dennis opened the car door, stepping out and squaring his shoulders. He knew what had to be done, and Kamau would be watching his back—from a distance.

"Be careful, Dennis," Kamau said, almost under his breath. Dennis grinned. "I always am."

Walking toward the warehouse, Dennis took a deep breath. Two men waited outside, both armed, their eyes narrowing with suspicion. One of them, stocky and sporting a scar above his eyebrow, stepped forward. "You the buyer?" His voice was gravelly, testing.

Dennis nodded, keeping his tone steady. "Here to talk business. I've got clients looking for quality, and I was told you might be the ones to help."

The man's gaze lingered on Dennis, calculating, before he gave a curt nod and motioned for him to follow. The warehouse was dimly lit, its floor cluttered with crates and sacks. Men stood in groups, their unblinking stares drilling into Dennis. He fought to keep his expression neutral, ignoring the itch of nervousness crawling up his spine.

A tall man with a sharp scar across his cheek emerged from the shadows, his skeptical gaze locking onto Dennis.

"You're the buyer?" the tall man asked, his gruff voice tinged with doubt.

"That's right," Dennis replied smoothly. "I've got clients looking for ivory and horn. High-end buyers who pay well for the right product. I was told you could deliver."

The man's eyes narrowed as he studied Dennis. After a pause, he motioned toward a secluded room in the back, concealed by a heavy curtain. "Come."

Inside, Dennis noted the makeshift office: a table strewn with ledgers, a satellite phone, and several bags, some visibly stuffed with cash. The scarred man gestured for Dennis to sit before leaning against the table, arms crossed.

"We don't work with just anyone," he said, his voice skeptical. "You say you've got clients, but talk is cheap. Prove you're worth our time."

Dennis reached into his jacket and set a small stack of cash on the table, fanning out the crisp banknotes. "I'm not here to waste anyone's time. My clients want consistency and quality. If you're as good as they say, we'll both be happy."

The scarred man eyed the money, then nodded to an associate who stepped forward with a small wooden box. He opened it, revealing a few ivory carvings—intricate pieces polished to a fine sheen. Dennis kept his face impassive, though the sight of the carvings twisted his stomach.

"This is just a sample," the man said, watching Dennis closely. "If your people like it, we'll talk larger shipments—but only if we're convinced you're serious."

Dennis leaned forward slightly, meeting the man's gaze. "I have buyers in the Middle East and Europe looking for a steady supply. No one-off deals. If you can deliver, we'll make serious money."

The scarred man exchanged a look with his associate before returning his attention to Dennis. "There's someone

higher up you'll need to meet if this goes anywhere. They don't make deals lightly. We're just the sellers. He's the one calling the shots."

Dennis's pulse quickened. This was it—the connection they needed. "I've heard of him," Dennis said casually. "They call him 'The Broker,' right?"

A flicker of surprise crossed the man's face. "Not many know that name." He paused, studying Dennis. "If The Broker's interested, he'll contact you. But he's careful. Until then, don't try to find him."

Dennis nodded, his expression steady. "Understood. I'll be waiting."

Suddenly, Dennis sensed a shift in the atmosphere. One of the men by the door was frowning, his gaze fixed on him. He leaned in to whisper something to the scarred man, whose expression immediately hardened.

"Who are you really?" the man demanded, his hand moving to the gun at his side.

Dennis's heart pounded as he raised his hands slightly. "I told you, I'm here to do business."

The man wasn't buying it. He stepped closer, suspicion darkening his eyes. Kamau's urgent voice crackled in Dennis's ear. "Dennis, get out. Now."

Dennis acted instinctively, flipping the table toward the man and diving to the side. A shot rang out, splintering the table. Dennis scrambled to his feet, shoving past one of the men and sprinting for the door.

"Kamau, I'm coming out!" he shouted, breathless.

He burst through the entrance, his pursuers' shouts and pounding footsteps close behind. Spotting Kamau's jeep speeding toward him, Dennis made a desperate dash.

"Get in!" Kamau yelled, the passenger door swinging open.

Dennis dove inside, slamming the door just as Kamau hit the gas. The jeep roared forward, tires spitting dust. Shots echoed behind them, and Dennis ducked instinctively, his breath ragged.

"That was close," Kamau said, his eyes fixed on the road.

Dennis nodded, swallowing hard. "Too close. But I got something. They mentioned The Broker. He's the one running things. All of this is connected."

Kamau's expression darkened. "The Broker—this mysterious operator. No one knows who's behind the name. But if he's involved, he's got his hands in everything."

Dennis exhaled deeply, the adrenaline slowly fading. "We need to find him. He's the key to all of this."

Kamau tightened his grip on the wheel. "We will. But first, we need to regroup. You almost didn't make it out of there."

Dennis leaned back, exhaustion washing over him. Kamau was right. They'd pushed their luck, but they'd confirmed a critical puzzle piece. The Broker was real—and now they had a name to follow.

Chapter 8: The Broker's Shadow

Tracking Mrefu

The following day, Dennis arrived early at the Wildlife Preservation Alliance's office to coordinate with Kamau. Morah, always smiling, led Dennis to an empty office he could use for the day.

Dennis had a probable phone number for Mrefu, which he had obtained from the poachers' phones. His first move was to contact an old acquaintance working in telecommunications in Nairobi. Dennis knew that getting information from a phone company was challenging, but it could be done with the right incentives and the right person. He made the call using an encrypted line, leaning back as he waited for his contact to pick up.

"Kioni, it's Dennis," he said when the line connected. "I need a favor—one that requires discretion."

Kioni's voice was warm, though tinged with curiosity. "Dennis Bellamy. It's been a while. What kind of favor are we talking about?"

"I need information on a phone number. Specifically, I need to know who the account is registered to and any address linked to it," Dennis replied, his tone serious.

There was a pause on the other end of the line, and Dennis could almost hear Kioni considering the risks. "You know this isn't exactly legal, right? If I get caught, it could end my career."

Dennis nodded, even though Kioni couldn't see him. "I know. But it's important. I could get it in a slower, official way, but lives are at stake. I wouldn't ask if it wasn't."

Kioni sighed, the sound of typing coming through the receiver. "All right. Send me the number, and I'll see what I can do. But Dennis, you owe me. Big time."

"I know. I'll make it up to you," Dennis promised, ending the call.

He sent the number to Kioni and waited, pacing the small room as the minutes ticked by. Finally, his phone buzzed with a message. He opened it, his eyes scanning the text. The account was registered to a man named Joram Wa-Mrefu Mwangi, with an address in a neighborhood on the outskirts of Kisumu—a low-income area known for its transient population and lack of official oversight. It was the kind of place where someone could disappear without a trace.

Now that he knew the phone was officially registered in Mrefu's name, Dennis's second move was to use IRIS's resources to pinpoint Mrefu's current location using tower information. He contacted the office back in the States, relaying the details and requesting a Stingray, a device that could intercept and locate mobile phone signals. It wasn't easy—the device was highly restricted, and using it in Kenya would require some delicate maneuvering—but Dennis knew that if anyone could make it happen, it was his handler.

"We need to find this guy, and we need to do it fast," Dennis said, his voice tense. "If we can track his phone, we can at least get a general idea of where he is."

His handler paused, then replied, "I'll see what I can do, Dennis. But it would be best if you were careful. If Mrefu is as connected as you think, he might already know someone is looking for him."

Dennis ended the call, his mind racing. They had a name and an address, and soon, they might have a location. It wasn't much, but it was more than they had before. With every piece of information, they were getting closer to unraveling the network that had brought so much death and destruction to the Mara.

Dennis looked at Kamau, who had been waiting patiently, his gaze steady. "We're close, Kamau," Dennis said, his voice edged with determination. "We just need the Stingray. It'll be here in a few days, and then we can track Mrefu down. But until then, we need to keep a low profile."

Kamau nodded, his curiosity evident. "So, this Stingray—how does it work?"

Dennis leaned back, his eyes narrowing slightly as he explained. "It's a powerful tracking device, officially called an IMSI catcher. It pretends to be a legitimate cell tower, so when a phone connects to it, it gives us valuable data—like the phone's unique IMSI number and a general location."

Kamau's brows rose. "So, it's like it's hijacking their signal?"

"Exactly," Dennis said, nodding. "Once Mrefu's phone connects to it, the Stingray can even intercept messages and, if needed, weaken his phone's security. The plan is to locate his device without alerting him. But we'll have to act fast

once we know where he is. We need to position the Stingray close to his phone."

Kamau's face hardened, understanding the stakes. "And if he moves?"

"We'll be ready to track him in real-time. This is as close as we've ever been, Kamau," Dennis said, the weight of their mission clear in his gaze. "We're one step away from Mrefu and dismantling his entire network."

Kamau nodded, his resolve as firm as Dennis's. Piece by piece, they were pulling Mrefu's operation out of the shadows.

Stingray on Mrefu

Kioni called Dennis early in the morning, the urgency in his voice clear. "I've got something for you, Dennis," he said. "The location tied to Mrefu's phone is in a neighborhood on the outskirts of Nairobi—a place called Mathare."

Dennis got an address and thanked Kioni, feeling a surge of determination. This was the break they needed. He turned to Kamau, who was already gearing up and ready to accompany Dennis on the next leg of the investigation. Together, they packed the Stingray device, which IRIS had delivered discreetly, and set off for Mathare.

The road to Mathare was filled with the bustling chaos of Nairobi's streets—traffic jams, street vendors, and crowds of people going about their day. When they finally arrived, the neighborhood was a maze of narrow, winding streets lined with small shops, homes made of corrugated metal, and

dusty courtyards. The air was thick with the scent of charcoal fires and the distant sound of children playing.

Dennis parked the vehicle in an inconspicuous spot, and they set up the Stingray device, positioning it to collect data from the surrounding area. The device was powerful enough to mimic a cell tower, forcing nearby phones to connect. Samuel watched as Dennis worked, the small screen of the Stingray lighting up with signals.

"Let's see what we can catch," Dennis muttered, adjusting the controls. Soon, Dennis noticed Mrefu's number. The signal was strong, and they now had a solid location to work with.

For the rest of the day, they monitored the activity, watching as phones connected and disconnected and data packets flowed in. It was tedious work, but the logs they were collecting could give them the information they needed—phone numbers, locations, and even messages. Dennis smiled, a sense of progress washing over him. "We've got him," he said, glancing at Samuel. "Now we know where he is. Let's pack up and get back."

Kamau nodded, his expression filled with both relief and determination. They had a location, and with it, they were one step closer to bringing down the network.

Studying the Stingray Logs

Dennis returned to the pension with a single-minded focus: track down The Broker. He knew they would unravel the entire operation if they could find this elusive figure. But The Broker was challenging to find. He was a ghost, and the trails were buried deep. Back at his temporary apartment,

Dennis set up his laptop, accessing the encrypted data they had pulled from the Stingray logs.

Dennis spent hours studying the data—contact lists and cryptic messages. He cross-referenced the numbers with the information they already had, trying to make sense of the connections. Slowly, a pattern began to emerge: several contacts in Somalia and South Sudan, where arms smuggling was rampant. It became clear that Mrefu was involved in other criminal activities beyond poaching.

Kamau entered the room with two cups of coffee. He handed one to Dennis and watched him work. "Any progress?" he asked.

Dennis nodded, his eyes still on the screen. "I think I've found something. These numbers that Mrefu talked to are linked to militia groups in Somalia and South Sudan. The Broker isn't just moving ivory and rhino horn; he's moving weapons, too. He's supplying militias across East Africa."

Kamau's brow furrowed. "So that's why they're so well-armed. The poachers aren't just working for profit—they're part of something bigger."

Dennis looked up, meeting her gaze. "It gets worse. Some messages allude to a shipment planned in a couple of weeks. It looks like it will combine wildlife products with a massive arms cache. They plan to use a ship going north to the Somali coast, a shipment for South Sudan, and then to the Gulf. If that happens, we're looking at a significant escalation in the region's conflict."

Kamau set his coffee down, his expression grim. "A good occasion to stop them. Do we have any idea where the shipment is going to be staged?"

Dennis shook his head. "Not yet. But I think I have a lead. There are mentions of a warehouse near the port in Mombasa. If we can get there before the shipment moves, we might be able to stop it—and maybe even find out who The Broker is."

Kamau nodded. "Then we'll have to head to Mombasa. But we need to be careful. If The Broker's involved, he'll have eyes everywhere."

Dennis got an offer

Later that afternoon, Dennis received an unexpected call. The number was blocked, but he answered anyway, his instincts on high alert. The voice on the other end was calm, almost friendly.

"Mr. Bellamy, I understand you've been asking questions," the voice said. "Questions that could get you into trouble."

Dennis stiffened. "Who is this?"

"Let's just say I'm someone who can make your life a lot easier—or a lot more difficult. You're meddling in affairs that don't concern you, Mr. Bellamy. But I'm willing to offer you a way out."

Dennis felt a surge of anger but kept his cool. "Really? What could make you think I would be interested?"

The voice chuckled softly. "Oh, but you haven't even heard the offer. A significant sum of money, Mr. Bellamy. Enough for you to walk away and forget about this…"

Dennis's jaw tightened. "I might be too expensive for you."

A brief silence followed before the voice spoke again, this time colder. "You should give us a number that would interest you. You're being watched, Mr. Bellamy. For your sake and for the sake of those around you, I suggest you make an offer."

"How would I contact you?" asked Dennis.

"We will be in touch." The voice on the other end hung up.

Dennis's heart was pounding. He looked over at Kamau, who had been listening. His eyes were wide. "What was that about?" he asked.

Dennis set the phone down, taking a deep breath. "They know about me. They're trying to buy me off. And they made it clear—they're watching."

Kamau frowned, his expression hardening. "That means we're getting close. But it also means we need to be more careful. We can't let them scare us off."

Dennis nodded, determination burning in his chest. "We won't stop. We will find The Broker and bring this entire network down."

Watching his Back

That night, Dennis couldn't shake the feeling of being watched. He knew that The Broker's influence reached far,

and the phone call confirmed they were on dangerous ground. He double-checked the doors and window locks, ensuring everything was secure.

At breakfast, Dennis sat at the table, his thoughts racing. The Broker wasn't just a trafficker—he was a power broker who thrived in the chaos of East Africa. And now, Dennis and his team were in his crosshairs.

As Dennis stared at the map before him, he felt the weight of what they were up against. This wasn't just about stopping poachers or saving wildlife. It was about dismantling a network that thrived on instability and profited from the suffering of others. And they had to move fast. The shipment was the key, and Mombasa was their next target.

Dennis looked up as Kamau joined him, his expression determined. "We need to leave for Mombasa soon," Dennis said. "We need to get there before that shipment does. But first, I need to be in the Mara."

Chapter 9: Enjoying the Maasai Mara

Back in the Maasai Mara

Later that morning, Dennis stood at the terminal of Wilson Airport, the smaller of Nairobi's two main airports, bustling but far quieter than the international hub of Jomo Kenyatta. Wilson mainly catered to domestic flights, chartered planes, and tourists heading into the wilds of Kenya—just what Dennis needed.

The air was warm, the late-morning sun casting a golden glow over the tarmac. Small and rugged planes sat in neat rows, their propellers still as they waited for their next flights to the coast, the Rift Valley, and the Maasai Mara.

His flight was scheduled for the early afternoon, one of the small, low-flying charters that ferried tourists and locals alike to the savannah. As the boarding call echoed through the terminal, Dennis grabbed his bag and moved toward the plane, a small Cessna Caravan with scuffed white paint and a tired but reliable look.

He had taken these flights before—an hour and a half over the rolling hills and plains, dipping in and out of clouds, the world stretching wide and open below. The plane was small, with just a few seats and little room for anything but the essentials. Dennis nodded to the pilot, who smiled briefly as he stowed his bag and settled into the narrow seat by the window. The engine roared to life, a familiar sound now, and soon they were taxiing down the runway, picking up speed.

As they lifted into the air, Nairobi fell away beneath him, the sprawling city quickly becoming a patchwork of roads, buildings, and green parks. The city's noise and chaos seemed to shrink with every minute, replaced by the steady hum of the plane's engine. Dennis watched as the landscape shifted—first the busy streets, then the outskirts, where the high-rises gave way to open fields, farms, and rolling hills.

The flight leveled out, and soon they were flying low enough that Dennis could see the earth below clearly, the land starting to stretch into the vast, untamed beauty of the Rift Valley.

The sky was a pale blue, dotted with clouds that cast shadows over the land, and the world felt peaceful up here, away from the noise of the city and the search for Mrefu. As the plane flew over the savannah, Dennis could make out the shapes of animals moving below—a herd of wildebeest crossing the plains in their long, graceful lines and giraffes standing tall among the trees.

He felt a familiar calm settle over him. Something was grounding about Mara, always reminding him why he was here and why he fought the battles he did. The flight was uneventful, with barely a few minutes of turbulence over the Rift. The pilot was steady and sure, and soon, the familiar outlines of the Maasai Mara began to rise in the distance.

The plane descended slowly, the vast expanse of golden grassland unfolding beneath them, broken only by the winding rivers and clusters of acacia trees. The familiar airstrip was little more than a dirt path; it was simple and functional but fit the landscape perfectly. As the plane

touched down, bouncing slightly on the uneven strip, Dennis felt that familiar surge of anticipation.

The Mara always had that effect on him—it was a place of raw, wild beauty, danger, and tension. There was always something waiting, just beneath the surface. The plane came to a stop, and Dennis grabbed his bag and stepped out onto the strip. The air was warmer and purer here, with the unmistakable scent of earth and grass. He took a deep breath, letting it fill his lungs, and looked around.

She stood a little ways off, leaning against one of the Land Cruisers parked near the strip. Naomi. Her dark hair was pulled back, her eyes scanning the horizon, but the moment she saw him, her face lit up with a smile. She pushed off the vehicle and walked toward him, her movements easy and confident, like she belonged to this land as much as the animals did. "Welcome back," she said, her voice carrying over the sound of the cooling engine.

Dennis smiled, slinging his bag over his shoulder as he closed the distance between them. "Good to be back," he replied, his eyes meeting hers. She tilted her head slightly, giving him that look—the one that said she had been waiting for him and had plenty to say when the time was right. "How was Nairobi?"

"Chaotic," Dennis said, shaking his head. "Didn't get as much as I hoped, but I'll fill you in." Naomi nodded, understanding without asking.

"Well, you're here now. We've got work to do." Dennis chuckled.

"I didn't think I was coming back for a vacation."

She smiled, her eyes bright in the afternoon sun, then turned toward the Land Cruiser. "Come on, I'll drive. We'll talk on the way." As they climbed into the vehicle, Dennis felt a sense of relief. Nairobi had its demands, but the Mara was different.

Here, everything felt sharper and more transparent. Dinner with tourists Dennis was glad to be back from Nairobi. He glanced at Naomi as they drove toward a nearby lodge for dinner. She was focused, as always, but she had a lightness in her that he had been missing in the city. They had agreed to take the evening off, to leave the world of poachers and danger behind, if only for a few hours.

Mara Sopa Lodge is nestled on the slopes of the Oloolaimutia Hills, offering panoramic views of the vast Maasai Mara plains, perched on a gentle hill overlooking the savannah. It was the kind of place where tourists came to marvel at the beauty of the Mara, to feel like they were part of something bigger. Acacia trees surrounded the lodge, and from the open dining area, you could see the endless plains stretching far into the horizon.

Tonight, as the sky turned pink and purple with the setting sun, the scene felt almost unreal in its perfection. Inside, the lodge was warm, with large wooden beams and stone walls giving it a rustic charm. Lanterns flickered on each table, casting a soft light over the diners, most of whom were relaxed after a long day of game drives. Dennis and Naomi found a table near the open balcony, where the breeze carried in the fresh scent of the grasslands.

As Dennis and Naomi settled into their seats, the last rays of the setting sun illuminated the landscape in soft pink

and purple hues. The vast expanse of the Mara stretched before them, dotted with acacia trees and the distant movement of wildlife. Dennis leaned back in his chair, breathing in the fresh, cool air that carried the scents of the grasslands.

"This place has a way of making you forget everything else, doesn't it?" Dennis remarked, his voice low and thoughtful. "It's like time stands still here." P a g e 149 | 268 Naomi smiled, looking around the Mara Sopa Lodge's rustic interior. "It does. There's something timeless about it," she replied, then added with pride, "Did you know this lodge was built in the early '80s? Back then, it was one of the first in the Mara." Dennis raised an eyebrow. "The '80s? It's held up well."

"It has," Naomi nodded.

"It was built by a small group of conservationists who wanted to create something sustainable but still welcoming for tourists. They were determined to showcase the beauty of the Mara while protecting the ecosystem. You see the wooden beams and stone walls?" She gestured to the sturdy, natural structure around them. "They used local materials, sourced from the area, to make sure the lodge blended into the environment." Dennis ran his hand over the smooth wood of the table. "It feels like the whole place grew out of the ground. A lot more character than the modern lodges." Naomi chuckled.

"It wasn't always this elegant, though. In the early days, the lodge was simpler—fewer rooms, no hot water, and no luxury amenities. But it had charm. Guests would gather around campfires, and dinner was cooked over open flames."

Dennis imagined it—tourists sitting in a small group, sharing stories of the day's wildlife encounters, the Mara unfolding in the background, untouched by time. "Sounds more rugged. Fitting, given the surroundings."

"Exactly," Naomi agreed. "But over the years, they expanded. Added the pool, updated the rooms, and made it more comfortable for tourists. Yet, they've kept the heart of it intact. See those lanterns?" She pointed to the dimly lit table decorations. "They still use them every night, just like when the lodge first opened. It keeps that sense of connection to the past alive."

Dennis glanced toward the balcony, where the breeze brought the distant sounds of the Mara. The stone walls around them exuded the history Naomi spoke of, and the open dining area seemed to invite the wilderness in rather than shut it out. "You can feel the history here," he said. "I bet the place has seen its share of stories." Naomi smiled softly. "It has. Some old guides who worked here during the first years would tell tales of how lions wandered closer to the lodge and how elephants would drink from the watering hole near the cabins. Things were wilder back then."

Dennis nodded, his gaze distant as if picturing the lodge in its earliest days, untouched by the conveniences of modern life. "I like that they've kept it simple. It's elegant, sure, but it still feels like you are part of something bigger out here in the wild."

"That's what they wanted," Naomi said, leaning back in her chair.

"A place where people could come, experience the Mara, and not feel cut off from nature. Even now, when they

expanded, they've stayed true to that vision." Dennis smiled, appreciating the lodge even more now that he knew its story. "Seems like they succeeded." He paused, watching the shadows lengthen across the plains. "This place... it's a reminder that there's more to life than what we're fighting. Naomi glanced around, her eyes softening. "It's nice here," she said. "Feels like a different world." Dennis nodded. "Yeah, it's good to be out of the thick of things for a bit. We've earned it."

They soon found themselves conversing with a group of tourists, happy and carefree, their faces lit with the excitement of a day spent in the Mara. Something was refreshing about seeing the Mara through their eyes—full of wonder, untouched by the grim realities that Naomi and Dennis faced daily. As the tourists shared their stories, they were enjoying the beauty and thrill of the wild, their worries far from the poaching threats that kept Naomi and Dennis awake at night. For a while, the troubles that followed them seemed far away.

And that, Dennis thought, was something to savor. The group of tourists gathered around the lodge's wooden table was diverse. A young family with two children sat closest to the fire, the kids wrapped in blankets, their eyes wide with excitement as they listened to the adults' stories. The father, a bearded man in his thirties, nudged his son and smiled as he asked, "Did you ever think you'd see so many animals in one day, buddy?"

The boy shook his head, his voice soft with awe. "No, Dad. I still can't believe we saw a lion." Next to the family, an older couple from Canada sipped their tea, their silver hair

glowing in the firelight. They had spent years traveling the world, yet they both agreed that the Great Migration was unlike anything they had ever witnessed. "We've seen wildlife before, but nothing like this," the man said to Naomi. You're lucky to work in such a place."

"I am," Naomi replied with a smile. "But it's not just luck—it's also a responsibility."

A younger couple sat nearby, hand in hand. They were newlyweds, still fresh from their wedding, and Kenya had been the honeymoon destination of their dreams. "We wanted something special," the woman said. "And watching the P a g e 152 | 268 wildebeest cross the Mara River today— it was beyond anything we imagined." Across from them was a solo traveler, a woman in her late twenties who had been hiking across Africa for the last month. She was sun-kissed and adventurous, a backpacker who thrived on experiences like these.

"I've heard about the migration all my life," she said. "Seeing it today was like watching a force of nature in action." The group had questions for Naomi, as was common when tourists found themselves in close quarters with a ranger who knew the land so well. One of the older men leaned in, his voice hushed. "Street peddlers have offered us some curios on the way here—small statues, jewelry, even some old bones. Is any of that legal to bring back to the States?" Naomi chuckled softly. "It's a good question. Kenya has strict laws when it comes to wildlife products. Anything that comes from an animal—bones, horns, even feathers—could get you in trouble with customs when you try to leave.

It's best to avoid those." The newlyweds exchanged glances, and the woman asked, "What about those carved statues? We saw some beautiful wooden carvings in the market earlier."

"Those are fine," Naomi assured them. "Wooden carvings, Maasai jewelry made from beads, woven baskets—these are all great souvenirs. You can also find items like soapstone carvings and paintings. As long as it doesn't involve animal products, it's a safe bet." One of the solo travelers, intrigued by the conversation, leaned forward. "And what about marijuana? Is it legal here?" Naomi shook her head firmly.

"No, marijuana is illegal in Kenya. There are some countries where the laws are more P a g e 153 | 268 relaxed, but Kenya isn't one of them. Possession, use, and trafficking of marijuana can lead to serious legal consequences, so it's best to steer clear of that." The older man from Canada nodded thoughtfully. "It's good to know what to avoid," he said.

"We don't want to ruin a beautiful trip with legal trouble." Naomi smiled, her eyes reflecting the flickering firelight. "Kenya is full of beautiful things you can take home with you—memories, photos, stories. Stick to the cultural souvenirs; you'll have plenty to show for it when you return." The conversation continued, but the mood remained light.

The tourists were enthralled by the landscape, the animals, and Naomi's stories about the land they explored. The children dozed off as the fire crackled while the rest of the group continued to savor the experience of being in the

heart of one of the world's most incredible natural wonders. The great migration had left its mark on them, and now they would carry a part of the Mara with them, safely tucked away in their hearts.

Naomi stood by the firepit outside the dining area, the embers glowing softly in the evening light. The sky had fully transitioned from pinks and purples to the deep blues of night, and the quiet murmur of the lodge's guests created a peaceful backdrop. She glanced over at the group of tourists seated near them during dinner. They were still chattering excitedly about the day's events, flipping through photos on their cameras and phones, their faces lit with enthusiasm. One of the guides, a tall Maasai man named Daniel, stood nearby, talking quietly with another staff member.

Naomi had known Daniel for years; he was one of the best guides in the Mara, respected by tourists and locals alike. She approached him with a warm smile. "Daniel," she greeted him. "How's the group tonight? They seem like they had a good day." Daniel turned to her and smiled, his white teeth gleaming in the firelight. "They did, Naomi. We saw the Great Migration today, with wildebeests crossing the river. It was spectacular. They'll talk about it for the rest of their lives." Naomi chuckled.

"It's always like that, isn't it? The first time seeing the migration—it leaves a mark." Daniel nodded thoughtfully. "It's what keeps people coming back. The Mara surprises them even when they think they've seen everything." Naomi looked over at the group again, their excitement contagious. An idea formed in her mind as she glanced back at Daniel.

"I was thinking, Daniel… would it be possible to bring someone with your group tomorrow morning?" Daniel raised an eyebrow. "Someone new to the group? Sure, we have room. Who's joining?"

"Dennis," Naomi replied, a smile playing on her lips. "He's had a rough few weeks, and I think a morning safari might do him some good. He could use a break from everything going on." Daniel's smile widened.

"Dennis, huh? I think that's a great idea. We'll leave early, right after sunrise. I'll make sure he gets a front-row seat." Naomi laughed softly. "Thanks, Daniel. He'll love it." She watched as Daniel returned to his conversation, then turned and headed toward the lodge, where Dennis was still sitting at the table, sipping his drink and staring out at the night sky.

She could see the tension in his posture, the way his shoulders were still tight from everything weighing on him. She knew how much he carried—the losses, the guilt, the endless cycle of danger—and she wanted to give him just a few hours of peace, a chance to reconnect with the beauty of the Mara. Naomi approached him quietly, sliding into the seat next to him. "Hey," she said softly. Dennis turned to her, a small smile appearing on his face.

"Hey. Where'd you disappear to?"

"I was talking to Daniel," she said, leaning in closer. "I arranged a little surprise for you." Dennis raised an eyebrow, curiosity flashing in his eyes. "A surprise?" Naomi nodded. "Tomorrow morning, you're joining the group for a short safari. Daniel's going to take you out with the tourists."

Dennis blinked, clearly taken aback. "Me? On a tourist safari?"

"Yeah," Naomi said, her voice soft and playful. "I figured you could use a break.

You've been in the thick of things for too long. A few hours of just enjoying the wildlife, seeing the Mara with fresh eyes—I think it'll be good for you." Dennis stared at her for a moment, then let out a quiet laugh. "You're serious."

"Very," Naomi said, her smile widening. "I know you don't take much time for yourself, but this could be fun. No poachers, no patrols, no danger. Just animals and the open plains." Dennis chuckled again, shaking his head. "I didn't expect this, but... yeah, I could use something like that."

Naomi leaned closer, her voice lowering. "It's my gift to you." Dennis looked into her eyes, his expression softening. "Thank you," he said quietly, his hand reaching out to gently touch hers. "I appreciate it." The Ivory Escape Dennis and Naomi sat at the small wooden table on the lodge's porch. The sky above the Mara was streaked with sunset's orange and purple hues. Dennis poured two cups of steaming tea, offering one to Naomi, who took it and wrapped her hands around it as if seeking warmth.

"Tell me a story, Naomi," Dennis said, looking out over the savannah. His voice was calm, but there was an edge to it, the kind that comes after too many frustrating dead-ends. Naomi sighed, her eyes distant for a moment, remembering. "All right. This case was not so long ago. It was about ivory smuggling. You probably heard of it. It involved two brothers, Nicholas and Samuel Jefwa."

Dennis nodded, a flash of recognition crossing his eyes. "I've heard bits and pieces. But I don't know the full story." Naomi leaned back in her chair, her gaze fixed on a point somewhere in the distance. "It started with a shipment of tea from Kenya to Thailand. The paperwork got changed halfway. Thai customs were tipped off, and they found over three metric tons of ivory when they opened the containers. Imagine that, Dennis.

Over three thousand kilos of tusks were packed between tea leaves. It was sickening." Dennis shook his head, taking a sip of his tea. "So, they caught them. The people responsible." Naomi gave a dry smile. "Yes, they did. At least some of them. Mahmoud Sheikh, his sons, and those Jefwa brothers. They even caught a few customs officers who'd helped them. They brought them in and charged them for dealing in wildlife trophies, for exporting wildlife without a license, and for organized crime. It looked like a success.

A real win for once." Dennis frowned. "Looked like?" Naomi let out a long breath, setting her tea down. "It was all smoke and mirrors in the end. The Jefwa brothers slipped out of the country before they even made it to trial. Authorities said they went to Tanzania first. Then they disappeared.

South Sudan, Congo, and maybe even the Central African Republic. Nobody really knows. The official story says they vanished, but…" she shook her head.

"They had help. Wealthy friends in Kenya. The kind of people who make phone calls that open borders." Dennis clenched his jaw. "And no one could do anything?" Naomi smiled sadly. "You have to understand, Dennis. These weren't small players. They were tied into everything— customs, transportation, banks. The brothers owned a company called Potential Quality Supplies.

Officially, it was just a business, but there was no record before or after those shipments. It was a shell set up to move the ivory. The connections ran deep. Too deep. They were former employees of companies with serious pull. People with influence."

"Money moves everything," Dennis muttered, his eyes narrowing. "Even the law." Naomi nodded slowly. "Exactly. The Kenya Revenue Authority got involved. They identified bank accounts, financial transactions, land, and vehicles tied to the brothers. Seven cars, land worth millions of shillings, and thirteen bank accounts.

They had the receipts, Dennis. It looked like they had enough to finally bring people down." Dennis raised an eyebrow. "But they didn't."

"No, they didn't," Naomi said softly. "They issued an international warrant for the Jefwa brothers, but it was too late. They were already gone. The assets were frozen, but we all know how it works. The bank accounts were probably emptied before anyone could put a hold on them.

The cars, the land, it's all in limbo, 'pending investigation.' The longer the case drags on, the more those assets disappear. Every time there was progress, a new magistrate would be assigned. Paperwork lost, momentum gone. It's like the system was built to fail. Or maybe it's just corrupted to the core." Dennis stared at her, his face unreadable. "And what about Mahmoud Sheikh?" Naomi shrugged.

"He faced questioning. They found an electronic cutter, some ivory chips, showing he had processed ivory, and even receipts that tied him to the shipments. He and his sons were arrested, but their trial… It's been years, Dennis. They're still out. Rumor has it that Mahmoud had connections, too. The kind of people who'd rather pay off an officer than see a courtroom. Some even say he's back in business. Not ivory, but something else.

You know how it is." Dennis clenched his teeth, the muscles in his jaw tightening. "So they got away with it. Even after all that." Naomi sighed, her voice soft. "They did. Or at least they got enough help to make sure they didn't lose everything. They left Kenya but took what mattered most: their money and power. It wasn't proven in court, but everyone knew. Corruption leaves no fingerprints, Dennis. Just a trail of people who stop asking questions."

They sat silently for a while, the sky's orange deepening to red as the sun dipped below the horizon. Dennis finally looked over at Naomi, his eyes hard. "But you're not one of those people, are you?" Naomi smiled faintly, shaking her head. "No, Dennis. I'm not. And I know you're not either. That's why you're here.

That's why we keep fighting." Evening with Naomi, They sat in comfortable silence for a moment, the lodge's sounds fading into the background as they focused on each other. There was an unspoken understanding between them, a bond that had deepened over the weeks of shared struggle and danger. Naomi could feel the warmth of Dennis's hand on hers, and she smiled softly. "Come on," she said, gently pulling him by the hand.

"Let's go somewhere quieter." Dennis followed her without hesitation as they drove to her room in the ranger camp. The room was simple but welcoming, with soft lighting and a large window that offered a view of the night sky and the distant savannah. Naomi closed the door behind them, the soft click of the lock signaling a moment of privacy. She turned to Dennis, her eyes searching his face. "You've been carrying so much lately," she said softly, stepping closer to him. "I want you to let it go, just for tonight."

Dennis smiled, though there was a sadness in his eyes. "It's not easy to let it go."

"I know," Naomi whispered, touching his face gently. "But you don't have to carry it alone." For a moment, Dennis hesitated, his gaze intense as he looked at her. Then, with a quiet sigh, he wrapped his arms around her, pulling her close. Naomi leaned into him, her head resting against his chest, the steady rhythm of his heartbeat calming her. They stood like that for a while, holding each other in the quiet room, the world's weight slipping away, if only for a few moments.

Finally, Dennis pulled back slightly, his eyes meeting hers. "Thank you," he whispered, his voice low and full of emotion. Naomi smiled, her hand sliding to the back of his neck, pulling him into a soft, lingering kiss. The tension between them for weeks seemed to dissolve, replaced by something deeper, comforting, and familiar. They moved to the bed, their movements slow and deliberate, savoring the quiet intimacy of the moment.

There was no rush, no urgency—just the simple pleasure of being together, of finding solace in each other's presence. As the night deepened, they held each other close, the outside world fading into the background. Safari The next morning, Dennis woke early to the soft light of dawn filtering through the window. Naomi was already up, standing beside him. He dressed quietly, preparing for the safari, the memory of the previous night still warm in his mind.

When Naomi dropped Dennis off at the lodge's main area, Daniel was already waiting with the group of tourists. Their excitement was palpable—cameras were at the ready, and they were buzzing with anticipation for the day ahead. "Ready?" Daniel asked with a grin. Dennis nodded, a smile tugging at his lips. "Let's do this."

They climbed into the open safari vehicle, Dennis taking a seat near the front as Daniel started the engine. The cool morning air brushed against his face as they drove out of the lodge, the vast plains of the Maasai Mara stretching out before them. The sun was beginning to rise, casting a golden glow over the landscape. As they drove deeper into the park, the wildlife began to emerge.

A herd of zebras grazed lazily near a cluster of acacia trees, their striped coats shimmering in the early morning light. Nearby, a group of impalas moved gracefully through the grass, their ears twitching at the sounds of the vehicle passing by. "There's always something magical about the early morning here," Daniel said, glancing back at Dennis. "The animals are active, and the light is perfect for photos." Dennis nodded, feeling a sense of calm wash over him as he took in the scene. It was a far cry from the chaos he was used to—no poachers, no danger, just the quiet beauty of the Mara.

They drove on and soon encountered a pride of lions lounging in the grass. The tourists gasped in awe as the lions, lazily basking in the sun, lifted their heads to observe the vehicle. One of the lionesses stretched, yawning widely before flopping back down, utterly unconcerned by the humans watching her.

"Lions are the kings of this land," Daniel said softly, his voice reverent. "They know they're at the top." As they moved farther into the park, they encountered a family of elephants crossing the road, their trunks swaying as they moved in perfect synchronization. Dennis watched them, marveling at their size and grace. The young calves trotted alongside their mothers, protected and safe within the herd. But it wasn't just the large animals that caught Dennis's attention.

They passed a small watering hole where a group of warthogs wallowed in the mud, their comical faces causing the tourists to laugh. Farther on, a pair of giraffes moved slowly through the trees, their long necks stretching to reach

the highest branches. Everywhere Dennis looked, there was life. The Mara was teeming with it, and for the first time in weeks, he felt a sense of peace settling over him. The world outside the park seemed far away with its dangers and betrayals. As they neared the end of the safari, Dennis spotted a cheetah in the distance, poised and ready to hunt.

The tourists were enthralled, cameras clicking as the sleek predator stalked its prey.

They watched in silence as the cheetah exploded into action, its muscles rippling as it chased down an impala in a blur of speed. "That's nature," Daniel said quietly as the tourists murmured in awe. "Life and death, always in balance." Dennis sat back in his seat, feeling a profound sense of gratitude. For the Mara, for the life it sustained, and for the moments of peace it offered, even amid chaos.

He knew the fight wasn't over and that there were still battles to be fought, but for now, he allowed himself to be fully present, to breathe in the beauty of the land he had come to love. As the safari vehicle returned to the lodge, Dennis felt a sense of renewal. He was ready for whatever lay ahead, but for now, he was content to simply be.

Chapter 10: Raid on the Maasai Mara

Preparing the next raid

Dennis sat on the edge of a wooden bench in the dimly lit briefing room, the scent of dust and sweat heavy in the air. He leaned forward, elbows resting on his knees, his mind whirring with calculations and strategies. The upcoming raid weighed heavily on him, not just because of its complexity but because of the stakes. This wasn't a group of desperate men with homemade rifles. These poachers were organized, heavily armed, and prepared to fight.

They weren't going to flee at the first sign of trouble. Across the room, Naomi was bent over a large map spread across a table, her fingers tracing the lines of the Mara as she spoke quietly with a group of rangers. Her voice was low and steady, and her demeanor was calm, but Dennis could feel the tension radiating off her. This operation had to be precise— there was no room for error.

Dennis stood, stretching his shoulders as he walked over to the map. "You ready?" he asked, his voice quiet but carrying the question's weight. Naomi glanced up, giving him a quick nod. "As ready as we can be," she replied. "We've got a solid plan, but these poachers aren't like the ones we've dealt with before." Dennis nodded in agreement. "I've noticed. They've got more firepower and equipment than usual. The informant wasn't lying when he said they had vehicles and a makeshift helipad. No helicopter right now, but visibly, they have used one."

Naomi's brow furrowed. "Yeah, it changes things. They've got resources, and they're not afraid to use them. If they're connected to a larger network, this could be a major operation." Dennis looked down at the map, his eyes tracing the routes they would take to approach the poachers' camp. "We need to know as much as possible before we move in. I'll run more drone surveillance tonight, see if I can pinpoint their sentries, and figure out their patterns." Naomi nodded, leaning closer to the map.

"Good. They've got at least one guard posted at all times, and they're rotating regularly. It's not sloppy either— they're methodical about it." Dennis sighed, running a hand through his hair. "Which means they're expecting trouble. We can't assume they'll scatter the moment we show up. If anything, they'll dig in and fight." Naomi's eyes flickered with concern, but she masked it quickly.

"Then we hit them hard and fast. No hesitation." Drones Later that night, Dennis sat in the passenger seat of a rugged Land Cruiser, its engine idling softly as they waited in the trees several kilometers from the poachers' camp. He adjusted the controls on his drone. His eyes were fixed on the tablet screen in front of him as the small device zipped through the night sky, its infrared camera scanning the terrain below. "Come on, show me something," he muttered under his breath, watching as the dark outlines of the camp came into view.

The drone flew silently above the cluster of tents and makeshift structures, its camera zooming in on a group of men standing near the vehicles parked on the camp's edge. Dennis counted at least five figures, their movements

deliberate. One of them was armed with an AK-47, pacing slowly along the perimeter. The others were talking, but Dennis could tell they weren't relaxed, even from the aerial view. They were on alert. "They're more disciplined than I'd like," Dennis said, his voice cutting through the quiet tension in the vehicle. "One guy is armed, patrolling. The others seem alert but stationary for now." Naomi, sitting behind the wheel, leaned over slightly to glance at the screen.

"Do you see any sentries farther out?"

"Not yet," Dennis replied, moving the drone to the western side of the camp. "But they've got a makeshift helipad here, no helicopter but traces of landing. They've used it recently. There are tire tracks from vehicles around the edges like they've been loading and unloading something."

"That means they've got another way out if things go south," Naomi said, frowning. "We need to account for that in the assault plan." Dennis maneuvered the drone over to the east side, where a guard stood near a clump of bushes. He was alone but armed with a rifle, and every so often, he'd turn to scan the surroundings. "They've got a sentry on the eastern side, too," Dennis noted, marking it on the map in his mind. "This isn't going to be easy." Naomi stayed silent for a moment, her eyes fixed on the screen.

"No, it's not," she finally said. "But we have the element of surprise. And you've got that other trick up your sleeve, right? The Stingray?" Dennis nodded. The Stingray, a device used to mimic cell towers and intercept phone signals, had become a crucial tool in gathering intelligence. "Yeah. Once we're in range, I'll activate it and see if we can capture any

communications. If they're using burner phones, we'll know who they're talking to and maybe get a better sense of the broader network." Naomi's eyes flickered with hope. "If we can link them to a bigger operation, this raid wouldn't just stop these poachers— it could cripple the whole syndicate." Dennis glanced at her, his expression serious. "That's the goal. But we've got to get out of there in one piece first."

Flashback: Mrefu's Path to Poaching Meanwhile, in the Poachers' camp, Mrefu was inspecting his final preparation for the attack. His informer had warned him of an attack the following day.

A gust of wind returned a memory that simmered just below the surface. In his younger days, Mrefu had been a proud cattle herder, a role that had been part of his heritage. His days were spent under the same sun, his hands hardened by work. But poverty and desperation had a way of corroding even the strongest traditions. The rain had stopped one season, and with it, the livelihood that his family had depended on for generations. Watching his livestock die, one by one had left him feeling stripped of everything that made him a man.

One day, when all seemed lost, Mrefu encountered a man with smooth skin and a silver tongue. His nickname was Shetani, but he was known in whispers as The Broker. He had appeared like a specter, draped in the soft folds of imported fabric, with promises of wealth and power that seemed beyond Mrefu's reach. Leaning against a tree, Mrefu allowed himself a moment of satisfaction. Shetani had seen something in Mrefu's desperation years ago. Their partnership had grown, and Shetani's influence opened

doors to a world Mrefu could barely imagine. Ivory, rare animals, even arms shipments. Shetani was the connection that brought it all together, and Mrefu was the one on the ground, making sure the goods flowed without a hitch.

Their business was dangerous, but Shetani had given him the resources to silence anyone who tried to interfere. Mrefu's Preparations for the Ambush In the early morning, Mrefu crouched near the cliff edge. His eyes narrowed as he surveyed the sprawling savannah below, shadowed by early morning fog. This wasn't a battle born of mere circumstance—it was a fight he had orchestrated with the precision of a chess master. With a slight nod to his lieutenant, Obasi, Mrefu motioned for him to sit by his side. Their conversations were few, but their shared understanding was all that mattered in moments like this.

The sky was quiet, but Mrefu could already envision the rangers' arrival, the sounds of their tires skidding to a halt, their steps tentative as they walked into the trap he had carefully laid. Mrefu's informer had promised to inform them when the rangers would leave their camp, but Mrefu's poachers were ready anyway for them. "Obasi," Mrefu began, his voice a whisper that seemed to blend with the rustle of the grass. "The rangers will come straight down this path, just as they did last time." He traced a line in the dirt with his finger, his eyes glinting with satisfaction. "But they won't know what's waiting for them now." Obasi nodded, his lips pulling back into a hard grin.

"The positioning is perfect, boss. By the time they realize it, they'll be trapped."

"You know," Mrefu said, turning to Obasi, "this isn't just about tusks and horn. It's about control. These rangers think they can come in and dictate what we do and who we are. But we're the ones who set the rules out here. We decide who lives and who dies. Obasi tilted his head, watching Mrefu with a mixture of admiration and fear.

"You think they'll learn their lesson today?" Mrefu's eyes gleamed with a predatory intensity. "They'll learn that we are the masters of this land, not them. Today, they lose more than their men. Today, they lose their fearlessness." A faint smirk appeared on Mrefu's face. "That's the plan. We don't want them running away too soon. We need them to see exactly what they're up against." He stood up, stretching his legs, his gaze turning serious. "

These rangers think they're saving lives by coming after us. They think they're heroes. Today, we show them that this land answers to different rules." Final Briefing Early that morning, Dennis and Naomi returned to the briefing room, this time with the rest of the ranger team. The drone footage from the previous night had provided invaluable information about the poachers' movements, and Dennis had spent the better part of the morning reviewing it with Naomi. "All right," Dennis began, his voice steady as he addressed the group. "Here's the plan. We've identified the sentries on the eastern and western sides of the camp.

They've got at least two guards rotating throughout the night, and they're armed. About a dozen poachers occupy the rest of the camp, but they're not just sitting around. They're organized and have vehicles—trucks, motorcycles, and a helicopter pad. This isn't a ragtag group. They're

prepared for a fight." The rangers listened in silence, their expressions grim but focused. Naomi stepped forward, pointing to the map. "We'll approach from the southern side, using the cover of the scrubland to get as close as possible without being seen. Once we're in position, we'll move in fast and hard." One of the rangers, a young woman named Asha, raised her hand.

"What's the objective? Capture or eliminate?"

"Both," Naomi replied without hesitation. "We need to gather intelligence, but if they resist, we neutralize the threat. We can't afford to let them escape. This camp is a key hub in their network, and if we let them scatter, they'll regroup and come back stronger." Dennis installed the activated Stingray in the rangers' lead vehicle, hoping to intercept any communications between the poachers and their command. Seconds later, his tablet lit up with a series of pings as the device picked up several phones in the camp. "I've got them," Dennis murmured. "Multiple devices, all in the camp."

"Anything interesting?"

Naomi asked. Dennis scanned the data, noting the patterns of the signals. "Looks like they're communicating with someone outside the camp. Can't tell who yet, but this isn't just internal chatter. They're in contact with a larger network."

"Good," Naomi replied. "Keep monitoring." Dennis stepped back, letting Naomi take the lead in finalizing the details with the team. He knew they were as ready as they could be, but the thought of going up against such a well-equipped group weighed on him.

These poachers weren't just opportunists looking for a quick score—they were professionals, dangerous and prepared. Dennis's war experience told him that attackers need at least a 3 to 1-numerical advantage on defenders. He was not sure that that was the advantage they had. The Poachers are ready. On the poachers' side, Obasi walked off to oversee the final placements, ensuring that the men were ready, hidden among the rocks and vegetation, their guns poised for the signal.

The air was thick with anticipation, and as Mrefu moved along the lines, he nodded at each man, his presence reinforcing their readiness. Mrefu laughs inside about the naivety of the rangers walking into his ambush. Soon, the informers called to signal the departure of the rangers' caravan. When the sun was fully up, they saw dust rising from the horizon, a sign of approaching vehicles. Mrefu's heartbeat was steady as he crouched low, his hand signaling his men to be ready.

This would be the day the Rangers remembered who truly controlled the Mara. The Raid is Starting As the raid began, Dennis's pulse quickened. The team moved silently through the brush, staying low as they approached the camp from the southern side. The rangers continued their approach, inching closer to the camp. The poachers were nowhere to be seen. The camp looked abandoned. "All right," Naomi's voice returned, this time with a steely edge. "We're in position. Let's move." The rangers swiftly surged forward. Suddenly, Chaos erupted in the camp. Shouts of alarm rang out, and the poachers started shooting from hidden positions. The eastern sentry spun around. The raid had begun smoothly—too smoothly, Dennis realized in

hindsight. The rangers had approached the camp with precision, the plan to surround and swiftly overwhelm the poachers seemingly falling into place. But all it took was a single gunshot, echoing through the stillness of dawn, to shatter the carefully orchestrated assault.

Dennis had barely registered the crack of the rifle when everything descended into chaos. His heart dropped as the camp erupted in gunfire. The poachers weren't fleeing, as the rangers expected; they were fighting back and with more firepower than expected. Naomi was beside him, her rifle up, her eyes scanning the perimeter. Her movements were fluid and calm, but Dennis could sense the undercurrent of tension. The poachers weren't just defending themselves—they were organized, well-armed, and coordinated. This was no ordinary group. "Go! Go!"

Naomi's voice cut through the noise as the rangers surged forward, trying to regain the upper hand. Dennis ducked behind a rock as bullets ripped through the air, kicking up dirt and debris around him. He activated his drone, sending it skyward to get an aerial view of the camp, but it was clear that their carefully planned element of surprise was gone. "Dennis!" Naomi's shout brought his attention back to the immediate threat.

She was firing, her focus unwavering as she kept the advancing poachers at bay. Dennis followed her lead, adjusting his position and scanning for an opening. It was then that he noticed something unsettling. The poachers were moving in coordinated groups, covering each other as they advanced, clearly trained for this kind of engagement. They weren't just armed with outdated rifles—they had

automatic weapons, and Dennis even caught sight of a rocket-propelled grenade launcher slung over one of their shoulders. This wasn't a small-time operation. These poachers were prepared for a full-blown battle.

"We need to fall back!" Naomi's voice rose above the gunfire, her face tense with the realization that their position was untenable. Dennis nodded, preparing to signal the others when it happened: Naomi jerked violently to the side, a pained expression crossing her face. "Naomi!" Dennis shouted, his heart leaping into his throat as she stumbled. Her hand shot to her side, where blood was already soaking through her uniform. She dropped to her knees, her rifle slipping from her grasp.

Without thinking, Dennis lunged toward her, his adrenaline spiking as he caught her before she fell completely. Bullets zipped past them, and Dennis could feel the dirt and grit flying up around him. He pulled her behind

a large boulder, his hands trembling as he inspected the wound. Blood oozed from her side, staining his hands red. "Naomi, stay with me!" Dennis's voice was hoarse, full-blown emergency mode creeping into his brain as he pressed his hand over the wound, trying to staunch the flow of blood. Naomi's eyes were half-closed, her breath coming in shallow gasps, but she was still conscious. "They got me," she rasped, though her voice betrayed her pain. But Dennis looked down.

The blood flowing through his fingers told him this was more than just a graze. He scanned the area, desperately looking for a way out. The rangers were pinned down, their initial assault falling apart under the poachers' relentless firepower and positional advantage. They had to retreat—now. "Captain Odhiambo, we're pulling back!" Dennis shouted into his radio, his voice strained. He didn't wait for a response. He pulled Naomi to her feet, not feeling his weight leaning heavily on him as he guided her toward the retreating rangers.

The rangers were falling back in groups, firing as they moved, trying to keep the poachers from advancing too quickly. Dennis and Naomi were at the rear, every step feeling agonizingly slow as the sound of gunfire filled the air. He could see Captain Odhiambo in the distance, shouting commands as he covered the retreat. But the poachers, feeling victorious, were still pressing forward, their determination unshaken.

Chapter 11: After the Defeat

Escape

As Dennis dragged Naomi toward the makeshift extraction point, where the vehicles were waiting, he caught sight of something that made his blood run cold. A ranger lay on the ground, motionless, his body disfigured by bullet wounds. He forced himself to look away, focusing on evacuating a possibly dying Naomi to safety, but the sight seared itself into his mind.

"Keep moving!" Dennis shouted, his voice raw, as he half carried, half-dragged Naomi toward the waiting vehicles. The rangers fired sporadically behind them, trying to slow the poachers' advance, but it was clear that this fight was lost.

Finally, they reached the vehicles, and Dennis heaved Naomi into the backseat of one of the Land Cruisers. His breath came in ragged gasps as he turned to Captain Odhiambo, who was already shouting orders for the remaining rangers to retreat.

"Get her in!" the ranger shouted, his rifle barking as he fired towards the poachers. Dennis pulled the door open, helping Naomi inside before scrambling in after her.

"Get them out of here!" Odhiambo bellowed to the driver, who slammed his foot on the gas, sending the vehicle lurching forward as the convoy roared to life.

Dennis looked back, seeing the other vehicles following, some with wounded rangers slumped in the seats.

The sounds of gunfire gradually faded as they sped away from the camp, the poachers receding into the distance. Dennis slumped beside Naomi, his chest heaving with exhaustion and relief. He glanced at her, his heart pounding as he saw how pale she had become. She was still somewhat conscious, but her eyes were half-closed, and her face was slick with sweat.

Dennis tore open a medical kit, his hands moving quickly as he applied pressure to the wound.

"Stay with me, Naomi," he said, his voice tight. "You're going to be okay."

"Naomi, stay with me," Dennis urged, his voice low and urgent. "We're almost there."

Naomi's eyes fluttered open, and she managed a weak smile. "I'm still here," she whispered, though her voice was faint. Dennis's mind raced as they sped through the Mara, the adrenaline fading and leaving behind a cold knot of fear in his gut. Several rangers were dead. Naomi was injured. And the poachers had been waiting for them.

Someone had tipped them off. As the convoy approached the ranger station, Dennis's thoughts were mixed: worrying about Naomi, evaluating how much blood she had lost, thinking that he should have listened to his intuition about the strength of this very organized team of poachers, and thinking about finding the informant. The poachers had been ready for them. They had been waiting. Dennis was ready when, finally, the vehicle skidded to a halt as they reached the ranger station. His focus was entirely on Naomi, her breathing shallow and labored, her face pale and glistening with sweat.

The back of the Land Cruiser felt like it was closing in on him, the cramped space amplifying his anxiety. His hands pressed firmly against the wound on her side, but the blood was still seeping through his fingers. It was worse than he had hoped.

"Medic! We need a medic here!" Dennis shouted, his voice breaking through the chaos as the rangers scrambled out of the vehicles. Within seconds, two medics were at the side of the Land Cruiser, their faces grim as they saw the blood staining Naomi's uniform and Dennis's hands.

They quickly assessed her condition, and one of them, a young woman with sharp eyes, immediately opened the medical kit she carried. "We need to get her out of here," the medic said, her voice steady.

"Help me lift her." Dennis nodded, swallowing the lump of fear in his throat as he and the other medic carefully lifted Naomi out of the vehicle and onto a stretcher. She groaned in pain, her eyes fluttering open for a brief moment before they closed again.

Dennis could see her chest rising and falling in shallow gasps, her breaths coming quicker. The medics laid her down on the stretcher, and the female medic immediately went to work, cutting away the fabric around the wound to get a better look. The other medic quickly hooked up an IV line, pushing fluids into Naomi's system to counter the blood loss. Dennis hovered close, his heart racing as he watched them work.

"It's a deep wound," the female medic said, glancing up at Dennis. "She's lost much blood, and the bullet seems to

have hit an organ. We need to stabilize her, but this isn't something we can handle here."

Naomi's breathing became more erratic, her chest rising and falling unevenly. Dennis felt his stomach twist. This wasn't just a flesh wound—it was severe, life-threatening. He felt the panic creeping up his spine, but he forced it down. He needed to focus. He needed to keep his head clear, for her sake.

"Can you stop the bleeding?" Dennis asked, his voice hoarse.

The medic nodded as she applied pressure to the wound. "We're doing what we can, but it's bad. The bullet likely nicked her liver, maybe her intestines. She's going to need surgery, and soon."

The other medic leaned over, checking Naomi's pulse.

"Her heart rate's dropping. We need to evacuate her to Nairobi. She won't make it through the night out here."

Dennis's heart pounded in his chest as he knelt beside Naomi, gently gripping her hand.

"Naomi," he whispered, his voice tight with emotion. "We're getting you out of here. Hang on."

Naomi's eyes fluttered open briefly, her lips parting as if she wanted to say something, but her voice was barely a whisper.

"Dennis…"

"I'm here," he said, squeezing her hand. "Stay with me. We're going to take you to a hospital." Naomi managed a faint smile, her eyes half-closed.

"Don't... let them win, Dennis. Promise me." Dennis swallowed hard, nodding. "I promise."

The medics worked quickly, stabilizing her as much as possible in the field. They wrapped her wound tightly, applied bandages to slow the bleeding, and started perfusions. But it was clear from their tense expressions that this was a race against time.

"We're ready to move her," the medic said, glancing at Dennis. "We've radioed for an emergency chopper. It'll be here in fifteen minutes to take her to Nairobi."

Dennis's mind raced as the gravity of the situation sank in. He knew Nairobi was their best chance, but fifteen minutes felt like an eternity. He nodded stiffly, watching as they lifted Naomi onto the stretcher again, securing her for the ride to the helipad.

As the medics rushed her toward the extraction point, Dennis jogged alongside them, unable to take his eyes off her. He could see the strain on her face, the effort it took for her to stay conscious. Every bump on the rough terrain made her wince, and the sight of her in such pain tore at him. They reached the helipad, the sound of the helicopter's blades cutting through the air growing louder as it approached. The medics continued their work, monitoring her vitals, but Dennis could see the concern in their eyes.

Naomi's condition was worsening—her breathing shallower, her skin turning paler by the second.

"Come on, Naomi," Dennis whispered, his voice cracking. "You're stronger than this. Hold on."

The helicopter touched down with a blast of wind and dust, and the medics wasted no time in transferring Naomi onto the waiting aircraft. Dennis felt helpless as he watched them secure her to the stretcher inside, his heart pounding in his chest. He wanted to go with her, to make sure she was okay, but he knew he could do nothing now. It was in the hands of the medics, and he had so much to do here. As they prepared to lift off, one of the medics turned to Dennis.

"She's stable for now, but it will be a rough ride. We'll do everything we can."

Dennis nodded, his throat tight. "Thank you." The rotors spun faster, and the helicopter began to lift off the ground, carrying Naomi toward Nairobi and the emergency surgery she desperately needed. Dennis watched it ascend into the sky, his heart heavy with fear and hope.

He could only pray that they'd gotten to her in time. As the helicopter disappeared into the distance, Dennis stood there for a long moment, the adrenaline still pumping through his veins. He turned slowly, his eyes narrowing as he recalled the raid. Someone had betrayed them and tipped off the poachers, and now Naomi was fighting for her life. He clenched his fists, his resolve hardening. Whoever was responsible for this wasn't going to get away with it. Naomi had risked everything for this mission, and Dennis would do whatever it took to ensure that betrayal was brought to light.

As he headed back to the ranger station, his mind was already racing with plans. He would dig into every communication they'd intercepted, trace every call, and find out who had fed the poachers information. The Broker's network was bigger and more dangerous than anticipated,

but Dennis wouldn't let them win. Naomi would recover. She had to. And when she did, they would finish what they started. Someone had betrayed them, and if they didn't figure out who, this wouldn't be the last time they walked into an ambush. Dennis stood back, his hands stained with her blood, his mind racing.

The raid had been a disaster—someone had betrayed them, and now Naomi was paying the price. He felt a surge of anger, his jaw clenching as he looked around at the rangers, their faces a mix of exhaustion and despair. One of the rangers approached him, his expression grim.

"We lost three men," he said quietly.

"They knew we were coming." Dennis nodded, his gaze drifting to the horizon and the bright morning sun. He had suspected as much, but hearing it confirmed only fueled his determination.

The Broker had eyes everywhere and the power to manipulate and corrupt even those who were supposed to be on their side. He stepped outside the medical building, where Captain Odhiambo was barking orders to the remaining rangers. The captain's face was dark with anger and frustration, and Dennis could see the same thoughts mirrored in his expression.

"We were set up," Odhiambo said, his voice low and furious as Dennis approached.

"Someone told them we were coming." Dennis nodded, his jaw tight.

"I am going to check what is in the Stingray logs," Odhiambo cursed under his breath, pacing angrily.

"We need to find out who's feeding them information." Dennis's mind churned with possibilities. There had to be a leak—someone on the inside who knew about the raid in advance. The poachers had been prepared, and if they didn't stop whoever was behind it, more lives would be lost.

"I'll start looking into the communications we intercepted during the raid," Dennis said, his voice cold with determination. "Maybe we can trace the calls, find out who they've been talking to. We need answers."

Odhiambo nodded sharply.

"Do it. I'm going to debrief the surviving rangers. We need to figure out how we will respond to this."

This raid could have provided Dennis with new evidence, perhaps documents or communications found at the camp that reveal connections to the smuggling operation. The failed raid emphasized their mission's complexity and danger, showing how powerful and well-connected their enemies were.

It motivated Dennis to dig deeper and take even greater risks, knowing that this network wasn't just poaching—it had the power to infiltrate and manipulate the authorities meant to protect Kenya's wildlife. With Naomi fighting for her life, Dennis knew he was on his own. He couldn't afford to wait—couldn't afford to let The Broker slip away. He looked towards the medical tent, his heart heavy. Naomi had risked everything for this mission, and now it was up to him to see it through.

The Traitor

The rangers' camp was quieter the following morning, the usual hum of activity replaced by a somber stillness.

The failed raid had left a scar on the surviving rangers and the resolve of their fight against the poachers. Dennis and Odhiambo knew that something had gone horribly wrong—someone had betrayed them, tipping off the poachers and causing the entire operation to descend into chaos. Three rangers were dead because of it, and Naomi was in the hospital, fighting for her life.

Dennis was monitoring closely the medical news from Naomi's doctors, while he tracked down the lead they had gathered. Using the phone numbers they had recovered with the Stingray the day of the attack, he managed to locate phone call metadata that suggested one of the local villagers, a man named Karani, was actively communicating with the poachers and had called them just as the rangers left the base to the Poachers' camp.

This late morning, they found him sitting outside his small home on the outskirts of a nearby village, a cigarette between his fingers as he looked out over the fields with vacant eyes.

"Karani," Odhiambo called, his voice low and tense.

The man looked up, his face a mask of indifference that cracked just slightly when he saw who had come for him. He stood slowly, his hands trembling, the cigarette falling to the ground. He knew why they were here and made no effort to run.

The raid had been meant to be a closely guarded secret, known only to the rangers involved. The plans had been discussed in hushed tones, away from the prying eyes and ears of anyone who could compromise their mission. But somehow, the information had leaked. It turned out that Karani had been present during a routine meeting at the ranger's station, working on maintenance for one of the vehicles. He had overheard enough to understand what was happening.

The rangers, trusting in their own loyalty, hadn't thought twice about Karani's presence. He was just a villager, someone they saw daily, working quietly in the background. But that small lapse in security had cost them dearly. Karani took what he had overheard and passed it along to the poachers.

"Why did you do it?" Odhiambo asked, his voice tight and barely contained anger, as they led Karani to one of the vehicles.

The ride back to the ranger's camp was silent, the weight of what had happened hanging between them like a dark cloud. Dennis watched Karani in the rearview mirror, his eyes searching for something—regret, fear, remorse. But Karani's face was blank, his gaze unfocused. When they arrived, Karani was taken to a small room for questioning.

Dennis and Odhiambo stood across from him, the air thick with tension.

"We know you warned them," Dennis said, his voice cold. "We lost three men because of you. Naomi is in the hospital. They didn't stand a chance because of what you did."

Karani swallowed hard, his eyes flicking up to meet Dennis's before darting away. "I didn't mean for anyone to die," he whispered, his voice hoarse.

"I just... I had no choice." Odhiambo leaned forward, his hands on the table between them.

"No choice? You had a choice, Karani. You chose to help those bastards. You chose to betray us."

Karani's eyes filled with tears, and he looked down at his hands, his fingers trembling.

"They came to me weeks ago. They knew I worked near the camp. They said they needed information, and if I didn't help them... they would kill my family. My wife, my children. They showed me pictures—they knew where they lived, where my kids went to school. I was scared."

Dennis watched him, his expression hard. He had heard this story before—fear used as a weapon, forcing good people to do terrible things. But it didn't change the fact that three rangers were dead, that Naomi might not make it, all because Karani had chosen to save himself instead of warning them.

"You could have come to us," Dennis said, his voice quieter now. "We could have protected you."

Karani shook his head, his tears spilling down his cheeks.

"I didn't think you'd be able to. These people—they have money, power. They said they had people on the inside who would know if I tried to betray them. I thought... I thought they would leave us alone if I just told them what

they wanted." Odhiambo let out a bitter laugh, stepping back and running a hand over his face. "And now three men are dead, and Naomi is fighting for her life because of you. Do you understand that, Karani? Do you understand what you've done?"

Karani's shoulders shook as he sobbed, his face buried in his hands. "I'm sorry. I didn't want anyone to die. I swear, I didn't think it would end like this."

Dennis looked at him, the anger in his chest simmering, tempered only slightly by the man's obvious despair. He wanted to hate Karani, to see him as nothing more than a coward who had cost them everything. But he couldn't. He saw the fear in Karani's eyes, the desperation of a man who had been pushed into a corner and made the wrong choice. "Sorry, won't bring them back," Dennis said, his voice flat. "But you can help us now. You can tell us everything you know about these people—names, locations, anything that can help us bring them down." Karani nodded, his breath hitching as he wiped at his face. "I will. I'll tell you everything. Just... please. I never wanted this.

.Dennis turned to Odhiambo, their eyes meeting for a long moment. Odhiambo's gaze did not show forgiveness, only the cold, hard resolve of a man who had lost friends and brothers because of the man sitting before them. But he gave a short nod, his voice tight. "Then start talking." The air in the small room was heavy, filled with tension that seemed to settle in the corners like dust. Dennis leaned against the wall, arms crossed. Karani was slumped in a wooden chair, his face pale and streaked with tears. Across from him,

Odhiambo paced slowly, his boots scuffing the floor as he tried to contain his frustration.

Karani, the man responsible for giving away the information that had led to the deaths of three rangers and Naomi's severe injury, was now their only hope of piecing together what had happened. "Start from the beginning," Odhiambo said, his voice hard but calm. "Tell us exactly how you got involved with the poachers." Karani wiped his face with trembling hands, his breath shaky as he tried to collect himself. "I... I didn't think it would go this far. They approached me a few months ago—some men I didn't recognize at first, but they looked like locals.

They said they needed someone on the inside to give them information about patrols and areas where the rangers were weak. They promised me money, said no one would get hurt, just... said it was to avoid conflict." Odhiambo's eyes narrowed as he leaned in closer, his voice sharp. "And you believed that?" Karani's shoulders sagged. "I didn't know what to do. I'm not like you, Odhiambo. I don't have your strength. They said they had connections and that they could make my life difficult if I didn't help. I was scared."

Dennis cut in, his voice low and steady, keeping Karani on track. "Who were these men, Karani? Give us names." Karani hesitated, rubbing his hands together as if trying to warm them though the room was sweltering.

"I didn't know most of them. But one... one I recognized. Mrefu."

Dennis exchanged a glance with Odhiambo: Mrefu again. "Okay," Dennis said, his voice firm but controlled.

"Mrefu is one. Who else?" Karani shook his head quickly. "I didn't get any other names. They were careful about that. But Mrefu handled me most of the time. He'd tell me what information they needed and where to meet him. Sometimes, he'd have others with him, but I didn't know them."

Odhiambo let out a frustrated breath but kept his focus.

"Fine. Let's talk about the information you gave them. You said they asked about patrols. What else did they want?"

Karani's voice was barely above a whisper. "They asked about the routes the rangers were taking. Especially the less-patrolled areas, places where they could slip through unnoticed.

They wanted to know when the rangers were spread thin, which zones weren't being watched."

"And you told them?" Odhiambo's voice had an edge to it now, a barely contained anger that made Karani flinch.

"Yes," Karani admitted, his voice breaking.

"I told them. I gave them maps of the zones that weren't covered well. They said no one would get hurt, just that they needed to avoid patrols." Dennis felt his stomach twist.

The betrayal was deeper than they had realized. Karani had handed over their operational weaknesses, giving the poachers exactly what they needed to strike without opposition. But there was more they needed to know.

"You said you met them a few times. Where?" Dennis asked, pushing Karani toward the details that might help them strike back.

"How did they pay you?" Karani licked his lips nervously. "We met mostly in remote areas, places where no one would see us. A few times, near the edge of the Mara. There's a spot off the main road near the old stone bridge. We met there a couple of times. But I overheard something, once, something about a safe house."

Dennis leaned forward, his interest piqued. "A safe house?" Karani nodded quickly, his eyes darting between Dennis and Odhiambo.

"Yes. I wasn't supposed to hear it, but one of them slipped up. They mentioned a safe house outside the Mara, a place they use when moving supplies in or out. I think it's close to the main road, but I don't know exactly where but probably close to where we were meeting."

Dennis locked eyes with Odhiambo. A safe house could be a goldmine of information. It could give them access to documents, weapons, and possibly even the location of other key players in the poaching network.

"Do you know how to get there?" Odhiambo asked, his voice tight with impatience. Karani shook his head.

"No, I swear. I only heard them talk about it. I never went there."

Dennis exhaled slowly, suppressing his frustration. "Fine. What else did you hear? Anything about their communications?"

Karani shifted uncomfortably in his chair. "They didn't talk much before me, but I know they use burner phones. Cheap ones, ones they can toss when they're done. Mrefu

had a couple of them. He'd give me one when he needed me to pass along information, but he'd take it back after."

"And the other men? Did you see how they communicated?" Dennis pressed. "I saw Mrefu meet with a couple of police officers once," Karani admitted quietly. "He gave them something—cash, I think. It was right after we met near the bridge. They didn't talk much, but I knew they were on the take.

They'd let the poachers pass without checking their vehicles. I think one works at the checkpoint near Talek, the other at the Narok post." Odhiambo muttered something under his breath, pacing the room again. Corruption ran deep, and they had always suspected there were compromised police officers in the area. This confirmed it, but it still wasn't enough. "Do you have names?" Odhiambo asked sharply, stopping to face Karani. Karani hesitated, then nodded.

"I think one of them is called Kiptoo. I'm not sure about the other one."

Dennis filed the name away, his mind already working through the possibilities. They could trace Kiptoo and maybe find more information about the safe house through his connections.

"What about upcoming operations?" Dennis asked.

"Do you know if they have anything planned soon?" Karani shook his head, a look of panic crossing his face.

"No. They didn't trust me with that. They didn't need to, not after I gave them the patrol routes. I think... I think that's why they used me. They didn't need inside

information about everything, just where to avoid the rangers. They have someone else handling the bigger stuff."

Dennis frowned. "Someone else? Another informant?" Karani's face twisted in uncertainty. "I don't know. Maybe. I don't think it's a ranger. If they had someone higher up, they wouldn't have needed me for the patrol information. But it could be someone else in the community, someone who hears things." Odhiambo's jaw clenched.

"Do you have any suspicions? Anyone else who's been acting strange?" Karani hesitated, glancing at the floor.

"There's a man in the village… Mutiso. He's been quiet lately and keeps to himself. He knows a lot of people, and he's been seen talking to strangers a few times. I'm not sure if he's involved, but… it's just a feeling." Dennis and Odhiambo exchanged a look. It wasn't much, but it was a lead. They would need to investigate Mutiso and see if he had any connections to the poaching network.

"What about money?" Dennis asked, steering the conversation back to Karani's personal involvement.

"How much did they pay you?" Karani's voice shook as he answered. "Not much. A few thousand shillings here and there. Enough to keep me quiet, to keep me feeding them information. They made it clear that if I stopped, they'd come after me." Odhiambo stepped forward, looming over Karani. "And now? Are they still in contact with you?" Karani shook his head furiously. "No. Not today after the raid. They disappeared after that. I think they knew something went wrong, and they cut me loose."

Dennis remained silent for a moment, his mind racing. Karani had given them valuable information, but there were still too many unknowns. They needed to act quickly before the poachers had a chance to regroup. Odhiambo crossed his arms, his gaze hard and unyielding.

"You're lucky we're not handing you yet over to the rangers who lost their friends, Karani. But if you're lying, if you're holding anything back, or if you try to flee, I will. You'd better remember more details."

"I'm not!" Karani interrupted, his voice desperate. "I swear, I've told you everything I know."

Dennis straightened, stepping toward Karani.

"We'll see. For now, you're staying under our watch. We'll deal with you later. But if you try to run, if you even think about it, you won't make it far." Karani's face crumpled as he nodded, his fear palpable. "I won't run. I promise." Dennis turned to Odhiambo, giving him a curt nod. "We've got enough to start with. Let's get moving."

Naomi's Injuries

Naomi had gone to surgery as soon as she reached Nairobi. The bullet wound in her side had caused significant internal damage and loss of blood, and she had undergone emergency surgery to repair the damage to her liver and intestines. After 5 hours of surgery, cutting, and sewing, the doctors managed to stabilize her, but her condition remained serious, and she was being closely monitored in the intensive care unit. The prognosis was cautiously optimistic—if no complications arose, she was expected to recover fully, but it would take time.

The doctors estimated she would need at least six to eight weeks of rest and rehabilitation before she could even consider returning to the field. The injury had left her physically weakened, and she would require months of physiotherapy to regain her strength. Despite the gravity of her condition, the doctors were hopeful that she would eventually regain full mobility and be able to resume her work as a ranger. It was now unlikely that she could be an active member of the team.

The news weighed heavily on Dennis beyond the affection he had for her. Naomi was a fighter, but seeing her incapacitated like this, knowing the risk she had taken, only deepened his resolve. She had been the heart of their team, the one who had pushed them all to keep going, even when the odds seemed impossible. Dennis knew that he had to carry on the fight, not just for the wildlife they were trying to protect, but for Naomi and for the rangers they had lost.

The Abandoned Camp

The afternoon sun was high in the sky when Dennis, Odhiambo, and the rangers returned to the camp with an ambulance and heavy escort. The air was thick with heat, the kind that clung to your skin and made every breath feel heavy. The place had been abandoned in a rush after the battle, but the memory of the ambush and the smell of the battle still hung in the air like smoke. Three rangers had died here. Naomi had been shot, barely making it out alive. The silence now felt like an insult.

The camp was just a scattering of broken-down tents, a few makeshift structures leaning haphazardly against trees. The ground was churned up, dry earth mixed with ash and

the remnants of a fire. Dennis scanned the place, eyes sharp, taking it all in. They had left in a hurry. Whoever was here didn't plan on sticking around once the bullets started flying. Odhiambo stepped up beside him, silent, his face hard.

The other rangers moved quietly through the camp, their rifles slung over their shoulders, picking through the debris.

"Looks like they didn't take much with them," Odhiambo muttered, kicking at an empty can that clinked against the hard ground.

"Left in a rush," Dennis said, his eyes falling on a garbage pile near the camp's edge. A heap of old food wrappers, bottles, discarded tools, and something else: papers. They were strewn across the ground, some singed, blackened at the edges.

A few fluttered in the breeze, still caught in the embers of a fire. Dennis crouched, picking up one of the pages. The corner crumbled in his hand, burnt to a crisp. But the rest was legible. His fingers brushed off the ash as he scanned the words. He couldn't make much sense of it—names, numbers, hastily scribbled notes. But it was something. Whoever had been here hadn't been careful enough to destroy everything.

Odhiambo knelt beside him, frowning as he looked over Dennis' shoulder. "What do you think?"

"Could be useful," Dennis said, collecting more half-burnt papers.

"They tried to burn this, but they didn't finish the job. Maybe we'll get something out of it."

He sifted through the pile, finding more scraps. Some were too far gone, just ash that disintegrated between his fingers. But others—there were fragments of maps, lists of supplies, schedules, even a few receipts.

Dennis's hands moved quickly, sorting the valuable from the useless, knowing that in this mess, there could be a clue, something that would point to where the poachers had gone or who they were working for. Behind him, one of the rangers was sifting through a bundle of clothing. It smelled foul, the stench of sweat and blood mixing with the heat. Dennis didn't pay it much attention. His focus was on the papers, the small fragments of truth left behind. "They didn't expect us to come to attack them this fast," Odhiambo said, his voice low, his eyes scanning the tree line.

"Thought they'd have more time to pack."

"They were sloppy," Dennis replied.

"That's good for us." The rangers moved through the camp, quiet, methodical. No one spoke much. There wasn't much to say. The ground beneath them had been soaked in blood that same morning, and it felt like the dead were still watching. Dennis stood, stuffing the papers into his pack. "We'll take this back, see if we can make sense of it." Odhiambo nodded, his face set in a grim line. "Anything else?"

Dennis looked around, scanning the camp one last time. He caught sight of a tree where the branches had been hacked at, leaves scattered on the ground beneath it. An old fire pit sat near the center of the camp, blackened and cold. He could

almost see the poachers sitting there, making plans, knowing they'd be gone before anyone could find them.

"No," Dennis said quietly. "Let's move out."

They turned and headed back toward the trail, the camp behind them, silent now. But Dennis knew they weren't done.

There was still something there, more half-burnt papers, in the ashes left behind. They'd figure it out. They had to.

Two Ethiopian Girls

Meanwhile, in Ethiopia, Meron and Tigist had been filled with hope and trepidation when they first encountered the man who promised them a better life. He was well-dressed, spoke their native Amharic, and seemed warm enough, radiating a sense of security that made the two sisters believe in him. Meron, the older of the two at fifteen, had been the one who convinced Tigist, barely thirteen, that they should go with him. He spoke about jobs in the Gulf, where many of their friends and neighbors had gone to support their families.

The promise of a modest wage seemed too good to pass up; they dreamed of helping their mother, of sending money back to their family. They had no idea this was only the beginning of a nightmare. After they agreed, things moved fast. Within a day, they were taken by bus to a crowded house on the outskirts of Addis Ababa, filled with young women like themselves. From there, they traveled under the cover of night, crammed into the back of a small, enclosed truck with a dozen other girls.

The journey was grueling, the air thick and stale, the space suffocating, but Meron held Tigist close, whispering reassurances as best as she could, even though her own fear gnawed at her heart. Once they reached the Ethiopian-Kenyan border, they were transferred to another vehicle and handed off to a new group of men. These men were not like the ones before; they were rough, harsh, and spoke in a language Meron barely understood. They seemed less interested in their destination than in asserting control, barking orders, and shoving the girls if they moved too slowly. The promise of work and safety began to fade, replaced by a cold fear as the sisters realized the intentions of these men were darker than they'd imagined. Their captors were careful, navigating through unmonitored border crossings at night, avoiding police and authorities. Days passed in silence and hunger.

The men showed no kindness, only cruelty, and any question was met with a slap or worse. Meron tried to shield Tigist, but it became harder with each day. Days later, weakened and broken, they were shoved into yet another truck heading toward Nairobi. They traveled silently, heads lowered, bruises hidden under thin, worn clothing, hoping the journey would finally end. They didn't speak to one another; their spirits were crushed by what they had endured. When the truck finally stopped, they were escorted out, blindfolded, and led into what they would later recognize as the safe house.

The men removed their blindfolds, and Meron glanced around, taking in their surroundings. It was a small, dingy room with a single barred window, reeking of dampness and dust. The door locked behind them with a loud, final click.

They were alone again, huddled in the corner, as Meron wrapped her arms around Tigist, doing her best to soothe her sister's trembling.

They stayed silent and watchful, waiting for whatever was to come next. The wear of their journey showed in every thread and seam of their clothing. Meron's kemis, once a soft cotton dress in earthy tones with intricate patterns around the collar and sleeves, now hung limply, stained by days of dust, sweat, and the grime of transport. The delicate embroidery that once marked the dress as a prized garment from home was frayed and pulled, the stitching weakened by relentless travel and rough handling.

Tigist clung tightly to her netela, her thin white shawl now smudged with dirt, wrapped protectively around her shoulders. Originally a comforting piece, it was now little more than a worn cloth, its edges frayed from being clutched and used for warmth on cold nights along the journey. Underneath, her loose skirt—a faded blue, once sturdy and practical—was mottled with dust and dirt, the waistband stretched and sagging from endless days of wear. Her sandals, a thin pair made from old rubber, were cracked and misshapen, offering little protection to her now-sore, swollen feet.

As they settled onto the sparse mat provided, they both tried to pull their clothing into some semblance of order, a small attempt to reclaim dignity in an undignified space. But the material, stretched and dulled by exhaustion, seemed to mirror the emotional weight they carried.

Their clothes, like them, bore the signs of survival. They clung to each other as the house's low murmur of voices and

occasional shouting sounded through the thin walls, the fabric of their worn clothing barely separating them from the cold, unyielding floor.

Bashir

Bashir closed the door behind him, taking in the two girls huddled close, their eyes wide with fear. He had already told them twice to sit apart, but they clung to each other as if their lives depended on it. He felt a surge of irritation, but he kept his voice low and controlled.

"Move. Over there," he said, pointing to the room's far corner.

His voice was firm, without patience. "Now."

They hesitated, exchanging a frightened look. The older one, Meron, took a shaky breath, pulling her sister closer. Bashir's eyes narrowed as he took a step closer, his presence filling the small room. He had no time for defiance. "You're in Kenya now," he said, his tone dripping with warning.

"This isn't your home. You follow orders, or there will be consequences." He paused, letting his words sink in. "Don't make this difficult. Do as I say." He could see Meron's jaw clench, her eyes betraying a flash of anger despite her trembling hands. But the younger one, Tigist, was already starting to shift, her body language tense with confusion and fear. "See? Your sister gets it," he said, a smirk flickering as he looked directly at Meron. "You might think you're strong, but that doesn't matter here. You do what I say, or you'll both regret it." But as he went about it, a curious thing happened: the older girl, Meron, didn't look at him in defiance or even with the fear he'd come to expect.

She looked… resigned but with something unyielding in her gaze, something that irked him. She was holding her younger sister's hand tightly, her expression somehow both protective and steely. Bashir watched, hoping to see her resolve waver, but Meron's reaction was unnervingly calm, as if she was determined to hold on to whatever shred of control she still possessed. This threw him off slightly; he'd expected her fear or pleading, something he could work with, not this quiet endurance.

In Bashir's mind, the younger girl, Tigist, was just as much of an unknown as her older sister. He imagined her fragile and fearful, perhaps even too frightened to resist or defend herself. But as he continued to observe her, he noticed something in her eyes that unsettled him. There was fear, yes, but also something fierce, a small spark that showed she had some fight left. She wasn't overtly resisting, but her gaze held a kind of silent rebellion, like she was trying to tell him that she wouldn't go down easily, no matter what he threw her way.

"You're going to follow my orders, both of you," he said, his tone hardening.

"Anything else, and I won't be so kind. You're not here to resist—you're here to obey."

"You're wasting your time if you think someone's coming to help you," he murmured, cold and direct.

"You're alone here. Do you understand?" He straightened up, letting his words linger, watching the defiance slowly dim in her eyes.

Tigist was making strange, sad noises and crying silently. He cleaned Meron's sex with the washcloth, his fingers delving into her sex and then her anus.

He couldn't help but smirk at her defiance as his fingers moved across her trembling body, his smirk a silent declaration of his control over her. But for now, he relished in his power over these two girls - one so innocent and the other so defiant. Finally, Bashir took out a small bottle of lubricant. His fingers glistened with the slick product as he slowly pushed his fingers into the girls' sex and anal cavities, their bodies tensing in response to the foreign intrusion. A faint, sweet fragrance of the lubricant mixed with the metallic scent of bodily fluids filled the air, making Bashir's actions seem even more predatory and sinister.

He enjoyed his fingers going easily in and out, their bodies yielding to his touch and the slickness of the lubricant. He relished in the control and power he had over them, "You are going to meet Mrefu, and you should be happy I took care of you." He told the terrified girls. He had seen so many terrified such girls and women that he had stopped looking at them as persons, just as cattle transiting through the facility, and sometimes just as toys for his lust. These were cute, and he was envious that they were for Mrefu.

Mrefu arrives

Bashir glanced at them with his usual dispassion, nodding toward Mrefu as he entered the room.

"They're all yours, boss. I washed them and got them ready," he muttered before moving to secure their bindings, his hands efficient and unfeeling.

Bashir tightened the rope around each wrist, ensuring they couldn't move or wriggle free. Meron winced as the rough fibers bit into her skin, but she said nothing, focusing on shielding Tigist, trembling beside her.

"Good work, Bashir," Mrefu replied smoothly, a hint of satisfaction in his tone.

"Now leave us." Without a word, Bashir nodded and stepped outside, the door creaking shut behind him.

The air felt heavier once Mrefu was alone with them, and he paced the room, his eyes gleaming with calculated interest as he assessed his new captives. Mrefu stood, studying the two girls, feeling the familiar mixture of power and control settle over him. Yes, he thought, they'll bring in good money and meanwhile give him so much pleasure. Too bad he was already so late in the day, too late to enjoy them. He took in their expressions—Meron's defiance, the slight tilt of her chin, trying to protect her younger sister. It intrigued him, this small act of courage. But courage would get them nowhere here; it was a luxury they couldn't afford, not in his world. He was used to this routine, to watching fear take hold. The younger one, Tigist, was visibly scared, her eyes darting between him and the door, searching for any escape route.

There was always one like her in each batch—new to the reality of their fate, still holding on to hope. But hope was something Mrefu knew how to extinguish. Meron, even trapped, still met his gaze, her eyes sharp, challenging. She didn't know who she was up against, but Mrefu found her defiance mildly amusing. It wouldn't last long, he told himself. He'd seen the same expression in countless others,

and then relaxing as he moved inside of her, the tightness of her flesh igniting a fire within him, and he was lost in the raw intensity of their carnal encounter. He came fast in the tight, somewhat dry sex, wiped himself, and left the room already thinking with pleasure about coming back the following day.

After Mrefu left, Meron and Tigist were left alone in the room to recover from their ordeal. Meron and Tigist huddled together on the thin mattress, their immature, strained bodies aching and violated, Meron's physical pain almost a relief compared to the anguish gripping her mind. Tigist clung to Meron, her small arms wrapped tightly around her, the only comfort she had left. Numb from the trauma, she looked to her older sister with a kind of quiet trust, holding onto her as though Meron were her only anchor in a world that had collapsed into horror. The older girl's heart broke as she looked down at her sister, guilt washing over her like a tidal wave.

All of this, she thought bitterly, was her fault. If only she hadn't made those choices. If only she hadn't believed the lies of the recruiter. How much more could they endure? Would the torment repeat endlessly, destroying their bodies, stripping them of everything they once were? She didn't see any way out. With every passing moment, hope seemed further out of reach. A part of her wished for death, a release from this agony. She wanted to let her soul cry out, to empty herself of all the pain, the regret, the dread of what was still to come. But she couldn't. She had to hold it together for Tigist.

Meron knew she was all her sister had, no matter what she felt. Tigist needed her strength, needed her to keep fighting, even if she had nothing left in her. Instead of succumbing to the despair clawing at her, Meron closed her eyes, her lips moving in silent prayer. She prayed with a fervor she didn't know she possessed, asking for a miracle, an escape, something, anything. "If there's a God," she whispered, barely a breath, "save us… or at least save her. I'll give anything, even my own life, my immortal soul, destroy me. Just let her be free." Her voice broke, and she felt Tigist's head burrow deeper into her shoulder as though she sensed her sister's despair even in her sleep. In that dark room, with nothing but each other, Meron clung to her prayer, clutching it as the only thing between them and the void. She would endure anything, even the depths of hell, if it meant her sister might one day be free.

Trash Dump Diving

Dennis crouched by the pile of damp papers, his fingers brushing through the half-burnt remnants. The stench of smoke and ash lingered, but last night's rain had saved some of the documents from turning to cinders. He smirked grimly. The rain had done them a favor. Whatever storm had hit the camp also ruined the poachers' half-hearted attempt to destroy their trail. These weren't just any scraps. There were far too many papers here for what should have been a simple poaching camp. Receipts, scribbled notes, maps—this wasn't the usual disorder he'd come to expect from men on the run. Whoever had been here, probably Mrefu, had been carrying an archive of some sort, maybe trying to sort it out before the ambush came down on them.

He sifted through the sheets, pulling out one that hadn't been completely ruined by the fire. It was crinkled and faded but legible enough. Dennis narrowed his eyes as he scanned it— numbers, bills for vehicle repairs, strange notes scribbled in shorthand. His gut told him this wasn't small-time poaching. This was part of something bigger. More digging turned up a name scrawled hastily in the corner of a receipt: Ziad, the Lebanese merchant. Then, there was another note listing payments in the same chaotic handwriting. Next to one of the larger figures was another known name: Otieno.

Dennis's heart skipped slightly at the sight of it. Someone high enough to grease the wheels of corruption and keep the poaching machine rolling. And then there was Mrefu. His name popped up in multiple places, always tied to supply chains, transport logistics, and payments made to middlemen. But there was something else. Dennis felt a chill as he pulled out another sheet, this one almost untouched by the fire. It listed a few code names—aliases, perhaps.

The Broker. Dennis's jaw tightened, but the real jolt came from the name scribbled beside it in bold, almost like an afterthought: Boniface Mathew Malyango, followed by "Shetani Hana Huruma"—The Devil Has No Mercy. "Shetani," Dennis muttered under his breath, his fingers tightening around the paper. He knew the name. The infamous poacher who had terrorized the elephant herds, leaving trails of blood and ivory in his wake.

The man who was once dubbed The Devil in poaching circles was convicted of being responsible for thousands of elephant deaths across East Africa. And yet, he had been

acquitted—his conviction overturned in Tanzania, a case marred by broken chains of evidence and weak police work. Dennis stood up slowly, his mind spinning with the significance of what he had in his hands. If Shetani, or Boniface Malyango, was connected to this network—and if his involvement was linked to both Ziad and Otieno—then this was much larger than anything they had thought.

Odhiambo was moving through the camp, his rifle slung over his shoulder, scanning the tree line for any movement. Dennis called him over, his voice calm despite the storm brewing in his head.

"You find something?" Odhiambo asked, eyes narrowing as he noticed the papers in Dennis's hands.

"Let's just say my luck in trash heap hunting paid off," Dennis said with a half-smile, though his tone was serious. He wasn't going to spill all the details yet.

"Tell me, have you ever heard of someone called The Broker?"

Odhiambo tilted his head, thinking for a moment. "Heard whispers. Not much, though. A middleman, from what I've gathered. Some say he connects poaching gangs to buyers overseas. But nothing solid." Dennis nodded. "What about Shetani Hana Huruma?" Odhiambo's eyes darkened, and he gave a slow nod. "Shetani? Of course. He's a ghost now, though. His conviction was thrown out in Tanzania— said the evidence wasn't clear. But he's a big name. Someone like that, if he's active in Kenya, people would notice. And believe me, we'd hear about it." Dennis glanced back at the papers, his mind working through the implications.

Shetani may have been acquitted, but if these papers were right, if he was still in the game, then it wasn't just about a few elephants anymore. This network was sprawling and dangerous, connected to powerful men like Otieno and farreaching criminals like Ziad. And The Broker—whoever he was—seemed to be the key to it all.

"We need to go through all of this carefully," Dennis said, his voice low.

"There's something big here, Odhiambo. Bigger than we thought." Odhiambo nodded, his face grim.

"I figured as much when we came back here. This isn't just poaching. It's something else."

Dennis looked across the abandoned camp, the burned papers fluttering in the breeze. They'd just stumbled onto something massive. The Devil had no mercy, but neither did Dennis. He wasn't going to stop until he uncovered the whole truth.

Mrefu at the Safe House

Mrefu's phone buzzed, pulling him from his planning. He glanced at the number, a smirk forming as he recognized the contact. Answering it, he listened carefully, nodding as a low voice on the other end described the situation at the safe house.

What should they do with the Ethiopian sisters? Mrefu's eyes glinted with dark satisfaction as he ended the call. He turned to his right-hand man, Obasi, who was double-checking their equipment.

"Change of plans, Obasi. I'm heading to the safe house." Obasi looked up, his brow furrowed with mild surprise. "Now? We're already stretched thin here with the recent movement."

"I have…personal business there," Mrefu replied, his tone cool but firm.

"There's a phone I left in my rush out. Don't want anyone sniffing around and finding it. And we're already set up to keep the new ones locked away. They'll be no trouble."

Obasi nodded, understanding the unspoken command in Mrefu's words. "I'll keep everything under control here. And if anyone asks, you're checking up on supply lines."

"Good man." Mrefu clapped him on the shoulder before turning away, already envisioning his arrival at the safe house, both for the items he needed to secure and for the added…entertainment waiting there. In this line of work, power was more than control—it was possession, complete dominance over everyone and everything.

Ambushing Mrefu

Karani had been lying low since the ambush that left three rangers dead, and Naomi wounded. His betrayal had haunted him, but after choosing to help Dennis and Captain Odhiambo, he found himself deeper than ever. He knew the syndicate wouldn't forgive him if they discovered what he'd done. Yet here he was, playing a dangerous game, pretending to be still loyal to Mrefu and his men.

The call came late in the afternoon, just as Karani was beginning to think they'd forgotten about him. Obasi, a close associate of Mrefu, was on the other end, asking how things

were going with the rangers. His tone was casual, but Karani could sense the underlying tension, the unspoken question hanging in the air: Were the rangers planning anything? Were they coming for revenge? Karani kept the conversation light, throwing in bits of harmless gossip he'd overheard, hoping to appear useful but not suspicious. They talked for a while, the poacher growing more comfortable, and eventually, the conversation turned to Mrefu.

"Mrefu's lying low, right?" Karani asked as if he didn't already know the answer.

"After the ambush, I figured he'd keep his head down," Obasi grunted in agreement.

"Yeah, but he's got some business to take care of. Going to stop by one of the safe houses soon." Karani felt his pulse quicken.

This was what he needed. But he couldn't push too hard or let them think he was fishing for information. "Oh? Which one?" Karani asked casually, knowing several safe houses were spread across the region. Obasi laughed.

"You know the one. Just a routine check. Nothing big."

That was all Karani needed. Indirectly, he could guess which safe house they meant from how the man spoke. It was the one they rarely used, deep in the bush, where they stashed essential things—things Mrefu didn't trust anyone to handle. And it wasn't just the location, he guessed.

From the tone and timing of the call, Karani knew when they would be coming. As soon as the conversation ended, Karani wiped the sweat from his brow and immediately called Odhiambo. His voice was tense but steady.

"They're going to the safe house," Karani said.

"Mrefu's heading there soon. This is our chance."

Odhiambo didn't hesitate.

"Where and when?" Karani gave him the details, his heart pounding as he realized what this meant. They had a chance—maybe the only chance they'd get—to take Mrefu down. He just hoped he hadn't miscalculated. There would be no second chances if they failed. The Safe House Dennis leaned against the side of the Land Cruiser, the dusty plains stretching out around them, the heat rising in shimmering waves off the ground. Beside him, Captain Odhiambo checked his radio for the hundredth time, eyes scanning the horizon. They were close—closer than they had ever been. And it was thanks to Karani, the low-level traitor who had switched sides, desperate to save his skin. Karani had given them everything they needed to track down Mrefu, the poaching ringleader.

There had been whispers of a safe house, a remote hideout where Mrefu occasionally stored weapons, ivory, and documents too dangerous to leave anywhere else. According to Karani, Mrefu needed to check on something important—perhaps a shipment being held up. That was their chance. Dennis glanced at Karani, sitting nervously in the back of the vehicle, beads of sweat forming on his forehead. He had agreed to help, though fear was clearly driving him. The promise of protection, of a way out, had been enough to make him betray Mrefu. It was up to Dennis and Captain Odhiambo to ensure this sting worked.

"You're sure he'll come?" Dennis asked, not taking his eyes off the horizon. Karani nodded quickly.

"He has to. There's something in the safe house. He needs to check it himself—he won't trust anyone else. The poachers told me that much."

"How many men is he bringing?" Odhiambo asked, his voice low and steady.

"Four. Maybe five," Karani replied. "They'll be armed, but they won't expect trouble here. They think this place is hidden."

Dennis nodded, eyes narrowing.

"Good. We'll be ready." The safe house stood near Maai Mahiu on the edge of a long, dusty road that stretched toward the horizon, seeming to lead nowhere.

The crumbling, forgotten structure was tucked behind a thicket of acacia trees, its cracked walls blending into the dry, desolate landscape. From a distance, it looked abandoned, the kind of place no one would give a second glance. But the place wasn't abandoned, not entirely. Dennis knew better than to think Mrefu would leave a safe house unguarded. There was at least one poacher inside. They'd seen glimpses of him pacing, watching the road. A small team went discreetly.

There was only one poacher inside, a middle-aged man named Bashir, who had been rapidly disabled. One of the rangers, whose voice was similar to Bashir, was ready to answer the phone in case of a call. Now ready, inside, Dennis, Odhiambo, and a team of rangers crouched low, rifles ready. They had surrounded the house, hidden among the trees and rocks, every sense tuned for what was coming. Dennis could feel the tension hanging in the air. This safe

house wasn't just another hideout but a vault of secrets. Mrefu's secrets.

Somewhere inside, there might be the evidence they needed to bring down Mrefu and the entire network. Karani had been right. Mrefu wouldn't trust anyone with whatever was stored inside. He would come personally to check on it. When he did, Dennis and Odhiambo would wait. Odhiambo crouched beside Dennis, his voice low. "As soon as Mrefu arrives at the front door, we hit the house from both sides. He won't have time to look for cover." Dennis nodded, his gaze never leaving the window.

Through a small gap in the shutters, he could see the road stretching out like a ribbon of dust. A cloud had appeared in the distance, growing larger as vehicles approached. Mrefu was coming, just as Karani had said. Dennis's heart pounded in his chest, adrenaline sharpening his senses. The rangers had taken positions around the house, hidden in the scrubland, every angle covered. They had been given strict orders—no one fires unless necessary.

They wanted Mrefu alive, wanted him trapped inside with no escape. "Get ready," Odhiambo muttered, his eyes narrowing as the vehicles drew closer. The plan was to wait until Mrefu and his men were at the door, distracted and thinking they were safe. Mrefu and his men would find themselves caught between the rangers at the back and Dennis's team inside. They would have no time to run, no place to hide. The vehicles slowed as they neared the house, the dust settling around them.

Dennis's pulse quickened. The moment was coming. Mrefu stepped out of the lead truck, tall and imposing, his

eyes scanning the area but seeing nothing suspicious. His men followed with rifles slung across their shoulders, casually confident. They thought they were alone. Mrefu walked toward the front door, his hand reaching for the handle. Dennis nodded at Odhiambo. "Now." Odhiambo motioned to the rangers at the front, signaling them to hold their positions.

Mrefu was still out in the open. They would strike the moment he stepped into the house, trapping him inside with no way out. The trap was set. Mrefu was walking into it, and there would be no escape.

Mrefu is Arrested

Everything happened fast. The rangers moved in from all sides, rifles raised, cutting off any escape route. Mrefu's men barely had time to react before they found themselves surrounded. One of the poachers raised his gun, but Odhiambo shouted, "Drop it! Or you die!"

The man hesitated, his eyes darting around as he realized how hopeless the situation was. Slowly, he lowered his weapon to the ground. Mrefu turned, his eyes widening as he saw the rangers closing in. There was no way out. He took a step back, his hand twitching toward the pistol on his belt, but Dennis stepped forward, leveling his rifle at him. "Don't," Dennis said, his voice calm but firm. "It's over, Mrefu. Put your hands up." For a second, Mrefu looked like he might fight, his eyes blazing with anger. But then he saw how futile it was. His men had already dropped their weapons.

There was nowhere to run. Slowly, grudgingly, Mrefu raised his hands, fury etched into his face. Odhiambo

stepped forward, securing the handcuffs around Mrefu's wrists.

"You're under arrest," he said, his voice laced with satisfaction. "For poaching, illegal arms dealing, and everything else we'll find in that safe house." As the rangers secured the area, Dennis couldn't help but glance at Karani, standing to the side, looking both relieved and terrified.

The man had helped them catch Mrefu, but he was still a traitor in many eyes. There was no telling what would happen to him once this was all over. But for now, they had Mrefu. And with him, the syndicate had lost one of its most important men. Dennis only hoped this would lead them to the next target—The Broker. As they loaded Mrefu into the vehicle, Odhiambo looked over at Dennis with a satisfied grin. "Not bad for a day's work," he said. Dennis nodded, though his mind was already moving forward. Mrefu was a big catch, but there might be something in the safe house that would help them take the syndicate down.

"I'm going to have a look at what I can find inside," Dennis said, nodding toward the safe house.

Odhiambo nodded. "Let's go. If there's anything in there, it'll help." Dennis walked toward the safe house, his mind already racing. Mrefu had been cautious, but not cautious enough. Whatever was in that building was important enough to draw him out personally. And if they were lucky, it might be the key to bringing down The Broker once and for all. Captain Odhiambo stood a few feet away, watching the road, his rifle slung over his shoulder.

The rangers had surrounded the place, making sure no one slipped in or out. Mrefu was in custody, but the

operation wasn't finished yet. Not until they found what they needed. "Ready?" Odhiambo asked, his voice low.

Dennis nodded. "Let's get it done."

The safe house looked dusty and neglected, but Dennis knew better than to trust appearances. There was always more beneath the surface. The safe house might look abandoned, but it was a critical piece in a much larger network, and that meant it couldn't be unprotected.

Dennis and Odhiambo exchanged a glance before stepping inside. The air was stale, thick with the scent of old papers and dirt, but Dennis's attention remained sharp. His eyes flicked around the room, searching for anything out of place—hidden cameras, motion detectors, traps. The room itself was bare— concrete walls, a single table in the center, and stacks of crates piled against one corner. Too simple. Too careless. "Be careful," Dennis muttered, his instincts on high alert.

"There's no way they'd leave this place unprotected." Odhiambo nodded, gripping his rifle tighter as he scanned the room. He gestured toward the corner where an antique safe was partially hidden behind a wooden shelf, not much defense in front of a motivated attacker, but enough to keep the poachers away. "There," he said quietly. Dennis moved toward it, but something caught his eye—a small, almost invisible wire running along the floor, just inches from the safe. He knelt down, examining it carefully.

"Trap," he whispered. "Tripwire. They didn't just leave this lying around."

Odhiambo crouched beside him, narrowing his eyes. "Can you disarm it?"

Dennis nodded, pulling a small multi-tool from his jacket. His hands moved quickly but cautiously, cutting the wire swiftly before standing.

"They wanted anyone who found this to think it was abandoned. Probably would've blown the whole place sky-high if we'd forced the safe without checking."

With the immediate danger neutralized, Dennis and Odhiambo returned their attention to the safe.

It took several minutes of precise work—Dennis prying carefully while Odhiambo used the crowbar for leverage. Finally, the heavy door creaked open. Inside, the contents were sparse but significant. A few faded maps, an old revolver—probably left as a diversion—but at the center of it all was a leather-bound ledger. Dennis reached for it, feeling the worn cover under his fingertips. His pulse quickened. He knew this was what they had been looking for. Dennis flipped the monthly ledger open, and the moment he saw the contents, he felt his stomach tighten.

Several pages of meticulously detailed records of the operations of the month. "Careful," Odhiambo warned, keeping a watchful eye on their surroundings. The safe had already yielded some clues—papers, ledgers—but Dennis had the sense there was something more hidden here, something Mrefu wouldn't want to leave behind. He pressed a little harder, and with a soft click, the panel shifted, revealing a small compartment beneath.

His heart rate quickened.

"There's something," he muttered, carefully pulling open the compartment. Inside, tucked away as though forgotten, was a satellite phone, its casing scratched and worn from years of use. It wasn't a new model—nothing fancy or sleek—but in this world, such phones were invaluable. Off-grid communication. Secure. Untraceable. The kind of phone you carried if you didn't want to be found. Dennis lifted it out, the device's weight far heavier than it seemed. He turned it over in his hands, looking for any identifying marks, but it was anonymous, just like its owner. Still, Dennis knew.

This was it. This was the piece Mrefu couldn't afford to lose.

"Why a phone?" Odhiambo asked quietly, leaning over Dennis's shoulder, his sharp gaze never leaving the room.

"It's not just a phone," Dennis said.

"It's his lifeline. His way of staying connected to The Broker, Ziad, and all of them. Mrefu doesn't trust anyone, not even his own men. That's why he uses this—keeps his conversations off the grid."

The phone came alive slowly; its battery was almost drained.

Dennis navigated through the simple, outdated menu with practiced fingers, scrolling through the recent call log. There were numbers—dozens of them—but they were all saved as code: random initials, digits, or symbols. Nothing that immediately gave away identities. Then, one entry caught his eye. Shetani Hana Huruma Three words. Simple. But Dennis's gut twisted at the sight of it. Shetani Hana

Huruma. The Broker. The elusive mastermind they had been chasing all this time.

Dennis stared at the words, the gravity of what they had just found hitting him like a punch to the chest.

"Mrefu wouldn't risk losing this," Dennis said, his voice low.

"It's his connection to The Broker. To everything. We've got him." Odhiambo crouched down beside him, his usually stoic face showing a flicker of recognition.

"That's The Broker," he murmured. "Mrefu's been calling him."

"What now?" Odhiambo asked, his voice low.

"We secure this and trace the calls. But Mrefu doesn't know we've got it, so we keep it that way."

Dennis pocketed the phone and prepared to leave when he noticed a barely visible locked door at the far end of the room.

His instincts flared. "Cover me," Dennis whispered, nodding toward the door. With a firm shoulder shove, he broke the lock. Inside, the air was stifling. In the shadows, Dennis could make out two naked young girls huddled together, visibly malnourished, their eyes wide with fear, handcuffed to a big metal ring in the wall. One looked like she had barely reached their teens.

The older girl, fifteen, maybe, held the younger one tightly, both frozen in place. Dennis knelt, speaking softly. "You're safe now. We're here to help you." And he rapidly freed their hands. They rushed to get their clothes that were

folded on a shelf, beside the door. The older girl's gaze shifted nervously between Dennis and Odhiambo, uncertain whether they were truly there to help or just another threat. She took a shaky breath before speaking in broken English, her voice thin and hesitant.

"They…brought us here from Ethiopia. Said we'd have good jobs and enough money to help our family." Her eyes filled with tears. "But then…they said we'd be sold."

Odhiambo's face darkened as he heard her words. "They've been kept here like cargo," he muttered, more to himself than Dennis.

It was clear now why Mrefu had returned—to keep a close watch on "goods" more valuable to him than anything else in the safe house. The younger girl looked up, her eyes filled with confusion and desperation. She leaned close to the older girl and asked, in a small, uncertain voice,

"Will… we go home?"

Dennis nodded gently. "We'll get you out of here, and we'll make sure you're safe."

The older girl, still wary but sensing their sincerity, nodded slowly. Dennis looked at them, annoyed, wondering how long they had been locked in this small, dark space, enduring fear and despair. They moved quickly after that, the urgency of the mission heightened by their discovery. The phone was no longer just evidence—it was a lifeline for these girls, a way to untangle them from The Broker's web.

Dennis nodded, but his mind raced. The criminals they were up against weren't amateurs—they were shrewd and calculating. If they had set a trap for anyone opening the safe,

there was no telling what else they had in place. There was no time to lose. They had to secure the ledger, but more importantly, they had to get out before anyone realized what they'd found.

"Let's move," Dennis said, his voice steady but urgent. "Should we leave a team here?"

"If there is no special reason, let's go. We recovered what we needed, and I don't want to put more rangers at risk," answered Odhiambo.

Meron and Tigist

The drive back to the camp was silent. The weight of the discovery pressed heavily on Dennis and Odhiambo as the two girls sat huddled together in the backseat. The older girl still clutched the younger one's hand tightly. Her gaze was vacant as she stared out the window, the passing landscape barely registering. Odhiambo glanced back now and then, his expression softening as he watched them. After a while, Odhiambo broke the silence, turning halfway in his seat to face them.

"You are safe now," he said gently, choosing his words carefully. "We are taking you to a safe place, back to the Maasai Mara. Do you understand?"

The older girl blinked, her eyes slowly focusing on him. She gave a small nod. "Maasai Mara?" she repeated, her accent light but clear, testing the unfamiliar words.

Odhiambo smiled gently. "Yes, Maasai Mara. It is a big, beautiful place. There are many animals, and good people too. You will be safe there."

The younger girl, her eyes wide and wary, looked up at her companion and then at Odhiambo, finally whispering, "My sister… Meron." Odhiambo's face softened further as he nodded. "Meron, that's a lovely name. And you," he asked gently, directing his gaze at the younger girl, "what is your name?" The girl hesitated, but after a moment, she met his eyes. "Tigist," she said quietly.

Odhiambo said their names reassuringly: "Meron and Tigist, you have both been very brave. When we reach the Mara, there will be people to help you, people who want to ensure your safety."

Tigist nodded slightly, still clutching her sister's hand. Dennis gave Odhiambo a glance of gratitude, the tension in the car easing as the girls began to understand their journey. As they continued down the road, Tigist's gaze softened, the faintest hint of relief showing in her eyes as she whispered to Meron. Her voice was too soft to hear but carried the weight of an older sister's comfort. With the Mara drawing closer, the landscape shifting to open plains and distant mountains, a quiet hope began to settle in the car, the promise of safety finally within reach. Odhiambo's sister, Nyambura, awaited outside as they pulled into the camp.

Her face reflected worry and compassion as she watched Dennis and Odhiambo gently guide the girls out of the vehicle. Nyambura was a nurse, and her presence here was not by chance; she had agreed to take care of the girls, offering a temporary refuge until further contact could be made. Her comforting smile reassured them as they shuffled toward the modest guest quarters she'd prepared.

"Come, my darlings," Nyambura said softly, extending her hand to the older girl. "You're safe now. We'll take care of you here."

She led them inside, helping them settle, a sense of warmth and calmness filling the room as she wrapped them in blankets and offered warm tea. Within minutes, Nyambura had a makeshift clinic ready in her small quarters, prepared to document any signs of abuse or trauma the girls might have suffered. Dennis waited outside, pacing, his thoughts dark as he considered what these girls had endured at the hands of the human traffickers. Odhiambo joined him, crossing his arms as he leaned against the wall.

"Nyambura's good with them," he said quietly.

"They're in the right hands here." Dennis nodded, his gaze fixed on the small window through which he could see Nyambura's silhouette as she worked.

"They've seen things no child should ever see, let alone experience. Mrefu's operation goes far deeper than we anticipated. But, of course, it is a global problem. Even in the USA, at any given time, there are 100,000 to 200,000 victims, A quarter of these children. Most of the victim's total numbers are women or girls."

Odhiambo's jaw tightened. "Once they're settled, we'll get these two children to a secure location. But for now, Nyambura will keep them safe. She's agreed to stay with them as long as they need her."

Dennis exhaled slowly. "At least here, they'll be treated with respect and kindness. After all they've been through, it's the least we can give them."

The Ledger

Dennis looked at the ledger at the Ranger's camp: dates, names, shipments. Ivory, weapons, drugs—everything that had passed through this safe house in the last few weeks. But it was the names that made his blood run cold.

"Ziad," he murmured, his finger tracing the ink. "And here— Mrefu."

He kept turning the pages, his breath catching in his throat. This wasn't just a ledger of minor operations. This was the entire network laid bare in front of them. Odhiambo leaned over, scanning the entries with a sharp eye.

"They didn't expect anyone to find this," he said. "We've got them."

Dennis started looking at the same names. This wasn't it. There had to be something more, something bigger. The safe house was just one piece of the puzzle. They needed something to link all the operations and tie it back to The Broker. And then he found it. Tucked between two entries, written in a rushed hand as though someone had meant to erase it later but hadn't, was a name. A codename, more like. "Shetani Hana Huruma." Dennis frowned, his brow furrowing. He'd heard the name before, whispered in dark corners.

It meant "The Devil Has No Mercy," and it was tied to a figure operating across borders, a ghost that no one had been able to pin down. The Broker. It had to be. He flipped the page, and there it was again. This time, it wasn't just a name. It was last month's set of transactions, carefully recorded, linking ivory shipments to arms deals. Whoever

had written this ledger hadn't just been tracking poaching. They were documenting the entire network—how goods flowed through the safe house, how they were split up, and who was in charge of moving them.

Dennis's eyes locked on a specific entry: Ziad, handling an arms shipment bound for South Sudan. And right beside it, in the same rushed handwriting, the initials B.M.M. Dennis's heart skipped a beat. Boniface Mathew Malyango, the man known as Shetani. "Jesus," Dennis whispered. "What is it?" Odhiambo asked. Dennis handed him the ledger, pointing to the entries.

"This is it. This proves it. Ziad works under Shetani, and Shetani is The Broker. This is the link we've been looking for."

Odhiambo's eyes narrowed as he studied the page. "We've got him."

Kamau

Dennis called Kamau on the satellite phone, keeping his voice low as Odhiambo listened beside him, ready to support him.

"Kamau, we've got him. Mrefu is in custody, and we've got the ledger—it's not just a list of transactions. It's a complete roadmap of the entire operation."

Kamau's voice crackled on the line from Nairobi, sharp and alert. "You got Mrefu? And what exactly did you find?"

Dennis glanced at the ledger in his hands, flipping carefully through the pages as he replied. "Everything's

here: ivory shipments, arms deals, even human trafficking routes. And it's not just about Mrefu or Ziad.

The initials B.M.M. appear repeatedly—Boniface Mathew Malyango. Shetani. He's The Broker. This is the connection we've been searching for." Odhiambo leaned in, his eyes on the ledger as Dennis explained. "Kamau, we also found two girls locked up in the safe house. Teenagers smuggled from Ethiopia. They're terrified, but one of them speaks some English. They're willing to help build the case against Mrefu if we can ensure their safety." Kamau let out a sharp breath.

"Having them is very important. Those girls could be critical witnesses. We must secure their statements immediately. And Dennis, about the ledger—we'll need an unbreakable chain of custody to make it stick in court. If we miss a step, Mrefu's lawyers will tear it apart."

"I know," Dennis said, meeting Odhiambo's gaze as he nodded.

"Odhiambo's photographing every page, documenting it carefully. He's prepared to secure it for clear proof of location and chain of custody, every step."

Odhiambo chimed in, his voice steady.

"We'll seal the ledger in an evidence bag, and I'll personally accompany it back to Nairobi. Every detail's being logged."

"Good," Kamau replied, his tone weighted.

"But listen, Odhiambo —don't let your guard down. Mrefu's arrest, this ledger, and these girls are all powerful

evidence, but they're also dangerous targets now. Shetani's associates won't hesitate to eliminate anything that could bring him down."

Odhiambo nodded, his grip tightening on the ledger.

"Understood. The girls are now with my sister, where they can receive medical care. I'll work on arranging their statements with you once they're ready. Meanwhile, I will organize a security detail."

As the call ended, Dennis took a steadying breath. Kamau's warning lingered. With Mrefu's ruthless network still at large, protecting the evidence—and the girls—would be as risky as going up against The Broker himself.

Shetani

Dennis had found the connection to Shetani, and he would probably learn more soon. After his quiet release in mid-2020, Boniface Mathew Malyango, known as Shetani, knew he could no longer operate openly in Tanzania.

His reputation had become too notorious, his face too recognizable after the documentary The Ivory Game had exposed his brutal exploits to an international audience. Yet, Shetani had no intention of abandoning his empire; instead, he saw an opportunity to reinvent himself and extend his reach. With years of experience, well-established networks, and connections spanning East and Central Africa, Shetani relocated, choosing Kenya and Ethiopia as his new base of operations. He slipped into Kenya's underworld, where his name didn't carry the same infamy.

He positioned himself strategically as "The Broker"— the unseen hand managing operations rather than the figure

on the ground. He had an eye for expansion and quickly aligned with local syndicates involved in arms and human trafficking, leveraging his logistical expertise to broaden his criminal empire. In Kenya, the illegal networks Shetani found were fragmented but powerful. He knew that to take control, he would need to integrate these disparate elements into a cohesive operation.

Slowly, he established connections in Nairobi's underworld and with key players along the smuggling routes through Ethiopia, Somalia, and down to Mombasa. These ports and border towns became the arteries through which his new ventures would flow. Shetani's role as The Broker made him nearly untouchable. He didn't need to be present to command respect and fear; he pulled the strings from a distance, overseeing the trafficking of an increased variety of items.

His knowledge of local systems and his talent for corrupting and influencing the authorities allowed him to expand his new empire in ways he hadn't imagined before. His relationships with corrupt officials and local leaders across East Africa allowed him to establish routes that went beyond animal parts — routes that now transported arms to militias, drugs to coastal cities, and even human lives to dark markets across borders. With Kenya as his new base and Ethiopia as his emerging network, Shetani now operated in shadows thicker than before, connected to the very systems that should have hunted him down.

Years of ruthless ivory trafficking had conditioned him for this new path. Every operation was meticulous, and each of his moves was calculated. Now, "The Broker" held a new

kind of power fueled not by poaching alone but by a network that spanned illegal trades, all flowing under his command.

His network stretched into remote African jungles, crowded Nairobi streets, and the bustling ports of Mombasa — a vast, lethal empire hidden behind the shadow of his infamous past.

Chapter 12: Final Preparations in Nairobi

Flight to Nairobi

It was time to return to Nairobi. The next phase of the fight would be fought in Nairobi and Mombasa. Dennis stood at the small landing strip in the Maasai Mara. The sun was barely up. The air was cool, the kind of crisp that promised heat later in the day. Around him, the savannah stretched out, golden and vast, with nothing but the distant shapes of acacia trees and the occasional movement of wildlife in the brush. The quiet was thick, broken only by the distant calls of birds and the soft hum of insects waking with the light.

Dennis picked up his small bag and walked toward the plane. The grass under his boots was still wet with dew, and his breath misted slightly in the cool morning air. The plane, a Cessna Caravan, was painted white and worn by years of dust and sun. It sat waiting, its propeller still. A few passengers were inside, and the pilot leaned against the door, checking his watch. He gave Dennis a quick nod when their eyes met. Dennis handed his bag to a flight attendant, who tossed it into the back without a word. Dennis followed, settling into his seat. The cabin was tight, the smell of oil and leather hanging in the air. The flight to Nairobi was short, just an hour or so, but Dennis was impatient to be in Nairobi with Naomi.

The pilot climbed. "Ready to go?" he asked, his voice gruff, practical.

The engine coughed to life with a deep rumble, and the propeller spun into a blur. All two of the ground crew waved lazily from a distance, and the Cessna began to bump and bounce along the dirt strip, picking up speed. As they lifted off, the Mara opened up beneath them, spreading out like an endless, untamed ocean. Dennis watched as the land fell away, the golden grasses fading into the horizon. For a moment, everything seemed small and peaceful. He caught sight of a herd of wildebeest moving slowly, following the ancient rhythms of migration. In the distance, a river snaked through the landscape, the water glinting like silver in the early morning light.

The plane climbed higher, and soon, the Mara was just a patchwork of browns and greens, distant and dreamlike. Dennis leaned back, his eyes half-closed. The loud noise of the engine was steady, lulling, and the miles between the Mara and Nairobi began to melt away. By the time they approached the city, the wildness of the savannah had given way to the sprawl of roads, buildings, and smoke. Nairobi's skyline rose ahead, jagged and gray against the morning sky. It felt like another world, so far removed from the quiet beauty of the Mara.

The plane descended smoothly, the landing strip at Wilson Airport growing larger in the windshield. They touched down with a soft jolt, and the plane rolled to a stop near the hangar. Dennis grabbed his bag and climbed out, thanking the pilot with a quick nod before heading toward the main terminal. Nairobi was already awake, the heat rising off the tarmac, and the smell of fuel and dust was thick in the air. He didn't linger long at the airport. The car from Bolt, the local Uber competition, was waiting for him, a

battered old sedan driven by a young man with a sharp, eager look in his eye. The city was alive as they drove through it—people on foot, matatus weaving dangerously among the cars, the markets already buzzing with life.

The noise, the movement, hit him hard after the silence of the Mara. The driver welcomed him with a nod, and soon, they were winding their way through Nairobi's bustling streets. Vendors were setting up their stalls, matatus wove daringly through traffic, and a steady hum of life filled the air, a stark contrast to the Mara's open plains.

Kenyatta National Hospital

His mind was focused on Naomi. He had been anxious to see her since hearing about her release from the intensive care unit, and he urged the driver to hurry as they neared Kenyatta National Hospital, the largest in Nairobi and known for handling serious trauma cases. After paying his fare, Dennis hurried inside, going to the room number he'd committed to memory.

The hospital corridors were a flurry of activity, with doctors and nurses moving briskly as patients and families filled the waiting areas. Dennis finally reached her room, pausing for a moment before he opened the door quietly. Naomi looked up from her bed, her face lighting up as she saw him. Though still visibly tired, she was alert, her natural strength and resilience evident in her expression.

"Dennis," she greeted him warmly, her voice a little soft but strong. "You finally made it."

"Naomi." He walked over, pulling up a chair beside her bed.

"It's good to see you like this. You look better already."

She laughed weakly, waving her hand dismissively. "The doctors fuss over me too much. I'd rather be out there, back in the Mara, than lying here."

He chuckled, "Somehow, I'm not surprised."

Naomi leaned forward, a spark of curiosity in her eyes.

"I've been hearing bits and pieces, but I want to know— what happened in the attack?"

Dennis glanced around. "It's been chaotic. We were set up; the poachers were heavily armed and waiting for us. They had backup and intelligence… someone named Karani tipped them off when we were going to arrive. We've been piecing together everything we could, but they were organized, Naomi. It's bigger than we thought."

Naomi's brows furrowed, her grip on the edge of her blanket tightening.

"So, the rumors about The Broker's network…"

"Real and more extensive than we thought. We recovered a ledger that links him to Ziad, Otieno, and even Mrefu. And it's not just about poaching, Naomi. We found two young girls at one of their safehouses, trafficked from Ethiopia. They were being held… part of a larger, dark operation."

Naomi's face paled as she took in his words. "They're trafficking people too?"

He nodded. "Yes. The ledger we found shows connections to everything—ivory, arms, people. The entire operation funnels through Nairobi and out of Mombasa. The

Broker has his hands in everything, and it's all interconnected."

Naomi leaned back, letting out a slow breath, her face etched with a mixture of horror and determination.

"It makes me want to get out of here even more."

He reached out, placing a reassuring hand over hers.

"The Mara isn't going anywhere, and neither are we. You'll get back; when you do, you'll be at your strongest. For now, just focus on healing. When you're ready, we'll take them down together."

Naomi sighed, her face softening as she looked at him gratefully. "Thank you, Dennis. It's just hard, knowing the fight is out there… but you're right. I'll rest. I'll do what I must, but don't be surprised if you find me in the Mara sooner than you think."

Meeting with Dr. Isaac Mugo

Dennis walked into the Wildlife Preservation Alliance (WPA) office with a sense of urgency. It was 3 PM, and the sun was casting long shadows across the streets of Nairobi. The office was quiet, save for the faint hum of the ceiling fan. He was scheduled to meet Dr. Isaac Mugo, the executive director—a man with a reputation for being relentless in the fight against poaching. Dennis moved past the faded wildlife posters on the walls, each one a reminder of the stakes they were up against: elephants, rhinos, and the vast plains of Maasai Mara. But behind the images of these magnificent creatures lay something darker—an entire network devoted to their destruction, and Dennis had finally started to piece it together.

"Dr. Mugo is ready for you," said Morah, the receptionist, gesturing toward the hallway.

Dennis followed her direction, entering the small office where Dr. Mugo sat behind a large desk cluttered with reports and documents. The air inside was thick with the gravity of their shared mission. Mugo rose to greet him, his sharp eyes taking Dennis in with concern and curiosity.

"Dennis," Mugo said, shaking his hand firmly. "Good to see you."

"Good to see you too, Dr. Mugo," Dennis replied, shaking his hand.

There was mutual respect between the two men, though they came from different worlds. Mugo gestured for Dennis to sit, and they both settled into the chairs across from each other. The doctor's desk was covered in papers, reports on wildlife trafficking, conservation projects, and scattered notes. In the corner, a map of Kenya pinned to the wall had several red dots marking areas of interest—hotspots for poaching activity, no doubt.

"I understand you're heading to Mombasa soon,"

Mugo began, his voice steady, though there was a weight to his words.

"But before you go, I wanted to discuss the situation in more detail. The Network you and Naomi have been tracking—it's more extensive than we first thought."

Dennis took a deep breath. The time had come to lay everything out.

"I've been digging deeper into the syndicate behind the poaching. There's more going on than just illegal ivory."

Mugo leaned forward, his expression unreadable.

"Go on." Dennis pulled out a folder from his bag, filled with notes and fragments of the documents he had recovered from the camp.

"The group we're up against isn't just a bunch of poachers. It's a complex, well-organized criminal syndicate. At the top of the chain is an elusive figure known only as The Broker."

Mugo's eyes narrowed. "The Broker?"

Dennis nodded. "I've heard whispers about him before, but the papers I recovered from the camp confirmed it. He's running everything. The poaching, the weapons smuggling, and, more than likely, drug trafficking. He's the one tying it all together, but he keeps his hands clean—no one's ever seen him."

Mugo sat back, absorbing the information.

"What else do you know?" "There are key players in this operation," Dennis continued. "Charles Otieno, the corrupt politician, is one of them. He's using his influence to shield the poachers and keep authorities off their backs. He's deeply embedded in the system, using his connections to keep the machinery moving."

Mugo's jaw tightened. "Otieno's name keeps coming up. He's dangerous."

"More than that," Dennis said, flipping through the papers.

"There's another key figure: Ziad. He's the arms dealer. The poaching profits are being funneled to him, and in return, he supplies weapons to militias in Somalia and South Sudan. He's not just profiting from the slaughter of elephants—he's fueling wars." Mugo exhaled slowly.

"And Mrefu?" Dennis nodded grimly.

"Mrefu was running the actual poaching operations, coordinating the poaching gangs in places like Nyawara. He was the one on the ground, but he's just one piece of the puzzle. We arrested him; he is not talking yet."

Dennis paused, letting the weight of what he was saying settle in. He pulled out the last sheet of paper, one that had sent a chill down his spine when he found it.

"There's one more name. Shetani Hana Huruma."

Mugo's eyes widened slightly at the mention of the name. "Shetani? The Devil?"

"The same," Dennis confirmed.

"He was supposedly taken down in Tanzania, convicted for trafficking ivory, but his conviction was overturned. Now, I'm not saying that's the same Shetani, but that name appeared alongside The Broker's in the papers I found. He might be The Broker himself. If he's involved, this operation is even bigger than we thought."

Mugo ran a hand over his face, thinking for a moment. "Shetani… I haven't heard any reports of him operating in Kenya recently. But if he's connected to this—if he's active again…"

"It would explain a lot," Dennis said.

"The sheer scale of the poaching. The way the operation spans across borders. It's not just local gangs. This is international, and it's being fueled by men like Ziad, Otieno, and possibly Shetani."

Mugo's face darkened. "What about evidence? Can any of this tie them together?"

Dennis tapped the papers. "We've got fragments. Receipts, notes, scribbled names. But it's enough to start pulling the threads together. The problem is that these men are well protected. Otieno's got a piece of the government in his pocket. Ziad operates in the shadows, and The Broker? He's a ghost. But we're getting closer."

Mugo was silent for a moment, then leaned forward, his gaze sharp. "And what's the next move?"

"I'm heading to Mombasa," Dennis said. "There are more leads there, particularly around the arms shipments. If I can track down Ziad's contacts, I might be able to get more solid evidence."

Mugo's eyes hardened. "I suspected as much. The level of sophistication we've seen—the poachers are too well armed, too organized. This isn't just local hunters trying to make a quick profit."

"No, it's not," Dennis said. "It's an international network. They're not just killing elephants for their ivory— they're funding militias in Somalia and South Sudan, selling weapons to whoever can pay. And now, with the drug trafficking mixed in, it's getting even murkier."

Mugo nodded. "You've uncovered a lot, Dennis. This isn't just about poaching anymore. This is a full-blown criminal empire."

Mugo sat back in his chair, his gaze drifting toward the map on the wall. "And Naomi? How is she doing?"

"She's recovering," Dennis said, his voice softening for a moment.

"She's out of the hospital and staying with me. It's slow, but she's tough. This fight... it's personal for her."

Mugo nodded. "It's personal for all of us. These men, this syndicate—they're destroying everything we've been working for. And they don't care. It's just money and power to them."

Dennis stood, meeting Mugo's gaze. "We're going to take it down. One way or another."

Mugo rose as well, shaking Dennis's hand again, more firmly this time. "Be careful in Mombasa. The deeper you go, the more dangerous this becomes."

"I know," Dennis said quietly.

"But we're in too deep to back out now."

As Dennis left the office, he felt the weight of the coming days pressing down on him. The network was vast, and the men behind it were dangerous. But they had made mistakes, and now Dennis had the trail. The question was, how long before they realized he was following it?

Naomi is Released

The past two days in Nairobi have been a blur of emotions. He had spent most of the time with Naomi, who had finally been released from the hospital. Though her condition had improved, she was still weak, walking slowly, needing support, and taking frequent breaks to catch her breath.

The doctors had insisted she stay close to the hospital in case there were any complications, and Dennis had stayed by her side, sharing a modest room in a guesthouse nearby. They had laughed together, reminiscing about old missions, and they had sat silently, Dennis offering his quiet support when Naomi's energy flagged. She needed someone with her, and Dennis gladly took on that role.

Visiting the David Sheldrick Wildlife Trust

The following day was bright, the kind of clear sky that made the world feel bigger than it was. Nairobi moved around them as Dennis guided the car through the streets, but it felt distant.

The city was a hum of people and noise, but here in the vehicle, it was just him and Naomi. She sat beside him, looking out the window, the breeze catching the strands of her hair. She was out of the hospital now, out of that sterile, too-quiet room. This was her first time back in the world, and she had insisted on coming here. The David Sheldrick Wildlife Trust. Dennis parked the car in the shade near the entrance.

The air was warm but carried that earthy smell of animals and trees, a reminder that they were far from the city's chaos. Naomi moved slowly, her steps measured, still

favoring her side where the wound had barely healed. But she moved with purpose.

"I needed this," she said quietly, almost to herself, as they walked toward the entrance.

Dennis nodded. "Yeah. I figured you did."

They stepped through the gates into the wide, open space of the orphanage. The air changed here, cleaner, filled with the low sounds of elephants grumbling, trunks brushing against the earth. They could see small ones in the distance, moving in herds, some no taller than Naomi's waist. Dennis knew why she had chosen this place. It wasn't just the elephants. It was about what had brought them here—the same thing that had put her in the hospital. A young woman with a worn safari hat and a clipboard greeted them.

She smiled, her eyes sharp but warm. "You must be Naomi and Dennis, right?"

Naomi nodded, her smile small but real.

"We've been expecting you," the woman continued. "You're just in time for the morning feeding. We've got a few orphans from Maasai Mara you might want to meet."

Dennis raised an eyebrow. "From the Mara?"

The woman nodded. "Poaching's been hitting hard there recently, as you know. We've got a couple of calves who lost their mothers just outside the reserve. They're still adjusting, but they're strong."

Naomi's eyes brightened. "I'd like to see them."

They followed the woman to the open area where the keepers were already setting out large milk bottles. The

elephants knew what was coming. They came in slow, lumbering lines, the babies leading, their trunks reaching out eagerly. There was a quiet joy in the air, a kind of peace from the routine of everything—the simple act of feeding something so vulnerable. Naomi leaned on the fence, watching them with a look Dennis hadn't seen in weeks.

One of the younger elephants, barely over a year old, moved toward them, its small trunk curling in the air. The keeper, a tall man with wide, kind eyes, handed Naomi a bottle.

"Go ahead," he said with a nod.

"He's from the Mara. His mother was killed near Talek River. He's still figuring things out, but he's got fight in him."

Naomi took the bottle, her hands trembling slightly, but she held firm. The calf approached, its trunk brushing against her arm before finding the bottle. She laughed, soft and surprised, as the little elephant latched on, drinking hungrily. For a moment, everything was simple. It was just her and the calf, and the world outside seemed far away. Dennis stood back, watching.

The sun was warm on his skin, but his thoughts were with Naomi. He hadn't seen her like this since before the ambush, since the bullet had knocked her down and left her clinging to life. Now, she was feeding a young elephant who had lost everything to the same darkness that haunted them both.

"They'll be all right," Naomi said quietly, her eyes on the calf.

"Yeah," Dennis said, stepping beside her.

"They will." The woman from the Trust approached again.

"You're welcome to stay for as long as you like. We're always looking for more support. Naomi handed the empty bottle back to the keeper and turned to Dennis.

There was a lightness in her eyes now, something that hadn't been there in weeks.

"Maybe this is the start," she said softly. Dennis knew what she meant.

This wasn't just about the elephants. It was about healing for both of them. They walked along the paths, talking with the keepers, learning about the orphans and the work being done. The experts were hopeful, but Dennis could sense the underlying tension. The battle against poaching was relentless. The elephants here were safe for now, but out in the wild, things were different. He knew that too well. As they made their way back to the entrance, Naomi stopped and looked out over the enclosure, where the young elephants were playing, pushing against each other with their trunks.

"They fight, but they keep going," she said.

"Just like us," Dennis replied.

Naomi smiled, a quiet strength in her expression. "Yeah. Just like us."

They left the Trust, and the world's weight was a little lighter than before. There was still a long way to go, but for

now, this was enough. The fight wasn't over, but they weren't finished either. Not yet

Chapter 13: Mombasa

Train to Mombasa

Dennis stood at the Nairobi Railway Station, surrounded by the hum of announcements and travelers' chatter. The station mixed old and new—high ceilings bearing history alongside modern ticket counters and digital displays. Vendors called out, selling snacks and water, their voices blending into the station's constant buzz. He glanced back toward the city, longing for Naomi, still recovering in Nairobi. Leaving her wasn't easy, but there was work to be done, and the lead about the Sea Dragon couldn't wait. Boarding the Madaraka Express, Dennis settled into a window seat, taking in the train's modern design—a gleaming symbol of progress financed largely by Chinese investments.

For some, it represented development; for others, it symbolized Kenya's growing debt. The train eased out of the station and soon sped through Nairobi's outskirts at over 120 kilometers per hour. As the cityscape gave way to fields of maize and clusters of acacia trees, Dennis watched herders with cattle and children waving alongside dirt roads. An eclectic mix of passengers—businessmen, families, tourists—filled the carriage. Dennis sipped tea from an attendant, his gaze drifting to the changing scenery as hours passed. The savannah gave way to a more tropical landscape, palm trees dotting the countryside as the air felt warmer and heavier, even inside the train.

Finally, Mombasa Railway Station appeared—a sleek, modern structure that surprised Dennis with its organization and cleanliness. Stepping into the humid coastal air, he

caught the salty scent of the ocean, mingling with vendors hawking fresh coconuts and roasted maize. The coast felt alive, bustling, and familiar as he began his work in Mombasa. Dennis stood at the Nairobi Railway Station, surrounded by the hum of announcements and travelers' chatter. The station was a blend of Kenya's old and new—a historical space with high ceilings juxtaposed against modern ticket counters and digital displays. Vendors called out, selling steaming snacks, cool water, and fresh fruit, their voices merging into the constant buzz of the busy terminal. Beside him, Kamau was reading over some documents, waiting for the train to Mombasa.

As they boarded the Madaraka Express and settled into their seats, Dennis took in the gleaming interior of the train—a sleek and modern symbol of progress, largely funded by Chinese investments.

"The Chinese have a real stake in Kenya, huh?"

Dennis remarked, glancing over to Kamau. Kamau gave a nod, leaning back thoughtfully.

"Yes, their influence has been growing rapidly, and not everyone sees it the same way. They've poured billions into Kenya—this train, for one. It's a flagship project, you could say. It's cut the travel time between Nairobi and Mombasa in half, which has been good for business, but…"

He trailed off, his gaze shifting to the countryside as it began to roll past them, Nairobi fading into the distance.

"But it's also a double-edged sword?"

Dennis guessed. "Exactly. Kenya's debt has ballooned as a result. This isn't just aid—it's a very calculated

investment, and if we default, our ports, like Mombasa, are the collateral. The Chinese-built Mombasa port facilities handle some of the highest cargo volumes on the continent. It's part of their Belt and Road Initiative, meant to link them to markets globally. But with it comes dependency."

As the train picked up speed, Dennis watched as the cityscape gave way to expansive maize fields, scattered acacia trees, and open savannah. Herder children waved as they passed, their faces lighting up as the sleek train sped by at over 120 kilometers per hour. Inside the carriage, families chatted, businessmen caught up on work, and tourists marveled at the passing landscape. Several hours later, the savannah had slowly transformed into a more tropical environment, marked by clusters of palms and a noticeable humidity in the air.

Finally, the modern lines of Mombasa Railway Station came into view—a sleek, organized structure that was a testament to the recent development. Stepping off, Dennis felt the coastal humidity settle around him, mixed with the distinct salty aroma of the Indian Ocean.

"Feels different already," Dennis remarked as they stepped out into the busy streets of Mombasa.

Tuk-tuks zipped past, their drivers calling out for passengers while vendors sold fresh coconuts and roasted maize from makeshift stalls. Women walked gracefully in bright kangas, balancing baskets on their heads, while children dashed down narrow alleys lined with Swahili-style buildings and newer high-rises. Kamau nodded, his eyes scanning the scene.

"Mombasa has its own rhythm. You'll see it in the harbor, the markets… everywhere. And we're just a stone's throw from Kilindini Harbor, where a lot of the action happens."

They soon made their way to the Wildlife Preservation Alliance (WPA) office, located conveniently close to the harbor. There, they were greeted by Aden Salim, a veteran investigator with a keen knowledge of the harbor's inner workings. Salim shook Dennis's hand firmly, his demeanor calm and measured.

"You must be Dennis. Welcome to Mombasa," he said, a slight smile breaking through his serious expression. Salim led them to a small local restaurant nearby for lunch, a place with painted walls and a faint smell of spices lingering in the air.

Seated at a wooden table, they ordered a spread of traditional Mombasa dishes—biryani, nyama choma (grilled meat), viazi karai (spiced fried potatoes), and samaki wa kupaka, a fish curry with coconut that was a coastal specialty. Salim served as their guide, explaining the nuances of each dish and how each one reflected the influence of Arab, Swahili, and Indian cultures along the coast. Between bites, Salim gave Dennis a primer on Mombasa.

"This city isn't like Nairobi. Nairobi's always moving fast, like it has somewhere to be. But Mombasa flows to its own beat, set by the tides. Even the way business is done here is different—it's about knowing the right people and having connections. It's more than just transactions."

Dennis took it all in, savoring both the food and the wealth of information.

"And the harbor?" he asked, keen to get a better sense of his target.

Salim's eyes narrowed slightly, his tone serious. "Kilindini Harbor is a maze of activity. It's one of the busiest ports on the East African coast, handling cargo from all over. But it's also a prime point for trafficking—ivory, drugs, weapons, even people. The port authorities are overwhelmed, and corruption runs deep. Smugglers know how to exploit every gap."

Kamau nodded in agreement. "Which is why we're here. It's a crucial point in The Broker's operations, and if we're going to make a dent in their network, this is where we need to start."

As they wrapped up their meal, Salim leaned forward, his voice dropping to a low tone.

"This investigation won't be easy, Dennis. The people who run things here have their eyes everywhere, and they don't take kindly to interference. But I'll show you what you need to know. If we're lucky, we might just find a crack in their operation."

Dennis met his gaze, feeling the weight of what lay ahead. He'd left Naomi recovering in Nairobi, but here in Mombasa, a different mission awaited him. And as he looked around at the bustling, vibrant city, he knew he'd have to adapt quickly to its rhythm if he hoped to bring down The Broker's network.

Mombasa Harbor

Dennis followed Selim as they navigated through the bustling maze of Mombasa Harbor, the air thick with the smell of salt, diesel, and the faint hint of spices.

They moved past towering stacks of cargo containers, their colors faded under the relentless sun, and toward a point where Selim could give Dennis a clear view of the port's operations.

"This, my friend," Selim began, gesturing to the sprawling complex before them, "is the beating heart of East Africa."

He pointed to the cranes, looming over them like giant steel skeletons, swinging containers with precision.

"Mombasa Harbor—it's not just Kenya's gateway, it's the link for Uganda, Rwanda, South Sudan, even as far as the DRC. Everything passes through here."

Dennis nodded, taking in the scale of activity around him. Ships lined the docks, some massive container vessels bringing in goods from far-off places, while smaller cargo ships serviced neighboring countries. Trucks queued along the roads, each one a small cog in the vast machine of East African trade.

Selim continued, "Most of what you see arriving here? Consumer goods, machinery, electronics, vehicles, and so much more. Most of it comes from Asia—China especially, followed by India, the Middle East, and Europe. And on the other end, we're exporting everything from tea, coffee, and minerals to fuel and agricultural products."

"China's pretty invested here, then?"

Dennis asked, glancing at Selim as they walked toward a quieter area of the harbor. Selim laughed, a hint of irony in his voice.

"Oh yes, you could say that. China's fingerprints are all over this place."

He waved his hand toward a newer part of the port, a modern section of container terminals gleaming in the sunlight.

"The upgrades, the terminals, even the Standard Gauge Railway linking Mombasa to Nairobi? All are backed by Chinese money. Through their Belt and Road Initiative, they've poured billions into Mombasa."

He paused, lowering his voice slightly, "Of course, there are concerns. Kenya's debt to China is staggering. Some say we're at risk of falling into a debt trap, that the country could lose sovereignty if we can't repay. But there's no doubt the investment has boosted capacity here."

Dennis frowned, watching as cranes swung containers with impressive efficiency.

"So China gets a logistical foothold in East Africa, and Kenya gets a modern port. High stakes."

Selim nodded, glancing around. "It's all very political. And if you ask me, it's not just about trade. China wants influence in the region, and Mombasa Harbor is key. They're involved in everything from the infrastructure to the daily operations. Do you see the goods coming in? A lot of them are from Chinese manufacturers, reinforcing the trade relationship. It's a global game, Dennis."

As they moved closer to the wharfs, Dennis leaned in, "And the Sea Dragon?"

Selim's face turned serious, and he gestured toward a quieter, heavily guarded area near the far end of the port.

"Down there, in Kilindini Harbor. It's a deep-water dock. That's where the Sea Dragon is supposed to dock later today. That part of the port is where a lot of, let's say, discreet business goes down. Some of it legitimate, some… not so much."

Dennis observed the area, noting the heightened security. He could see dockworkers and containers, but this part of the harbor had a different energy, a slightly sinister undertone. Selim glanced around, lowering his voice.

"The Sea Dragon's crew is rumored to be mixed up in more than just regular shipping: drugs, contraband, maybe even human trafficking. People don't ask questions there. Chinese investment may run the port, but some corners? They've got their own rules."

Dennis nodded the weight of the mission settling over him.

"Thanks, Selim. Looks like this is where we'll start."

Selim gripped his shoulder briefly. "Keep your eyes open, Dennis. And watch your back down there. Not everyone in Mombasa wants this part of the operation exposed."

The Docks

Dennis was looking for the Sea Dragon, an aging freighter docked at the port, which had come onto their radar

thanks to intercepted communication from Ziad Farah's network. The logs they had pulled from the Stingray in Nairobi had revealed coded references to a shipment—a combination of illegal ivory and arms destined for a buyer in Somalia.

Cross-referencing the details with information from IRIS's network, Dennis had narrowed it down to the Sea Dragon, a vessel known for its shady dealings, an owner with ties to the suspect underground, and maybe to The Broker's network. Dennis, trying to look inconspicuous, wore a faded uniform, indistinguishable from the workers moving crates and loading goods onto ships. He was still quite noticeable among the mostly black crew. He kept his head down, his eyes constantly scanning the area as he moved along the docks.

It was a labyrinth of shipping containers, forklifts, and cargo vessels, the perfect place for someone like The Broker to conduct his business away from prying eyes. Dennis hadn't taken long to identify the ship he was looking for. The Sea Dragon was definitely old; its hull rusted in places, sitting low in the water as it was loaded with cargo. He had watched from a distance as men in plain clothes—clearly not dock workers—oversaw the loading process, their eyes constantly sweeping the area.

They were careful, but they weren't invisible. Dennis could see the subtle bulges beneath their jackets where they carried weapons. Dennis approached the ship cautiously, carrying a clipboard he had taken from one of the storage areas. He moved purposefully, trying to appear as if he belonged to the background like he was just another cog in

the massive machine that was Mombasa's port. As he got closer, he could see the crates being loaded onto the Sea Dragon—some marked with symbols that indicated their contents were wildlife products, others marked with nothing at all, their anonymity more telling than any label could be.

He moved closer to one of the cranes, the noise of machinery providing cover as he slipped behind a stack of containers. From there, he had a clear view of the loading operation. He could see the crates being stacked, and from the way the men handled them—gingerly, with extra care—he knew they held more than just ivory or horn. They held weapons, likely bound for militias in South Sudan or Somalia, ready to fuel more violence.

Dennis pulled out a small camera, carefully recording the men, the crates, and the ship. He needed proof of what was happening here, something they could use to expose The Broker's network. He was just about to move to a different position when he caught sight of a familiar face. His heart skipped a beat as he recognized one of the men overseeing the operation—Mutua, Charles Otieno's bodyguard who had intercepted him in the Nairobi gala. The politician was more deeply involved than Dennis had even imagined.

The Chase

Dennis felt a chill run down his spine. He had uncovered crucial information, and now he had to return it to Kamau, his handler, and anyone else who could help use it. But as he turned to leave, Mutua, Otieno's bodyguard, glanced in his direction, his eyes narrowing. Dennis forced himself to stay calm. Every instinct screamed at him to run, but he knew better. He had to walk away slowly without drawing

attention. The docks were a labyrinth of containers and cranes, the air thick with the smell of salt and diesel.

He quickened his pace, blending into the shadows, but his heart raced as he heard raised voices behind him. They had spotted him. He sprinted, weaving through stacks of shipping containers, his boots slamming against the concrete. His breath came in sharp, controlled bursts. Footsteps pounded after him—heavy, aggressive, closing in. Dennis darted between rows of crates, the clatter of metal and the shouts of his pursuers echoing in the night. He cut a sharp corner, nearly colliding with a stack of wooden pallets, his shoulder grazing the rough wood. His eyes darted around, searching for cover.

A narrow alley between two rows of containers caught his eye. He slipped into it without hesitation, pressing his body flat against the cold metal. The alley was tight, the scent of rust and oil thick in the air, but it took him a few seconds to catch his breath. The men were close now. He could hear their voices—frantic, searching, barking orders. They didn't know where he was but would find him soon if he didn't move.

Dennis's mind raced, his thoughts calculating the next move. He needed to lose them or find a way to throw them off. Then he spotted it—a forklift parked a few meters away, its engine cold but the keys dangling from the ignition. It was risky, but it was all he had. He dashed towards it, keeping low, and vaulted into the driver's seat. The engine sputtered to life with a growl, shattering the night's stillness. Dennis slammed the forklift into gear, the machine lurching

forward. He aimed for a stack of empty containers, lifting them with the metal forks.

The grinding of the machinery was deafening, but it served his purpose. He shifted the containers with a calculated twist of the controls, creating a crude barrier between him and his pursuers. He leaped from the forklift, not bothering to check if it had worked, and took off in the opposite direction. His phone buzzed in his pocket as he ran. Kamau's name flashed on the screen. Dennis answered, his breath ragged.

"Kamau, I need backup. They're onto me."

Kamau's voice, always calm under pressure, came through the earpiece.

"Where are you?" "Docks," Dennis panted, dodging behind a stack of barrels as he spoke.

"South loading area. They've got eyes everywhere. I need to know where that ship is headed."

There was a brief pause, the sound of furious typing in the background.

"The Sea Dragon," Kamau said.

"Bound for Kismayo, Somalia. Dennis, it would help if you got out of there now. They won't let you walk away if they catch you."

"I know," Dennis replied, glancing over his shoulder as he slipped through a narrow gap between two containers.

He could hear the men closing in, their voices louder, more urgent.

"I've got the intel. I need a way out."

"Head for the main gate," Kamau said.

"I'll have someone there to pick you up. Just stay alive, Dennis."

Dennis ended the call, his mind laser-focused on escape. His muscles burned from the sprint, but he kept moving, his legs churning with purpose. He darted through the maze of containers, using the noise and bustle of the dockworkers as cover. He saw the main gate in the distance, illuminated by harsh yellow lights. The pavement shimmered under the glow. He was almost there. Suddenly, a gunshot tore through the air.

The sharp crack of the bullet ricocheted off the container beside him, sending a shower of sparks. Dennis ducked, instinct taking over, his pulse hammering in his ears. He could hear his pursuers now, their boots pounding the pavement, their shouts growing more frantic. He pushed harder, his legs screaming for relief, the main gate just a hundred yards away. Another shot rang out, whizzing past his shoulder. His breath came in ragged gasps, the adrenaline surging through his veins.

Then he saw it—a black SUV idling near the gate, its engine purring, ready for him—Kamau's contact.

"Come on," Dennis muttered, his chest tightening as the footsteps behind him quickened.

He could feel the heat of their pursuit, the weight of danger pressing closer. The gate was within reach, and Dennis forced every last ounce of energy into his legs. With a final burst, he slammed open the SUV door and threw

himself inside, his breath ragged and heart pounding. The driver didn't wait for orders.

The tires screeched as the SUV peeled away, leaving the shouts and gunfire behind. Dennis slumped back in the seat, his breath coming in ragged gasps. The tension was still coursing through him, but for now, he was safe—safe, with the intel that could take down The Broker. Dennis looked back, seeing the men disappear into the distance. Their figures grew smaller as the vehicle put more distance between them. He pulled out the camera, checking the photos he had taken. They were clear evidence of the weapons, the ivory, and the involvement of Otieno's men. It was enough to make a difference and bring The Broker's operation to light. The driver glanced at him, his expression unreadable.

"You, okay?" Dennis nodded, still catching his breath.

"I will be. Just get me somewhere safe."

The SUV sped through the streets of Mombasa, the city's lights blurring past. Dennis knew they had won a victory tonight, but it was only the beginning. The Broker was still out there, and the shipment was going to Kismayo. They had to act fast if they were going to stop it—and Dennis knew this was far from over. Introduction to the Police Force Dennis stood in the dusty yard of the Mombasa police headquarters, the sun beating down relentlessly. He wiped a bead of sweat from his brow and glanced around.

The scent of saltwater lingered in the air, a reminder that the docks weren't far, and soon, they'd be heading back there for the final takedown. He knew this was the moment they had all been working toward—bringing down Shetani, who

had caused untold suffering across East Africa. But they needed help, and Dennis couldn't do it alone this time. Captain Odhiambo, the tall, wiry ranger who had been Dennis's trusted contact, emerged from the building, flanked by Kamau.

Following closely behind them were a group of officers from the Kenyan General Service Unit (GSU), their boots crunching against the gravel as they approached. These men weren't the regular beat cops—they were the country's elite paramilitary force, trained for counter-terrorism, high-risk operations, and exactly the kind of takedown they were about to execute. Odhiambo gestured for Dennis to step forward.

"These are the men who'll help us bring in Shetani," he said, his voice steady with confidence.

"I've worked with them before. They're the best we've got."

Kamau, ever the quiet observer, nodded in agreement.

"They've been briefed. We know Shetani—The Broker—will be heavily guarded. This won't be easy."

Dennis looked at the officers, their faces hard and focused. Each one was geared up, ready for the fight ahead. Assault rifles slung over their shoulders, body armor strapped tight, and helmets that would soon be buckled down. These men were prepared for a full-blown battle, not just an arrest. One of the officers, a sergeant named Moses, stepped forward, his expression serious.

"We've seen the intel. If Shetani's on that ship, he won't go down without a fight. His bodyguards are mercenaries— well-armed, well-trained."

Dennis nodded, appreciating the bluntness. "We need to hit them hard and fast. I've planted explosives on the ship as a last resort. But the goal is to arrest him alive. He's more valuable to us breathing."

The sergeant gave a slight smile.

"We'll ensure he's still breathing, but his men might not be so lucky."

Odhiambo clapped Dennis on the shoulder. "We're ready when you are."

Dennis looked back at the group. This was it—the final push. They had the men, the firepower, and the plan. The only thing left was to execute it.

"Let's get to the docks," Dennis said.

"We don't have much time."

The Sea Dragon is Spitting Fire Dennis stood in the shadows of the Mombasa docks, the salty air thick with tension. He watched the Sea Dragon, a massive freighter, its rusty hull rising like a behemoth from the water. The ship was scheduled to leave for Kismayo, Somalia, laden with illegal ivory, weapons, and enough firepower to fuel violence across East Africa for months. Dennis knew this was their one shot to stop The Broker—now identified as Shetani— and cripple his entire operation. If they failed tonight, it would all slip away.

He adjusted his earpiece, Naomi's voice crackling through. "Dennis, are you in position?" she asked, her voice steady despite her recent recovery. She had insisted on supporting the operation, monitoring from a safe location. "I'm here," Dennis whispered, his eyes fixed on the figures moving near the ship. A team of well-armed men moved in and out of the freighter, loading the final crates. Dennis's breath caught when his gaze locked onto one man standing near the ramp, overseeing the operation.

Shetani. The man was rarely seen in public, preferring the shadows. But tonight, he was there, ensuring the shipment left smoothly.

"Security is tight, but I see him—Shetani's overseeing everything," Dennis whispered, trying to contain the surge of adrenaline. Naomi's pause was heavy.

"You're sure it's him?" Dennis nodded, even though she couldn't see him.

"I'm sure. He matches the description—tall, gray hair, sharp features. He's giving orders."

Dennis felt a wave of realization hit him. This wasn't just another shipment. It was the shipment—the lifeblood of Shetani's operation. Rumors had swirled about internal tensions in the syndicate, whispers of betrayal between Ziad, Otieno, and Shetani. The Broker didn't trust anyone anymore. The stakes were too high, so he had to be here himself. One slip and his empire could crumble. Dennis clenched his jaw, determination flooding him. It was time.

He moved through the shadows, keeping low, using the noise and activity on the docks to mask his approach. Shetani

stood near the ramp, eyes sweeping the area, confident yet wary. Dennis could sense the underlying tension in Shetani's stance—he knew he was taking a risk by being here, but he couldn't leave this shipment to chance. Dennis reached into his pocket, his fingers brushing against the small device—a remote detonator linked to explosives he had planted near the freighter's cargo. The plan was to destroy the shipment and take down Shetani alive. He took a deep breath, finger hovering over the button. Before he could press it, a cold voice behind him made his blood freeze.

"Drop it, Bellamy." Dennis turned slowly, seeing Mutua, Otieno's bodyguard who had recognized him, with his gun aimed directly at him.

His mind raced. He hadn't expected to be discovered so soon. The bodyguard gestured with his weapon.

"Hands up." Dennis raised his hands, hiding the detonator.

His eyes darted to Shetani, who was now watching them, a curious look on his face. Dennis knew he had to act fast. In a split second, he lunged forward, knocking the gun aside as he tackled the bodyguard. They hit the ground hard, the weapon skittering across the pavement. Dennis scrambled to his feet, detonator in hand, just as Shetani barked orders.

"Get him! Don't let him near the ship!"

Without hesitation, Dennis pressed the button. The docks shook as a series of explosions tore through the side of the Sea Dragon. The blast threw Dennis off his feet, the shockwave rattling his bones. The freighter lurched

He adjusted his earpiece, Naomi's voice crackling through. "Dennis, are you in position?" she asked, her voice steady despite her recent recovery. She had insisted on supporting the operation, monitoring from a safe location. "I'm here," Dennis whispered, his eyes fixed on the figures moving near the ship. A team of well-armed men moved in and out of the freighter, loading the final crates. Dennis's breath caught when his gaze locked onto one man standing near the ramp, overseeing the operation.

Shetani. The man was rarely seen in public, preferring the shadows. But tonight, he was there, ensuring the shipment left smoothly.

"Security is tight, but I see him—Shetani's overseeing everything," Dennis whispered, trying to contain the surge of adrenaline. Naomi's pause was heavy.

"You're sure it's him?" Dennis nodded, even though she couldn't see him.

"I'm sure. He matches the description—tall, gray hair, sharp features. He's giving orders."

Dennis felt a wave of realization hit him. This wasn't just another shipment. It was the shipment—the lifeblood of Shetani's operation. Rumors had swirled about internal tensions in the syndicate, whispers of betrayal between Ziad, Otieno, and Shetani. The Broker didn't trust anyone anymore. The stakes were too high, so he had to be here himself. One slip and his empire could crumble. Dennis clenched his jaw, determination flooding him. It was time.

He moved through the shadows, keeping low, using the noise and activity on the docks to mask his approach. Shetani

stood near the ramp, eyes sweeping the area, confident yet wary. Dennis could sense the underlying tension in Shetani's stance—he knew he was taking a risk by being here, but he couldn't leave this shipment to chance. Dennis reached into his pocket, his fingers brushing against the small device—a remote detonator linked to explosives he had planted near the freighter's cargo. The plan was to destroy the shipment and take down Shetani alive. He took a deep breath, finger hovering over the button. Before he could press it, a cold voice behind him made his blood freeze.

"Drop it, Bellamy." Dennis turned slowly, seeing Mutua, Otieno's bodyguard who had recognized him, with his gun aimed directly at him.

His mind raced. He hadn't expected to be discovered so soon. The bodyguard gestured with his weapon.

"Hands up." Dennis raised his hands, hiding the detonator.

His eyes darted to Shetani, who was now watching them, a curious look on his face. Dennis knew he had to act fast. In a split second, he lunged forward, knocking the gun aside as he tackled the bodyguard. They hit the ground hard, the weapon skittering across the pavement. Dennis scrambled to his feet, detonator in hand, just as Shetani barked orders.

"Get him! Don't let him near the ship!"

Without hesitation, Dennis pressed the button. The docks shook as a series of explosions tore through the side of the Sea Dragon. The blast threw Dennis off his feet, the shockwave rattling his bones. The freighter lurched

violently, flames spreading across its deck, and chaos erupted. Shetani's men scattered, shouting orders, desperately trying to control the situation. Dennis pushed himself up, his ears ringing from the explosion. Through the smoke, he saw Shetani, his face contorted with rage, shouting at his men. This was his moment. Dennis sprinted through the confusion, dodging containers and debris, eyes locked on Shetani.

The Broker saw him coming, his expression shifting from anger to cold calculation. He reached for a gun at his side, but Dennis was faster. He tackled Shetani, slamming him against a stack of crates. The two struggled, and Shetani's strength surprised Dennis. He could see Shetani's hatred and the cold realization that his empire was crumbling.

"You think you can stop me?" Shetani snarled.

"You have no idea how far this goes. Kenya is just the beginning. I have ties across continents. People will pick up where I left off."

Dennis drove his fist into Shetani's side.

"Not if I have anything to say about it."

But two of Shetani's henchmen appeared before he could subdue him, guns drawn. Dennis barely had time to dive behind a stack of crates as bullets tore through the air, splintering wood and metal. Shetani Arrest The roar of gunfire echoed across the docks, the crack of rifles mingling with the shouts of men and the hum of the freighter's engines. The Kenyan GSU officers were locked in a fierce firefight with Shetani's bodyguards, bullets ricocheting off

steel and concrete, sending sparks flying. Dennis clenched his jaw, his grip tight on the walkie-talkie.

"Odhiambo, what's your status?"

Odhiambo's voice crackled through the speaker, strained but determined.

"We're pushing through. Shetani's guards are dug in, but we've pinned them down. It won't be long."

Dennis glanced toward the Sea Dragon, the freighter looming in the darkness, its deck lit by the flash of gunfire. The plan had been simple—overwhelm the guards, take Shetani alive. But nothing about this operation had ever been simple. The GSU officers moved with precision, advancing in small groups using containers and crates as cover. Dennis saw Sergeant Moses leading his team, barking commands over the battle's din. Dennis regrouped with Kibet, ready to go on board as soon as humanely possible. Suddenly, explosions rocked the docks, sending plumes of smoke and debris into the air. Dennis ducked instinctively.

The explosions weren't from the charges he had set. This was Shetani's desperate final stand. Dennis pressed the walkie-talkie.

"Odhiambo, I'm heading to the boat. Keep pushing forward!"

Odhiambo's response was immediate.

"Go! We've got this."

Dennis and Kibet moved quickly, taking advantage of the chaos. They sprinted toward the Sea Dragon, dodging stray gunfire and ducking behind containers. As they

reached the ship, Dennis caught sight of Shetani—his face twisted with fury as he struggled against Odhiambo's team. But that wasn't Dennis's concern right now.

"We need to get inside," Dennis said, his eyes scanning the freighter's side.

They found a narrow access point and slipped aboard, moving swiftly through the corridors. The sound of gunfire echoed in the background, but Dennis forced himself to focus on the task at hand. Kibet moved to a locked door leading to the captain's quarters. "This is where they'd keep anything important," he said, pulling out a set of tools. Within moments, he had the door open, and the two of them stepped inside. Stacks of documents, ledgers, and a laptop sat on a desk, untouched by the flames outside. Dennis felt a surge of relief. This was it—the proof they needed to tie Shetani to the network.

"Kibet, grab everything," Dennis ordered. "We don't have much time."

Kibet worked fast, carefully placing the documents and electronic devices into evidence bags. The fire outside was spreading, but the room remained untouched for now. Dennis glanced at the ledger—page after page detailing shipments, names, and dates. Shetani's entire operation laid bare.

"Ziad, Otieno, Mrefu...and Shetani," Dennis murmured, running his finger down the page.

"We've got them." Kibet looked up, his expression grim but satisfied. "This will put him away for good."

Dennis nodded, but he knew they weren't out of danger yet.

"Let's move. We need to get this out of here before the fire spreads."

With the evidence secured, Dennis and Kibet made their way back to the deck just as Odhiambo's team closed in on Shetani. The Broker was cornered, snarling orders to his men, but the fight was over. Odhiambo and his team breached the last line of defense, slamming Shetani against the freighter's hull and locking him in handcuffs.

"We've got him," Odhiambo's voice crackled through Dennis's earpiece.

"Shetani is in custody." Dennis let out a breath he hadn't realized he was holding.

The arrest was important, but the documents Kibet now held would be the key to keeping Shetani behind bars for a long time. As they made their way back to the boat, Dennis couldn't help but feel a sense of finality. Shetani had been brought down, and the evidence was secure. They had struck a blow against the network, and for the first time, Dennis felt the tide turning. He stepped onto the boat, the sea breeze cooling his skin as they pushed away from the dock. Behind him, the Sea Dragon was in flames, but the fire hadn't reached what mattered. They had won.

For now. With a swift motion, Odhiambo slammed Shetani against the steel, locking him in handcuffs. Shetani struggled, but it was over. The Broker was finally caught, the man who had caused so much destruction. Odhiambo's voice crackled through Dennis's earpiece.

"We've got him. Shetani is in custody."

Dennis glanced back at the Sea Dragon. The firemen and police team were already extinguishing the flames— sirens from approaching police and ambulances cut through the night. The battle was over, but the long fight to dismantle Shetani's network had just begun. Dennis stepped onto the dock, the sea breeze cooling his skin. Shetani was in custody, but there were still secrets left to uncover. For now, though, they had won.

Epilogue

The sun was rising over Nairobi as Dennis stepped out of the car, his face drawn and exhausted. He had been up all night coordinating with Kamau, Kibet, Odhiambo, and a network of trusted contacts, ensuring the evidence they had gathered was safely in the right hands. It was time to bring everything to light and expose The Broker's network of crime and corruption for all the world to see.

Dennis entered a small, discreet office in the city center the following day. He was greeted by a journalist from an international media outlet, her eyes widening slightly as she saw the camera and documents Dennis placed on the table. He explained everything, recounting the details of The Broker's operation, Charles Otieno's involvement, and the shipment that was meant to fuel the violence and chaos across East Africa. The journalist listened intently, her expression growing more serious as she understood the gravity of what Dennis was revealing.

"This will shake things up," she said quietly, glancing at Dennis. "The people involved won't go down without a fight. Are you ready for that?"

Dennis nodded. "I know. But this is the only way to stop them. We need the world to see what's happening here—to understand the consequences."

The journalist agreed, taking the evidence with a promise to get it into the hands of people who could make a difference. Dennis knew that once the story broke, there would be a storm— political repercussions, backlash from those implicated, and perhaps even retaliation from remnants of The Broker's network. But it was a storm worth facing.

The following days were a whirlwind. The media reports spread like wildfire, the shocking images, and documents laying bare the scale of the smuggling ring and the corruption that had enabled it. International news outlets quickly picked up the story, spotlighting the Kenyan government harshly. Charles Otieno, once seen as an untouchable politician, was named a key figure in a smuggling operation that stretched across borders. Public outrage followed swiftly, and his political rivals seized the opportunity to expose more of his misdeeds. With his reputation in ruins, Otieno was stripped of his position, his once-promising political career left in tatters.

Dennis could finally return to the Maasai Mara. Naomi was waiting for him at the airport.

"You did it," she said as he sat beside her at the coffee stand. "I saw the news. It's everywhere."

Dennis smiled faintly, nodding. "We did it. The world knows now. Otieno's finished, and The Broker has lost much power. But we both know this isn't the end."

Naomi looked down at her hands, her expression thoughtful. "It's never really over, is it? There's always someone else willing to step in, to take advantage of the chaos." She glanced at Dennis, her eyes serious. "But what we did—it matters. We made a difference, even if it's just for a little while."

Dennis nodded, feeling the weight of her words. The battle against corruption and crime was never-ending, requiring constant vigilance. But as he looked at Naomi, he felt a sense of purpose, a reminder that the struggle was worth it, even if the victories were small and temporary.

"Thank you, Naomi," Dennis said quietly. "For everything. I couldn't have done this without you."

Naomi smiled, a hint of warmth returning to her eyes. "You would have done the same for me. We're in this together, Dennis. Always."

The sun dipped low in the Mara, casting a golden glow over the open plains as Dennis and Naomi sat quietly with Odhiambo and his sister, Nyambura. The small group shared a quiet camaraderie, their spirits lifted by the peaceful scene around them, a welcome contrast to the chaos they had endured. Just then, Meron and Tigist joined them, and both girls looked more like the carefree teenagers they were meant to be.

Meron's face brightened when she spotted Dennis. She walked up to him, a soft smile gracing her face, suddenly

mature beyond her age. And spoke quietly, "When you saved us, I had welcomed death. I didn't think there was anything left for us in this world." Her voice caught, her eyes shimmering with unspoken emotion. "But now, every day I wake up here in the Mara, I pray for you, Dennis, for what you have done for Tigist and me. I know God sent you, and now I can be happy again and trust life." Her eyes watered as she held his gaze, her gratitude and resilience shining.

Tigist squeezed her sister's hand, nodding silently, and then, with a shy smile, said, "We are so happy here!" The two slipped away toward the kitchen, offering to fetch refreshments for everyone.

Nyambura watched the girls go, her expression soft. "They've come a long way," she said. "The therapy has helped, but their love for each other has really pulled them through." She glanced back at Dennis and Naomi, a smile tugging at her lips. "Meron's taken to working in the reserve. She's got such a gift with the animals. And Tigist? She's excelling in school—both of them are. They're among the top students in their class. Without you all, they would be sex slaves in some brothels for what would be a short, miserable life. I am deeply grateful for them and all the souls you saved, Naomi, Dennis, and Odhiambo."

Naomi's face softened as she listened. "They're remarkable, and they've had to be so strong. But now they have the chance just to be girls, to live the lives they deserve."

Dennis nodded, a quiet pride filling him as he looked over the plains. The sound of laughter from the kitchen

floated to them, and Dennis smiled, feeling a warmth settle over him.

As the stars blanketed the sky over the Mara, Dennis and Naomi sat together in the quiet of the evening, a comfortable silence settling between them. The sounds of the savannah at night—the distant calls of wildlife, the rustling of leaves in the gentle breeze—filled the space around them. Dennis felt a bittersweet heaviness, aware that this would soon come to an end and he would have to leave.

Naomi turned to him, her gaze softened by a mix of gratitude and something deeper. "I always thought I'd be alone out here, just me and the Mara. But you..." she paused, her voice quiet but resolute, "you changed that, even if it's only for a while." Her hand rested gently on his, her warmth grounding him to this moment.

Dennis took a deep breath, searching for the right words. "Naomi, you're going to do amazing things here. The Mara is lucky to have you." He hesitated, a slight smile playing on his lips. "And maybe... maybe one day you'll share it with someone standing by your side. Someone who'll be with you for the long run."

A glimmer of hope flickered as she looked out over the darkened plains. "Maybe I'm ready for that. Children, a family here in the Mara. It's something I've been thinking about." she turned back to him, her voice dropping to a whisper. "But tonight... tonight, let's just be here together."

They moved slowly, rediscovering each other as if for the first time. Naomi leaned into him, and Dennis held her, feeling the lingering fragility beneath her strength. "Be tender," she murmured, her hand resting on his chest. The

intimacy felt both familiar and new, a quiet acknowledgment of what they'd shared and the paths they were about to take apart.

As dawn approached, they lay quietly; each lost in thought, the weight of parting a silent presence between them.

The following day, Dennis sat with Naomi outside the camp. She was healing, her bandages barely visible under her loose shirt. Kamau had joined them, carrying the latest news about Shetani's upcoming trial. The air was cool, and the sense of victory was tempered by the gravity of what they had uncovered.

"You did it," she said as he sat beside her. "I saw the news. It's everywhere."

Dennis smiled faintly, nodding. "We did it. The world knows now. Otieno's finished, and The Broker has lost much power. But we both know this isn't the end."

Kamau leaned back in his chair, his face thoughtful. "You know, Shetani is finally going to trial," he said, glancing at Dennis. "It's official. The Special Crime Prevention Unit found a money trail between him and Otieno. Everything's falling into place."

Naomi looked up, her eyes lighting with interest. "So, they've got him? For good this time?"

Dennis nodded, resting his hands on his knees. "We found the documents in the safe house. Kibet and his team did a fantastic job securing the evidence during the raid on the Sea Dragon. We have enough to bury Shetani for a long time."

Kamau smiled faintly. "Mrefu's testimony sealed the deal. When he realized he was facing the death penalty for the rangers' murders and for human trafficking, he flipped. He's testified that Shetani and The Broker are the same person. That, plus the documents we recovered from the abandoned poacher camp and the safe house and the testimony of the two sisters, gave us the smoking gun we needed."

Naomi leaned back, visibly relieved. "So, Mrefu actually came through as a witness? I thought he'd never talk."

Dennis chuckled. "Desperation changes things. He knows there's no way out unless he cooperates. And he wasn't the only one. Samuel convinced several poachers from his village to come forward, too. They all gave statements that tie Shetani directly to poaching, arms smuggling, and drug trafficking. We've got witnesses and the paperwork to back it all up."

Kamau added, "The financial records are solid. The SCPU traced the money flowing from Otieno straight to Shetani's accounts. There's no denying the connection anymore. Otieno's corruption was bad enough, but tying him to Shetani's network... that's the nail in the coffin."

Naomi's eyes glinted with satisfaction. "It sounds like there's no way out for them this time."

Dennis nodded slowly, looking out over the camp. "Shetani was caught overseeing the entire operation at the Sea Dragon. He can't wriggle his way out of this. We have him on the illegal operations, the money trail, and the murders. It's over for him."

Kamau smirked. "And when the trial begins, it's going to shake Kenya's political and criminal landscape. It's not just about Shetani anymore. Otieno's fall is just the start. Once this goes public, there'll be others scrambling for cover."

Naomi, her voice calm but serious, asked, "So what's next? What are we expecting once this trial starts?"

Dennis looked at her, his face hardening. "The trial won't be easy. There'll be plenty of pushback. Shetani has friends in high places, and they'll do whatever they can to disrupt things. But we have enough to convict him now. The documents from the safe house, Mrefu's testimony, the financial evidence—it's all there. If the prosecution does their job, Shetani will be locked up for life."

Kamau leaned forward, his tone conspiratorial. "And don't forget, this isn't just a local trial. International eyes are on this. Shetani's network reached across borders. They'll want to see this through, make sure the message is clear—no one is above justice."

Naomi smiled softly, her relief finally sinking in. "It's incredible. After everything, he's actually going to face justice."

Dennis sat back, letting the weight of the moment sink in. "It's not over yet. We've brought down Shetani, but his network is still out there. We've cut off the head, but plenty of others will want to take his place. We'll need to stay vigilant."

Naomi's smile faded slightly, her eyes reflecting the truth in Dennis's words. "It's a never-ending fight, isn't it?"

"Yeah," Dennis said quietly, "but this victory matters. Shetani's going to trial. We've broken his hold on Kenya, and Otieno's finished. We did what we came to do."

Kamau stood up, looking between Dennis and Naomi. "We've struck a blow, that's for sure. Shetani might be the big fish, but his capture will ripple through the entire network. It's only a matter of time before the rest are flushed out."

Naomi nodded, satisfied. "We'll be ready when that time comes."

As the sun continued to rise, painting the sky in hues of orange and pink, Dennis allowed himself a rare moment of peace. They had done it—brought down The Broker, exposed Otieno's corruption, and disrupted the smuggling network that had caused so much suffering.

But as he looked at Naomi, he knew the battle was far from over. There would always be more to fight, more shadows to bring into the light. For now, though, they had won.

Naomi squeezed his hand, and Dennis smiled. They had made a difference, and for the first time in a long while, that felt like enough. The sun was rising over Nairobi as Dennis stepped out of the car, his face drawn and exhausted. He had been up all night coordinating with Kamau, Kemet, Odhiambo, and a network of trusted contacts, ensuring the evidence they had gathered was safely in the right hands. It was time to bring everything to light and to expose

The Broker's network of crime and corruption is for all the world to see. In December, the Director of Public

Prosecutions in Kenya issued an arrest warrant against Otieno on multiple corruption charges from his tenure as the Governor of Nairobi County. He was arrested in Voi and, after being detained at Kamiti Maximum Security Prison for a few days, was released on a cash bail of Sh15 million or a bond of Sh30 million, as set by the anti-corruption court. One of the conditions of his release was that he was barred from accessing the Nairobi County governor's office until the case was resolved.

By late December, the Kenyan Senate had impeached Otieno. His fall from grace continued when the U.S. Department of State issued a travel ban on him, his wife, Miriam Otieno, and their two daughters, Nyambura Otieno and Amani Otieno, designating them ineligible for entry into the United States due to their involvement in corruption. The once-powerful politician faced a future shrouded in scandal, with his legacy irreparably damaged.

The Broker's network, though still partially intact, was crippled. The wildlife trafficking routes had been disrupted, and the shipment that Dennis had destroyed was a significant setback for those involved. But Dennis knew that the fight was far from over. The syndicate was still out there, beheaded and weakened but not defeated, and they would likely regroup and try to recover. They sat in silence for a moment, watching the sun dip below the horizon, the sky painted in hues of orange and pink. The world felt different and lighter, even if the fight was far from over. They had struck a blow against The Broker's empire and given hope to those who had lost it.

Dennis knew that his time in Kenya was coming to an end. There were other battles to fight, other places where people like The Broker needed to be stopped. He stood, looking down at Naomi.

"Take care of yourself. And if you ever need me, you know how to find me."

Naomi nodded, her eyes meeting his.

"Likewise. And don't forget—you still owe me a proper safari."

Dennis chuckled, the tension easing from his shoulders. "One day, Naomi. One day." As he walked away, Dennis felt a sense of closure. He had done what he had come to do, and though the road ahead was uncertain, he knew he would keep moving forward. The fight wasn't over, but he was ready for whatever came next. The lights of Nairobi flickered to life as the city settled into the night, a reminder that even in the face of darkness, there was always light.

Dennis glanced back at the camp one last time before disappearing into the shadows, knowing that he had made a difference—and that, for now, was enough.

www.ingramcontent.com/pod-product-compliance
Lightning Source LLC
Chambersburg PA
CBHW061547170626
46811CB00001B/116